D1140483

Plea·

Yc

Yo··

‹

I2501516

THE BLACK MONASTERY

by the same author

THE DEVIL'S PLAYGROUND

STAV SHEREZ

The Black Monastery

faber and faber

First published in 2009
by Faber and Faber Ltd
Bloomsbury House 74–77 Great Russell Street London WC1B 3DA

Typeset by RefineCatch Limited, Bungay, Suffolk
Printed and bound in the UK by CPI Mackays, Chatham ME5 8TD

A CIP record for this book
is available from the British Library

ISBN 978–0–571–24481–2

2 4 6 8 10 9 7 5 3 1

For Dennis
1976–2006

Though there is a designation of priest/monk in the Greek Orthodox Church, I have used it to my own ends. Similarly, certain methods and procedures of both the Orthodox Church and the Greek Police force I have altered for the purposes of plot.

We read signs as promises

Donald Barthelme

Two months earlier

She wakes him with kisses. She wakes him with coffee. The slap of her feet against white tiles pulls him out of dreams and into this burning day. She's singing now. Her voice a beat behind the words like an echo from a distant station. She tries to keep up with the lyrics, but she stumbles, and it makes him want to take her into his arms and crush her against him until neither of them can breathe.

This is what he wakes up to every day. This is the sound of his wife making coffee and the smell of frying butter on a sun-sizzled morning. This is the taste in his mouth, left over from dreams; that sudden disorientation on waking, the not knowing who or where, the moment of panic – then relief, as memory comes tumbling back. This is like every other morning except this morning it's his birthday.

He goes to the bathroom. Silently watches himself in the mirror. Every year seems to take more away, as if gravity was something you forgot how to fight after a while. He puts the razor to his throat and carefully shaves around the moustache. He trails his fingers through the dry bristle and tapers the ends. It's his one vanity, he knows, but it's a small one, and though he suspects the other officers make fun of him, well, it's a lot better than them making fun of his work or his wife.

She's hunched over the sink like a parenthesis. She contains his life. Her black hair rolling down her neck. Her arms sunk deep in the dishes, the kiss of glass against glass in the early morning silence.

She hums under her breath. Old songs he vaguely remembers from another time. She turns, her arms glistening with water and soap, foam clinging to her dress. 'I thought you were sleeping in?'

'Headache.' He doesn't need to say more. It's the shorthand they've developed over the long years, the way of saying things without saying them.

'You've always got a headache on your birthday. Oh, Nikki, maybe next year will be different, no?'

He shrugs. It's his last year as a policeman. Back on the island again. Back where it all began. 'I had them before I joined.'

'Maybe it's birthdays you hate.' She places the glass of orange juice in front of him.

He stares at the bright liquid, the constellation of pulp fragments clinging to the side of the glass. 'It's just another day. I don't see why everyone makes such a fuss.' He strokes his moustache. She looks at him, all glare and frustration. She knows this is what he does when he doesn't want to talk about something. When his mind takes one of its frequent detours into the past.

The country she left behind so long ago still lays its claim on Nikos. In the melody to a song, in the smell of a campfire, in the red-soaked sunset on a certain November day he will be reminded, and the whole weight of years will collapse down upon him. It's best to leave him alone when he gets like this. She can only be another reminder.

He watches her clean the sink. The dishes are done and piled up high. The floor is swept, apart from a few spilled drops of orange juice. The town is quiet; only the sound of birds and cicadas, the pull and crash of the sea, wind fluttering the leaves. These are moments he wishes would last for ever. But there are fewer of them every year.

The smash of breaking glass rips him from his thoughts.

'I'm sorry,' she whispers, 'it just gave me a fright.'

He gets up, carefully navigating around the scattered slivers of glass, like teardrops, spotting the floor. 'What did?'

4

But, before she can answer, he sees the cause of her fear.

He's staring down into the sink. It is empty apart from two orange centipedes rising from the plughole. Their antennae twist and flicker in the air. They turn towards Nikos, and twitch. It's this last movement that makes him step back. Murders, bodies and bruises he's fine with. The crescent-shaped scar made by a dagger, the shadow of fingers on a broken neck – these are his day-to-day. But insects and crawling things he's never been good with.

He stares at the shiny torsos, the twirling legs and black eyes. He watches as the centipedes crawl out of the drain and slither across the bottom of the sink, their legs like tiny hairs, black against the white porcelain.

'Don't worry, I'll deal with it.'

He nods, aware of how neatly she phrases things. Not saying, I know you're scared of them, I know how much they make you squirm. Just telling him it'll be OK by the time he gets home.

'God. They're huge.' He's transfixed. As you only are by the things which scare you. He watches them scale the walls of the sink. Their movements so precise and efficient like strings of miniature soldiers.

'Go,' she says. 'You've got a big day ahead of you, and I want you all fresh when you come back for dinner.'

He pulls his gaze away from the sink. He can still hear the scrape of their legs against the ceramic. They sound like a thousand tiny screams.

'I thought we agreed, no surprises.'

'Making you dinner is a surprise now?' She smiles but doesn't turn her head all the way towards him. She's watching the centipedes. Her fingers tapping against her leg.

He kisses her lips. She pulls away, her breath heavy and dry, 'Later,' she says, placing her finger against his mouth like a full stop only he is meant to hear.

It takes him ten minutes to walk to the police station. It's his favourite time of day. The tourists all asleep, the clubs and bars shut, the ferries still an hour away – it could almost be forty years ago. It could almost be the island he remembers.

He stops for coffee. He stops to chat to the old men in the taverna. They tell him stories about what their wives said to them the night before, the trouble their kids have got into, the antics of the crazy tourists. He sips his coffee and nods. It's a small island, and he needs to be as much priest or councillor as policeman.

Then it's a breakfast of *kourabides*. Those sugar-dusted cookies that his wife's banned him from eating in the house. More for the mess they make than the damage they'll do to his heart. They taste of his childhood, of his father going out on Sunday morning and coming back, a tower of white boxes from the bakery in his hands. She always knows when he's been eating them. There's sugar dust all over his clothes. His moustache is flecked white.

The street is quiet. The boats rock and tap each other in the current. He nods to the men walking their dogs and the fishermen sorting their catch. He looks up at the dazzling white villas hugging the western ridge, the sun breaking on their swimming pools and Japanese gardens. He's fifty-five today, but those houses are still as far away from him as they were forty years ago when he stared at them every morning on his way to school. It's one of many things he's learned to adjust to. He thinks of secrets and dark years and wonders at the possibilities his life once held.

The police station sits between the fish market and a shop that sells erotic Greek art to tourists. It used to be the smaller of the island's two churches but no one goes to church any more. The conversion was done quickly. There are corners dark with the ghosts of whispered confessions. Empty shadowed niches that once housed crumbling saints and martyrs. Fragments of frescoes still haunt certain walls. The smell of incense has never really gone away.

His secretary, Marianna, smiles when he enters. She's all lipstick and face powder. She's on the phone, nodding, chewing a pencil, checking her nails. Elias, his deputy, sits astride her desk. He's doing something with her computer, a cigarette poking through his thin grey lips. His other hand rests on her thigh.

'I'll tell him. Just stay where you are, please.' She swivels the chair towards Nikos. Elias' arm gets trapped between chair and table. His face flushes red. Nikos tries to bury his smile.

The secretary, pencil in mouth, passes over the note to Nikos.

'Just tell me,' he says.

'I know it's your birthday,' she replies, missing the way Nikos's forehead creases, 'but I think you'd better check this out.'

Elias is still moaning about his hand as they peel away from town. He's moaning about the heat, the long climb up to the ruins, the broken window on his police cruiser. Nikos lets him kvetch. These are Elias's last chances. In a few months, he'll be chief, and there won't be anyone to complain to. It's also a necessary distraction. A way for Nikos to stop thinking. To stop remembering.

He avoids the ruins if he can. He's never liked them. Not even as a child when every village boy would come up here at night, flasks and torchlight, fear and excitement, sleeping bags and cookies. But there's other history here too. A year ago and thirty-three years ago. Every bend of the mountain is a glimpse back into his younger self. Into things better left forgotten.

The old man is exactly where he said he would be. Nikos knows him from the market but he looks smaller today, as if what he had seen had somehow diminished him.

They can't make out what he's saying. His body shakes so much he looks as if he's out of focus. His words rush out tangled and twisted in their attempt to get to the punch line. But there's no punch line. There's only the old man's arm pointing towards the circle of rocks. The certainty in Nikos's blood. The knowledge of what they'll find.

Nikos leaves Elias with the old man. He wants to do this himself. He wants no distractions. He walks slowly. Each footstep bringing him that much nearer. He thinks about his wife's smile this morning. She's drifting away from him, he knows, but he can't find the way to bring her back. The sun burns his neck. Not yet nine, and already it's sizzling away.

The ruins stand before him. It's what people used to come to the island for. Now, they lie neglected and broken, unvisited and forgotten. Better that way, Nikos thinks, so much better.

There are stories and legends surrounding these woods, dark tales told to children on cold nights, but Nikos has never believed them.

The stones reflect the sun back into his eyes. They seem white as bones in the morning light. Once, they were the walls of an ancient temple. Providing cool and dark shelter from the weather. Privacy and isolation. Now they lie dotted and broken.

At the centre stands the altar. He can't see it from where he is but it's something he can never forget.

The voices of Elias and the old man are almost inaudible. The birds have stopped singing. The wind has died. There is always such stillness and quiet at the ruins. It doesn't make him calm. It only makes him tense.

He sees the body from fifty feet away. Flashbacks spin, flicker and fade. He closes his eyes down hard. Opens them to dancing motes and shadow ghosts, but this is no illusion. This is the past come back to haunt the present.

The boy lies on top of the altar. No amount of blinking or head-shaking will change that.

Nikos takes out his camera and reels off several shots. Concentrate on what's in front of you. The clues and traces. Forget everything else. Treat this as if it's the first crime scene you've ever come across. The camera shakes in his hand, and he takes several more shots to be sure.

The boy lies staked to the altar. His white skin reflects the sun as if it were made of marble. The altar is made of stone. There are carvings on it, but no one can say what they mean. Experts from Athens and the British Museum spent years trying to decode them but the islanders knew it was pointless. There's only one meaning to an altar.

Nikos scans the ground, the surrounding trees, anything to put off the moment he'll have to look down at the body. He stares up at the sky as if looking for an answer, but it is only the sky. He stopped believing in God a long time ago.

The altar is covered in orange markings, fresh and wet, daubed on the ancient stone. The skull of a cow lies on the ground next to it. Red ants and grey spiders crawl through the hatch-work of bone and tooth. Nikos's toes curl up inside his shoes. His breath turns short and shallow. The air feels raw against his skin.

He takes a deep breath. Waits until his heart slows down. Plants his feet deep into the soft earth beneath him. There's a trick to this, he knows. A way of cutting off everything but what's in front of you.

The boy lies on his back, eyes staring up into the empty sky. A ghastly mausoleum carved in living flesh. His arms and legs have been crudely tied to stakes in the ground. His skin is more red than white. The fingers on his hands are curled in tight against the palms. The nails, broken and bloody.

Centipedes surround the altar. Not the small, house cen-tipedes he saw this morning but a larger, more ferocious vari-ety. Their backs soak up the sun. Their legs susurrate in the still air. He swallows down his revulsion, the taste at the back of his throat he's learned to associate with irrational fear.

He recognises the boy. A local. Sixteen or seventeen years old. No one's reported him missing yet. It's the phone call he doesn't want to make. The voice on the other end of the line you don't want to hear. It's Elias's job in a few months' time, but now, this is all on him.

The rope binding the boy to the altar is thick and oily. The cuts on his abdomen are precise and professional. They traverse his stomach and groin. The stitching is jagged and rushed. The orange thread contrasting with the white skin.

Centipedes crawl across the boy's chest. Wriggle through the dark tangles of his hair. They snake out from under his limbs and between his feet. They seem to be coming from the body itself, as if in death it's given life to them.

There is no blood on the altar. None on the ground directly around it. There are splashes of red on the surrounding stones. Whether they are accidental or not, he can't tell. They seem to describe a pattern, but they could just as well be random.

He takes more photos, feeling better with the barrier of the camera pressed up against his eye, as if this were something watched late at night on television. The camera clicks and whirs in the dry air.

Elias is shouting from the other side of the ruins, but Nikos can't hear him any more. He can't hear the buzzing of the flies or scratching of the centipedes. His ears are filled with screaming. Shrill and vibrant. Coming from the forest around him. From the rocks encircling. From deep inside his head.

He places his hand on the altar to steady himself. He leans down and stares at the boy's face.

But there's only the tangle of ligament and muscle. The staring eyes. The receded gums and skeleton teeth. The mess that skin hides.

He looks up, dizzy. The sky seems closer. He breathes deep and tries to regain his balance. Elias is shouting. The wind is howling. The cicadas buzz and roar. He looks back down at the boy's body, the mutilated skin and cracked bones, and he gets to his knees.

There's no mistake. No conjecture or speculation. There's only what's in front of him, and it's no less shocking because he's seen it before.

He could be looking at a photo from last year. The boy. The altar. The centipedes. Tremors run through his arms and legs. They'd got it wrong, as he knew they had. They'd thought it was over. Looking down at the ravaged corpse, Nikos knows this is only the beginning.

I

ONE

The rain made it easier. A stroke of luck on a night so dependent on it. It was the middle of summer, but a thunderstorm crackled overhead, a muffled detonation poised above the city's roofs. The rain rendered him invisible.

He stood across the road, shrouded by an umbrella, pretending to talk on his phone but keeping his eyes on the doorway and the street ahead. There would only be one chance to get this right.

He let the first group go by. Their clothes were wrong, their hair, the way they held their bodies. He could never pass for one of them. So he waited, talking into the phone, making up stories no one would ever hear. It was the action, not the words, that was important.

They came out of a cab parked on the other side of the street. They were perfect. The denim jackets, slouched shoulders and messy hair. He watched them as they buckled against the wind and rain, unsheathed umbrellas and lit cigarettes. They were all smiles and chatter. Two or three drinks in, oblivious to all around them. He checked both sides of the road and made his move.

They didn't even notice as he crossed the street and fell in behind them. The wet pavement muffled his footsteps. The umbrella hid his face. He slowed when they slowed, then sped up as they climbed the marble stairs and approached the doorway. He could see the bright lights from inside and hear the spilled sound of laughter as it rushed out towards him.

This was the crucial moment. Everything depended on the next two minutes. His body shook. His mouth was dry. He'd never done anything like this before.

They stopped at the door. They fidgeted and searched pockets.

They're looking for their invites. They can't get in without them. A chorus of despair rattled through his head, but the men were only taking off their coats, stubbing cigarettes, straightening their ties.

He took a deep breath and closed the gap to only a few inches. He could hear them talking about football scores, smell the mix of aftershave and beer on their coats. He kept the phone to his ear and his eyes fixed straight ahead as he passed the sullen bouncer and gilded door frame, almost stumbling on the steps, nerves and panic fighting like two faded boxers inside him.

The lobby was brightly lit and thronged with people. His heart pounded like a train piston. The hand holding the phone was slicked with sweat. But he was in. That was all that mattered. That and the backpack which rested heavily on his shoulder. A reminder of why he was here.

He'd imagined this moment countless times since seeing the event advertised. But he'd imagined humiliation and shame. A hundred excuses for not having an invite. A room full of staring eyes. A quickly ushered exit. He'd never for one minute thought he'd be successful.

The crowd flowed through the club's lobby and into the main ballroom. He followed them, past portraits of greying lords on their last hunt, crumbling country houses and rows of dusty books with crimson covers. It was too hot in the room. His clothes stuck to his skin. The lights were too bright. His head was pounding. He could leave now. Save all the stress and hassle. The inevitable disappointment too.

He could hear champagne bottles roaring, glasses crashing, folk music playing, people laughing and chatting, a white noise of repeated remarks and feigned surprises. He tuned it out. He wasn't here for that. He'd come for only one reason.

He scanned the room, looking for her.

He wasn't sure he'd even recognise her. He knew her only from photos.

At first, there was nothing. A blur of people, suits and haircuts, greetings and kisses, noise and chatter. Then he saw her. A flash of black hair, the angle of a cheekbone but, when she turned, the girl was much younger and didn't look like Kitty at all. His breathing returned to normal. His heartbeat began to slow. A voice in his head told him to leave before he made a fool of himself. But there were other voices too, saying the signs were right, that this was his best and only hope. He stood there and concentrated on his breathing. Slow and deep, like something you have to learn how to do. He was relieved he couldn't see her. It delayed the moment of action. There was plenty of time, and there would be a more propitious moment. It was all in the choosing. A wrong choice could damn a life. He'd made one before, he wasn't going to make another.

He walked over to the publicity table, and there she was. Black and white and seven foot tall. A blow-up of the photo used for her last novel. He stood there and stared at it. He knew every inch of the photo by heart but the magnification had caused certain things, previously occluded, to emerge. He noticed the chipped nail on her left hand, the smudge of lipstick on her bottom lip, an expression in her eyes he hadn't caught before. It was like looking at a totally different image. He wondered which of her three photos she would most resemble.

He was breathing too fast. He fought back a flutter of nerves. Tonight he would finally see her. The real Kitty Carson. Not the photo reflected back from of a million paperbacks, their spines bent and broken on a beach in the midday heat. Not the face of a thousand Tube posters staring out into the sooty gloom. But Kitty as she was, stripped of flashlights, poses and Photoshopped edges.

A thread of hope wound through his body, detonating in his head. His excitement surprised him – he'd never felt this way before nor done such a thing; there were no rock stars or actresses on his walls – but he didn't think about it for long because there were things to do.

He scanned the table. Press releases and mock covers for *Holland Heart*, Kitty's new Lily Lombard novel. He took the press release and carefully folded it before putting it into his pocket. It would make a nice addition . . .

'Hey . . . I know you, right?'

Jason spun around, startled. A girl was staring at him. Her hair was like a flame about to go out, the last blaze of blood before it's snuffed. Her eyes searched his face. He nodded, not recognising the girl, wondering if his cover was about to be blown. If she began asking who he worked for, why he was here . . .

'That's it!' she smiled, all teeth and crinkled eyes, 'The gallery on Marylebone High Street. Didn't you used to run that? The one with the café?'

His heart crashed against his ribs. He thought of long days and unslept nights. The fires and winter floods. He wanted to lie, tell her she was wrong, but she seemed so sure of herself and so happy to have remembered that he didn't want to disappoint her.

'A long time ago.'

She laughed. He thought perhaps she was attracted to him. Or maybe he was wrong, maybe she was just being polite. He could never tell with these things.

'What happened? I noticed it closed down a couple of years ago.'

He shrugged. His mind flashed back through those last months. The constant letters and bills, demands and buzzing of the door. A year of being afraid of the morning post.

'I'm doing other things now.' He tried to keep his voice steady and his eyes locked on the girl's. 'For a long time I thought it was who I was and then one day I knew it wasn't.'

The girl nodded sympathetically, 'I used to like going there. You never knew what would be on the walls.'

'Thanks.' It touched him that she would remember, that anyone would, something he'd tried so hard to forget.

'Um . . . would you like to join us?' She placed her hand on his arm. It felt warm and familiar. 'It's about to begin.' She pointed across the room to a table with two other girls sitting around it. Jason started to say no, thanks but I'm waiting for someone, when he spotted Kitty. She was sitting at a table adjacent to the one the girl was pointing to. She was smiling and sipping white wine. She looked nothing at all like her photos.

'You're a fan, I assume?'

Jason swivelled round. He'd been staring at Kitty. The redhead smiled. He realised she'd asked him a question.

'Very much so.'

'Who isn't?' The girl on her left said, and they all laughed.

'We all work for her in one capacity or another. Ignore us.' The third girl added.

They introduced themselves, and the redhead, Marissa, shuffled closer to him. Her skin smelled sweet and flowery. If he hadn't come here for a purpose, he would have enjoyed talking to her, maybe swapped numbers, and, if he was lucky, she would call him and they would see a film together.

He angled his seat so he could see Kitty and Marissa at the same time. It seemed the best compromise. In the lulls of conversation he could hear the talk from Kitty's table, her accent much more clipped than he'd imagined, her voice full and throaty like someone who smoked, though, of course, he knew she never smoked. The backpack was placed safely between his feet. The thing inside nestled against his left shin, a reassuring presence but also a reminder that he hadn't achieved anything yet. Every minute it sat there felt like a tiny failure.

He looked across at Kitty and imagined his opening line, the way she'd be stand-offish at first and then something would pass between them, some shared recognition that lies beyond language. Only then could he give her the manuscript of his novel and she would remember him and start it later that night, calling him after finishing the last page, her voice husky and sleep-deprived, saying how she couldn't go to bed, how she . . . he crushed his hand into a fist. His eyes watered. He was back in the room. The girls were talking about some film he'd missed the name of. Kitty was sitting at her table, sipping wine, less than five feet away. He leaned towards her table, concentrating until he could make out the words she was saying.

'I'm so sick of all this.' Kitty sighed, and Jason wondered whether she meant the champagne glass she was holding, the launch, or something else. There was a tremor in her voice, a touch of sombre weight, the way some words slowed down almost as if hitting a wall. He hadn't expected her voice to be like this at all.

'It just feels so pointless these days. Most of the time, I don't even want to turn on the computer. I've never felt like that before.'

He noticed it again. A ghost flicker across Kitty's face. Something which looked very much like boredom when she thought no one was watching.

'This one's going to take you all the way.' The man on her left, her agent, replied.

'To where?' Kitty asked, and the other two laughed but Jason didn't think she was making a joke.

'You'll feel different after your holiday.'

'Will I? I'm stuck on this new book. I shouldn't even be going away.'

The agent turned towards her, and his eyes caught Jason's. Jason quickly looked away. 'That's exactly why you need this. Unwind. Get out of the country for a few weeks. It was so daring of you to have just gone in there this morning and booked it.'

Kitty shrugged. She downed her drink and was immediately poured another.

'The Greek Islands.' The agent continued, caressing the words as if they were a swallow of ancient, oak-casked Scotch. 'Which one? Mykonos? Antiparos?'

'Palassos,' she replied, and something crept into her voice; something like hope, excitement? Jason took out his pen, unfolded the press release, kept listening.

'The travel agent recommended it. It's quiet, not too many nightclubs. Places for walking. I . . . I think it's what I need. I feel so tangled these days.'

'There's always something magical about your first time in the Aegean.'

Kitty laughed, but Jason could tell she didn't mean it. 'I went as a student with some friends. We were doing Classics. We thought we were the first ones to discover Greece.' She took a sip of wine and stared at the wall, 'God, that seems a lifetime ago.'

'You told Don yet?'

She shook her head, 'I'm going to be missing his reunion gig.'

There was a silence in which everyone set about refilling their glasses or playing with the silverware.

'When are you leaving?'

Kitty turned towards her agent, relieved at the change of topic. 'Saturday. They booked me on an afternoon flight, can you believe it? By the time I arrive it'll be the middle of the night and I'll have to find the hotel in the dark. You'd think they'd plan these things a bit better.'

'So, what do you think about the film?'

It took Jason a few seconds to realise Marissa was talking to him. He didn't know which film she meant. 'It's OK, nothing special.'

'Nothing is these days.'

But his mind wasn't on the conversation, or on the girls sitting across from him, but on what he'd just heard. She was going away. If he didn't do it now, he'd miss his chance. He stared up at the swirling ceiling and made his decision.

But not yet. A few drinks first.

He realised he wasn't going to get her alone; she probably couldn't remember the last time she was alone in a public place. He needed to bump into her in a corridor or lift. But there was no time for that now. He'd have to hand it to her in front of whoever was there, her agent, editor, the whole bunch of them.

He looked back down at his watch, no time for fantasy scenarios now. He told himself, ten minutes, then no matter who she's talking to he'll get up, walk over and . . .

'She's halfway through the next one,' the girl who worked with Kitty said in reply to a question he'd missed.

'I heard there were problems,' Marissa replied.

'People love rumours, you know that.' The girl tilted her head, 'Believe me, this one's going to be better than anything she's done before.'

'You know, I once sent her a draft of my novel.' It was the girl who hadn't said much up to now. Jason's heart rammed his chest. His attention swooped back down to the table. 'Before I realised I wasn't a writer but an editor, that is. It was a pretty awful take-off of what Kitty was doing. I'm so embarrassed she'll link me up with that one day.'

'I wouldn't worry about it,' Kitty's secretary replied.

'Why's that?' It was the first unprompted thing he'd said all evening.

'Oh,' she smiled, 'she gets so many manuscripts every week. If she even bothered to read them, God knows how she'd have time to do her own work.'

'What does she do with them?' He tried to keep the emotion out of his voice, but he ended up sounding like someone with a speech impediment.

'She uses them to line her rabbit cages.' She looked at the girl who hadn't said much, 'Sorry, Danielle.'

'That's OK, that's all it deserved anyway. I'm actually relieved she didn't read it.'

'Nothing personal. She doesn't read any of them. Maybe the rabbits do, who knows?'

The girls disappeared. The room fell away. He felt like people must feel in an earthquake; that first disorientating moment when the Earth shifts beneath your feet and you no longer know which way is up. He'd been so sure she would read it if he could only get it into her hands. He could still try and give it to her, but he couldn't bear the thought of her smile, her *thank you*, and the idea of his novel sitting at the bottom of a rabbit cage, being shit on and torn by small, sharp paws.

Fuck.

He couldn't understand what the girls were saying. He watched their lips move, their arms arc and circle, but he couldn't hear anything. Only the blood pounding through his ears. The rat-a-tat rhythm of his heart. The clamour of everything promised and gone.

He excused himself from the table, said he felt unwell and got up. The bag felt like a weight on his back. He took one last look at Kitty and left.

He walked through Soho. The rain was gone, but the street shimmered with reflected neon and the strobing of traffic lights. He stared down at his feet as they splashed against the ground. People passed him, their arms heavy with shopping, their faces smiling and happy, a black mirror reflecting all he'd lost. He thought of all the days leading up to this one. His plans and hopes and dreams.

When he'd seen the notice for the launch he'd known it was meant to be. That he'd been granted a last chance. Maybe if she read and liked the book, she'd pass it on to her agent. He'd spent three years trying to be a writer. He'd staked everything on it. He'd borrowed money, lost friends, mortgaged his flat. The money had allowed him to write the novel. The money was running out. Barely enough to see out the month.

He hunched his shoulders against the wind. He walked for hours, crossing and recrossing familiar streets, one minute hoping he'd bump into her as she was about to get into a cab, the next kicking himself for such groundless hope. He knew where it would leave him. He'd blown his chance like so many times before. He'd waited for the perfect moment which never came, and he'd missed all the other possible moments.

He lit another cigarette and turned down Piccadilly. At the corner of Haymarket he stopped for a traffic light when something caught his eye. He crossed the street, drawn by the vista of blue and white, so clean and precise and different from everything around him in the London night.

He stood in front of the shop window. He stared at the poster. At the sun-blasted beach and landscaped hills. The white monastery in the top left-hand corner. And if he looked really close, he could see two figures, their backs turned, hand in hand, walking along the beachfront under unfamiliar stars and, looking even closer, his face pressed up against the glass, he could make out the outline of Kitty's hair, her hand in his, the silence of an island evening, the feeling that there's no one else in the world but the two of you.

TWO

The cab dropped her off at the far end of the street, a winding foliated cul-de-sac hidden somewhere in Kew. As she got out she felt the pain in her chest. The telltale fist that closed around her heart. She took deep breaths. Palpitations rumbled, and she fought hard against the screaming voice inside her head. It was the panic and excitement, she knew. The strain of these past few hours. The dread at having to tell Don. The secret pleasure too.

How he would react to this, she didn't know. Well, maybe she did. She'd never done such a thing in six years of marriage, never been away without him, though he, of course, could be away for months at a time when his band sporadically reformed and toured.

She walked slowly up the street, the quiet houses winking with switched lights and family warmth. She sometimes thought they were the only house in the road without kids and Christmas trees. Other times she knew it was so.

She reached the gate and stood there for a moment staring at the thin yellow rivulet of light emanating from the living room.

He would rage.

She knew that. Expected it. Especially with the concert next week. The comeback he'd been waiting for. She'd promised she'd be there. Had she forgotten? No, the holiday just seemed more pressing. She would explain to him why she had to go, why when she saw the poster showing the mysterious hills, skull-like monastery and sun-blasted beach, it was like everything she ever wanted but never knew she did. He would get angry, storm out, not talk to her. The routine was familiar, she could go through it once more.

Her nose immediately wrinkled at the smell of cigarette smoke. She hated it when he smoked in the house. That's what the conservatory was for. She worried about how the smell would seep into their rugs and curtains. She could see thin tendrils of smoke creeping into the frames of pictures and yellowing the spines of her books.

She walked into the room, and there he was, on the sofa, wearing nothing but his puke-green Stratocaster, an overfilled ashtray keeping him company.

At that moment she both loved him fiercely and hated him furiously. And she hated herself for not being able to make up her mind. He was the one thing in her life she hadn't immediately been able to decide – bad for me or good for me? – and it worried her, that she couldn't have certainty, even in this.

She picked the ashtray off the sofa, upended it into the bin, then quickly wrapped the bin plastic around the ash so it wouldn't infuse the air. She bent down and kissed him on the cheek.

'Hi,' he said, raising his head, which was as big as one of those Middle Eastern watermelons she saw in the grocery shops of Queensway. She loved his head, its stature and authority. It was like something off Mount Rushmore.

'How did it go?'

He never forgot to ask her about herself, and, even though she wasn't entirely sure he wanted to know the answer, she liked him for that, for taking the time, for realising small things mattered.

'Good,' she lied.

His eyes crinkled. She called it his mole look, but she'd never told him this. He put the guitar down. Frowned. Looked at her as if searching for someone he used to know.

'Anything wrong?' It was casual but it was also not so casual.

'Why do you say that?' She looked away from him. She hated how easily he could read her.

He laughed. 'You want to tell me?'

'The usual,' she sighed. There were no secrets she could keep from him. 'I'm just so tired of it.' She sat down beside him but then noticed another ashtray. She got up, picked it off the floor, undid the plastic, scooped it and buried it. She noticed that several of the cigarette butts were much thinner than the Camels Don normally smoked. She wondered about that. Examined them, but there was no tell-tale lipstick smear. Maybe he'd had a friend round. Maybe it was just that.

She boiled the kettle, set his espresso machine to 'on' and tried to decide between the fourteen different types of herbal tea that loitered in her cupboards. She hadn't drunk coffee for years.

'Have you seen the news?' Don said, taking the espresso and lighting a Camel at the same time. She scanned his face for any change but there was nothing she could see. She wondered when would be the best time to tell him. 'You know I haven't.'

'There was a train crash in Bangladesh; two hundred dead.'

He liked pointing the worst things out to her. The horror and atrocity neatly framed by the black edges of the television screen. He loved programmes on Africa.

'I really don't want to know.'

'No, of course not.' He took a deep drag off the cigarette, and, as he exhaled, she could see the coiling snakes of smoke sneak up to blemish her books.

He turned the TV on. A woman was crying, trying to speak, but all that came out were sounds, unmediated language. The syntax of shock and disfigurement. Kitty looked away. 'For God's sake!'

He snorted, exhaling a precise amount of tobacco smoke.

'Just turn it off, please. I've seen enough.'

'Enough of what? You never watch the news, never pick up a paper. You're so scared of confronting the world you'd rather make up your own world.'

'Since when are you mister amateur fucking psychologist?'

He didn't say anything to that. His head sagged, and his chin touched the top of his collarbone as he went back to the guitar. Kitty took a sip of her tea; it tasted like boiled water with some faint flavouring scraped from the pipes. She put it down.

'I'm going to Greece.' And there it was. Unloosed between them, landing with an almost palpable plop. Don looked at her as if waiting for the punch line to some obscure joke.

'On Saturday. I need to get away.' She wanted him to say something, to react. His silences scared her more than anything. 'Did you hear me?'

He rubbed his chin. She noticed he'd shaved that morning, cut himself too.

'That's a great idea.'

It was so unexpected, it left her breathless. She was so stunned she didn't know what to say. She knew how much the gig meant to him. 'I have to go, Don, I really do.'

'A holiday would do you good.'

She wanted an argument. The Don she knew. 'Is there something wrong?' She looked at him. Wanted him to say, *please stay*, even though she knew she wouldn't.

'Why would anything be wrong?' He got up. 'You're always thinking the worst, Kitty. Sure, it would have been nice for you to come . . .'

'Like you were there for me tonight?' She couldn't resist it, and if she'd thought about it she would have held back, but now that it was out she was pleased. 'You never come to my events. Not once in the past five years, and yet you expect me to come to every little gig you play.' She felt good saying it. Good and bad. Good for herself but bad for them. It was the conversation that hovered over the edges of their marriage, from that day in the emergency room until now.

'You don't need me,' he replied, still barely raising his head from the guitar. 'You're famous. Everybody loves you. Your books sell to countries I've never even heard of.'

'That's not the point.' She was amazed at how little he really knew her and how long it had taken her to realise this.

She climbed the stairs, past their bedroom, the radio sending out wisps of melody and static, and round the corner, through the extension and into the white room. She knew Don wouldn't follow her in there. He hadn't been inside for five years. 'It's just plain morbid,' he'd told her. 'It's an excuse for you to not let go,' he'd added when that hadn't worked. But here she was.

She sat on the floor, feeling its cold prickle against her legs. There was no furniture. There was nothing but the room and her thoughts. The one uncluttered space in her life.

They'd painted the room during her sixth month. It would be perfect for a nursery they both knew the first time they saw it. The window overlooking the park. The quiet and high ceilings. The comforting sense of proportion.

A couple of months after it happened, a moving company had come and taken the cot, the mobile of spinning dogs, the blankets and the playpen. Now it was just a room.

It had taken her fourteen months to step over its threshold again. She'd often opened the door and stood staring across the border, watching the trees change colour through the window. And then, one day, she stepped in. And found that the place she'd so feared was now the only place she could find respite. Don wouldn't come in. The room was far away from the pull of the ringing phone. It was a room without memory, without a present or future.

She stared at the walls and thought about her trip. She could see the small island, the sleepy bays and rustic shops, the long walks she would take through the forested hills, the silence and peace and beauty of it all. She willed the sea and shoreline until it rippled against the white wall. Until she felt she was coming back to herself again.

THREE

They blamed it on a drifter. One of the many who surfed through the Greek Islands on a search for women and prolonged ecstasy in the summer months. He fitted the profile. He was already what everyone expected him to be.

It was over almost before it began. The newspapers had their front pages. The island got back its nights of unbroken sleep. The companies began booking tourists again. Another murder successfully solved. Nikos had arrived a few months after the arrest. It was all over by then, the island returned to its normal self.

Now he's on the promontory again. Standing in the circle of ruins again. Staring down at a body again.

Two months before, it had been a local boy. Two months before, it had been the start of the season. Now there was no doubt. Now they would have to eat their words.

The girl lies staked to the altar. It is exactly the same as before. And before that.

Last year, before he came back to the island, they found a tourist girl and then, a month later, a local boy. This year it's the other way around, but in all other respects it's the same. The centipedes. The carvings. The body torn and stitched. The faceless skull staring up into a yawning sky.

He knows it's wrong to feel like this. To stare down at the body of a young girl and be thankful the killer's resurfaced. But it provides him an opportunity. A way of settling obscure debts and uneasy years. He's been given another chance, he knows, and the fact this girl had to pay for it with her life only makes him more determined.

* * *

'Same as the last one.'

'You're certain?'

The coroner turns away from the teenager's body. He shrugs. 'What? It doesn't look the same to you?'

They're in an annex of the police station. A temporary morgue on loan from the fish market. Plenty of ice and long, flat tables. The stink of fish guts and blood mixes with the corpse smell. That sweet and sickly delicacy which will take days to leave Nikos's nostrils.

'I know it looks the same, but is it the same?' He strokes his moustache. The smell of stale cigarettes rises from his fingers. It's better than the smell of the room.

'Nothing is exactly the same.' The coroner sighs, tired and worn out from a night at the table.

Nikos checks his frustration. Breathes out slow. 'Would you say it was the work of the same person then?'

The coroner looks back down at the body of the girl as if to remind himself, but his findings are etched as deep into his brain as they are on the strip of tape wherein he records them. 'Absolutely,' he says. 'Unless, of course, it's a copycat. Someone who knew the details of the previous murders.'

Nikos stares down at the girl. The Y cut not sewn back up yet, she looks like a mannequin, dressed awkwardly in a suit of blemished skin.

'Is there anything significantly different about this one?' He's still catching up. He remembers reading the reports on the bodies found last year, a tourist and a local. About the age they should be driving in cars to dark, deserted parks, necking boyfriends, drinking under lights, making plans for the future.

The coroner's shoulders turn into each other as he leans over the body. He sniffles, takes a handkerchief out of his pocket and wipes his nose. 'I'd say this one was faster.'

'Faster?' Getting information from the coroner was harder than extracting angels from a piece of stone. Nikos understands the old man's reticence. How these are the highlights of his working life. Moving around the small islands grouped in the Aegean, how it's mostly heart attacks and strokes and lung infections. He's loathe to let this one go, like a hunter come upon a rare and fantastic lion.

The coroner stuffs the handkerchief back into his pocket. 'The two last year seemed more deliberate. He took more time over them. Same with the boy a couple of months ago. This one was quick. There was less bleeding before death. No signs of struggle at all. Maybe the killer got bored.'

'Or maybe he's just got better at it.'

The old man takes Nikos through his findings. It's all on tape, and Nikos will review and transcribe the evidence from there, but the coroner wants to show off. He doesn't want the tape to get all the credit.

His fingers are fine-boned and curved like baby bananas. The nails cut short and square. Liver spots and wrinkles create a topographic map on the old man's hands as he slowly runs them across the dead skin.

'These were made post mortem.' His fingers trace the line of incision across the girl's torso. The cut begins about an inch above the navel. It falters at first then gains precision as it spans her stomach, turning down at right angles just in front of the kidneys. The incision winds its way around the pubis and the two ends meet under the girl's sex organs.

'See where he slipped.' The coroner's pointing to the faltering line above the navel. 'It would be logical to assume that's where the killer started. He was probably still shaking from the adrenaline of killing the girl and couldn't get a good grip. He made three points of entry before he got control of his hands. See how after that the line is true, all the way down to the bottom? Once he got going he finished quickly. There's no marks to indicate he stopped.'

'He made the whole cut in one go?' Nikos swallows down the taste of the girl's fear, the look in her eyes, the sound of her screams.

'It's easy,' the coroner replies, his eyes glinting, 'anyone who can carve a roast could have made those cuts. Didn't need to have any specialist knowledge, before you ask.'

'You're saying it's the work of an amateur.'

'Well, if this is his fourth body, I'm not sure we can still call him an amateur.'

'And the centipedes?' It's the part he doesn't want to get to. The part that freaks him out the most. Murder he can handle – but this? This is beyond mere murder. This is showing-off time. Some psycho's version of installation art.

'The centipedes were all dead when they were placed inside the body. There's no eggs, no sign they were still alive.'

'Anything on the centipedes themselves?'

'I'm not an entomologist but they look like normal island centipedes to me.'

Nikos nods. He already has several of their carcasses sealed and bagged and on their way to a specialist at the University of Athens.

'Same with the mouth?'

The coroner grins. His teeth look green under the flickering fluorescent. 'Those centipedes were also dead. Stuffed deep into the throat cavity. He stitched the mouth back up with the same thread as the torso.'

'Same thread we found last year?'

The coroner nods, 'Pretty much. A different batch perhaps but the same type. Basic hardware thread.'

This is a dead end, he knows. Last month Nikos pinned his hopes on the thread. But results came back disappointing. There were no fingerprints. The thread could be bought at any hardware store or fishing supply on any of a hundred islands. Three weeks of inter-office memos and questioned shopkeepers failed to bring up any mention of someone buying a large quantity. He'll send this thread off to Athens too, but he knows it's pointless.

They've left the face till last. Even after the centipedes and the gouged-out pelvic area, this is worse. Nikos stares at the red and yellow mess of muscle and capillary. The eyes protuberant and lidless. The peeled back mocking smile and pink gums.

'Again, same as the others.' The coroner traces a bony finger under the neckline. 'He cut the throat first. Then used that aperture to peel back the skin. It's pretty easy actually, no medical skill involved, make the cuts in the right place and it's like peeling a banana.'

'Why do you think he removes the faces?'

The coroner smiles gnomically, 'That's your job, inspector. All I can say is I don't know why the killer would go to so much trouble when the victim's already dead.'

Nikos has his ideas, but he keeps them to himself. He looks down at the neck, the wide-open scarlet smile halfway down the throat. 'He cut their throat first – you're certain about this?'

'Before any of the other cuts.'

'And there's no signs of struggle?'

The coroner nods.

'Do you think he lures them up to the ruins? Or does he just wait, hoping someone will show up? Either he came up behind them, surprised them, or he knew the victims. They felt safe with him.'

'As I said, that's your end of things.'

Nikos thanks the old man. He goes to the sink, strips off the latex gloves and washes his hands three times until the soap burns his skin.

The phone call comes half an hour later. Nikos sits at a taverna smoking away the smell of death and disinfectant. He's on his third coffee when Petrakis calls. It's the call he's been waiting for and the call he's been dreading. The one he knew would come as soon as he found the body up by the ruins.

'So?' Petrakis's voice is sharp and edged, as if honed like a trusted blade. He's no longer Police Chief; Nikos has that job now. He's the Mayor. Which means he's Nikos's boss again.

When Nikos started out, a twenty-two-year-old rookie, Petrakis was the legendary police chief of Palassos, more arrests to his record than Eliot Ness. He left in a flurry of disgrace and cover-up. Five years later, he's running for mayor and wins in a landslide. By then Nikos was back in Athens, working robbery and homicide. Trying to forget everything that happened in the summer of 1974. He thought he'd never see Petrakis again, but then he thought he'd never return to Palassos either.

'So,' Nikos repeats, knowing where this conversation is heading, 'I went over the coroner's findings.'

There's the sound of clacking ice cubes on the other end of the phone, and Nikos remembers Petrakis's habit of stirring the ice in his Scotch with his fingers. 'And?'

'It's the same as last year. Same as the boy two months ago.'

Nikos hears Petrakis drawing breath, then the gurgle of the whisky. 'You can't come out and say this is the work of the same perpetrator as last year.'

'But it is.'

'Are you one hundred per cent sure?'

'Absolutely,' Nikos replies.

'Nevertheless, we can't say that. We can't admit we sent the wrong guy to prison.'

'You.'

'What?'

'*You* sent the wrong guy to prison.' Nikos flashes back to the drifter. He'd seen his picture in the Athens papers. A skinny Macedonian, out of work and haunting the beach resorts in search of easy pleasure. The previous Chief of Police, Nikos's predecessor, was under house arrest, pending trial on twenty-seven charges of corruption. Petrakis had taken over. Petrakis had extracted the Macedonian's confession.

'We needed to close this thing.' Petrakis's voice is raised a couple of notches, whether because of the whisky or the conversation, Nikos can't tell. 'People were already cancelling their bookings. We lost Thomas Cook and the Russians when the second body was found, and we still didn't have a suspect. We needed to put people's minds at ease.'

'You needed to find the murderer,' Nikos replies, his jaw clenched. 'Once you arrested the drifter, the case was dropped. You let him get away with it.'

'You know what this means now, two years in a row?' Petrakis interrupts, 'Someone's trying to tell us something. You were there too.'

'This isn't 1974.'

'I know that,' Petrakis sneers, 'but someone wants us to think it is. We need to catch him before . . . we need this contained. No press. No fanfare. This is something we have to deal with privately. When you release the information to the press this afternoon, tell them there are similarities with last year's cases but that this year's killings seem to be the work of a copycat.'

'That isn't my conclusion.'

Petrakis takes another sip of whisky. The ice cubes rattle against the empty glass. 'That's *my* conclusion, and, in case you've forgotten, I'm still your boss. You want this killer? Then play it cool at the press conference. Otherwise you'll be watching from the sidelines, got it?'

Nikos wishes he could slam the phone down but it's a mobile. He stabs the *end* button with his forefinger and places the phone back inside his jacket. He takes a sip of his coffee but it's cold and bitter.

FOUR

She was so shocked by her first sight of the island that she almost turned back towards the boat. But there were people behind her, urgent and ready to disembark; the night had swallowed the ocean, and they were tired and crabby and wanted to get to their homes, hotels, the rest of life.

The harbour was a bouquet of light and sound. Mirror balls flashed. Strobes strobed. Brain haemorrhage-inducing beats boomed from every taverna. She could feel the vibrations, tangible in the air as the heat which still covered the land even though the sun had been down for a good few hours.

In front of her, awaiting the disembarkees, were gaunt men holding up small rectangular pieces of card with names scrawled upon them and forced smiles planted on their faces. She scanned the names as she dropped her bag but couldn't see hers anywhere nor any strange variant on it which might have relieved her in its wrongness.

'Carson? Pantheon tours?' She asked a small man holding a card with *Baz* scrawled on it. He shook his head and looked away.

'Madam?' Someone was waving at her from the other side of the group of men. She sighed, relieved. Perhaps his pen had run out or he didn't know how to spell her name. She walked towards him, past the spilling passengers and fried-food stink.

'Madam, I'm afraid there is no one here from Pantheon.'

She looked at him as if not understanding at first, not wanting to.

'But I'm supposed to be met,' she said, remembering the same sinking feeling she'd had at the airport when her taxi driver hadn't shown up. 'I don't know where to go.' She repeated the sentence in Greek. Her university Greek still lived somewhere in her head. The words felt strange and newly discovered in her mouth.

The man smiled, and she thought she could see sympathy there, maybe an understanding of what it means to be a single woman alone on a strange shore.

'The name of your hotel?' He replied in English.

'The *Argo*.'

'You can get a taxi.' The man pointed to small lay-by in the road which had already filled up with a scrum of tourists. 'But you might be waiting an hour, maybe two. Only three taxis on island, so they have to make round trip.'

She nodded, showing she understood, but began to feel scared, hopeless, as if the whole thing were damned from the start.

'Lady, you can walk if you feel up to it. Only twenty minutes up the hill, your bag it has wheels, no?'

She stared back, as if to check, though she'd bought it especially for the trip and knew its wheels were good. She began to wonder if perhaps this man who seemed so understanding only understood he had an easy one here, and she thought she could see something in his eyes she didn't like.

'No taxis?' she said, almost desperately, wondering if she'd made a huge mistake and how this would all be just another adventure if Don was with her.

He shrugged.

'And if I wanted to walk, how would I go?' she asked, realising she had no option now, not wanting to stand amongst the others, broiling in the heat.

He pointed towards town. She saw a line of tavernas all draped in marquees that closed them off from this side of the harbour. Behind them, streets wound uphill, narrow and twisted as a crash victim's spine.

'You go, you go, you go . . .' he said, pointing towards the dark street and then turning his hand up as if he were trying to reach the moon which hung over the island like a dim streetlight. 'Up and up and up, then you will see the sign. The hotel is at the top of the hill. Very expensive. Good views.'

She thanked him and began walking. She looked back to see if the man was following her but he'd disappeared.

The main street consisted of identical tavernas; blackboards with misspelled English delicacies outside each one. There were shops selling sun hats and inflatables. Racks of obscene postcards twirling in the early evening breeze.

She'd thought she would come to the island and hear the plucking of *bouzoukis* and the strained singing of Greek fishermen, but instead all she could hear was the thock and scream of electronic music emanating from the dark insides of bars. Red, green and blue lights flickered and drowned out the stars. Men sat on the pavement, drooling drunk, singing football chants. The smell of fried bacon and vomit mingled and saturated the still air.

She walked by a group of Australians laughing uncontrollably. She caught something about a mangled hand, centipedes, a story from the Outback no doubt, and passed them. To her left, a man in a shiny football shirt was lying face down on the cobbles. She heard him cough and saw a thin stream of vomit escape his mouth and roll down the cobblestones. With one shaky hand he tried to extract a cigarette from a crushed packet lying next to him. She held her breath and negotiated the trolley past him and into the snaky alleyway that led upwards.

The street of tavernas seemed the only flat area of the island. Hunched on its shoulders, the land reached up towards the black sky, punctuated by the lights of houses like fallen stars.

The walk wasn't as hard as she'd imagined, the dark giving the street the impression of a much steeper angle than it actually was. She pulled her luggage behind her, the wheels bouncing and cracking on the old surface and thought about how she was going to call her travel agent first thing in the morning and give him hell. Twice now she'd been stood up, left to fend for herself, and, from the few glimpses she'd seen, the island wasn't the quiet paradise he'd attested to.

She stopped and had to gulp at the air to catch her breath. No, it wouldn't do to get angry like that now. Not when she still had a way to go.

She continued up, past windowless houses and the crackle and buzz of cicadas somewhere in the distance. The streets turned unexpectedly into blind alleys or hidden restaurants, everything stooped and broken. There was no logic or order to it, and it made her feel dizzy, her heels unsteady on the cracked cobblestones.

She finally came upon the hotel sign and followed it to the left, through a small street where the houses seemed to have collapsed into each other like shoulders turning in from a blow. She heard something scampering behind her, but when she turned around she could see only darkness where the street disappeared.

The road wound round and back up, and she was climbing again, out of breath. In the distance, bright like a satellite, she spotted the neon letters spelling the name of the hotel, and she felt ecstatic, like an explorer come upon a ruined city of such fantastic design that it stopped one dead in its tracks.

She heard something shuffling off to her right, a cat or dog, and continued now she had a beacon to guide her, a promise the hotel was indeed real and not some figment of the travel agent's imagination.

She stopped abruptly when she saw them. A group of shadows, standing in the road, drinking and laughing. She knew the type. Their football shirts glistened in the moonlight. Their shaved heads made them look like a bunch of convicts on day release. They shouted and cursed and chanted terrace hymns. They fell over and punched each other on the shoulder. She quickly turned and took a parallel street, relieved they hadn't seen her.

The road kept twisting and turning. Her heart pounding. Her breath trembling. She'd come all the way here to avoid drunken English yobs; she couldn't believe it. She kept climbing, looking back all the time, so that she didn't spot the two men until she was nearly on top of them.

She thought maybe they were locals getting ready for a night on the town and made a promise to herself to smile when they went past, searching her memory for the phrase for *good evening*.

They stopped a couple of feet in front of her. She considered turning back, running, but that was silly. The boys had probably just stopped to light a cigarette but there was no telltale sizzle of tobacco nor flash of light to calm the beating of her heart.

She straightened up, determined to walk by them, to make as if this was just another passing in the night and nothing more, but when she got to where the two men stood she saw that they'd positioned themselves so she couldn't get past them.

'Excuse me,' she said, her voice floating away on the wind.

They looked at her, their faces dappled in moonlight. Young men in their twenties, dark and stubbly, smiling as they reached out and grabbed her, holding her shoulders rigid, chuckling to themselves.

'Please,' she said, but the tremor in her voice made her ashamed.

The taller of the young men put his hand on her breast. He grabbed her shirt and pulled it roughly out of her skirt. The other man gently unclasped her hand from the suitcase and grinned.

FIVE

Friday night in Palassos. The tubercular rasp of scooters and the relentless concussion of dance music. The peeling skin and six packs. A whole day and a half before Kitty was due to arrive. Jason double-checked the press release where he'd scrawled the name of the island. Had she known he was listening at the launch? Given the name of the wrong island? He shook his head. It was exactly that kind of thinking which had stopped him from doing so many things in the past.

He had a backpack with him. A few changes of clothes, toiletries and a copy of his manuscript. In his hand he held the new Lily Lombard novel, thick as a loaf of Polish bread, spine uncracked, half the way through. He stared at the photo on the back. The strange scenes around him. He couldn't quite believe he was here. He'd booked the trip the night of the launch, before doubt and fear could get the better of him. He knew she wouldn't talk to him any other way. Their positions in life were too far apart, almost like different species, unable to communicate. He stared at Kitty's face, remembering how he'd come across *Crime Novel*, her debut, in a Notting Hill charity shop. He'd read it in the dark months after giving up the gallery, those days when he rarely went out, when the city seemed to be a mocking chorus to his failure. Reading her, he'd felt something so familiar, as if she reflected the parts of him he was unable to see. As if the words were a blinking light guiding him to safe shores. Somewhere in the second reading he'd known this was what he wanted to do. To sit in a room alone. To write these kind of novels. The Gallery had been a nightmare from the start. Too many people to deal with, too many faces to remember, too much exposure. Writing a book meant you could hide yourself from the world.

The club was small and stuck at the back of his hotel. His ears were already screaming with feedback as he hunched over his second ouzo. The club was packed and pulverised by dancing bodies, glowing with sunrays and bronzing lotion, whooping and screaming and kissing and smiling. Their jaws grinding and gurning to the beat. This was not his scene. Too loud. Too tiring. Besides, he couldn't dance. Not worth a damn. Looked like he was an electrical toy whose wires had got crossed. So he sat at a small table at the far end of the club and watched them gyrate under the stuttering lights of the dance floor. The clubbers were mostly in their early twenties and looked like any of their ilk across the world. Cultural differences had been erased, and only the hooded tops, day-glo hats and trainers made by four-year-old cripples branded them. Their faces were tight and bug-eyed. They seemed lost in a mediocre dream.

By the third drink he was feeling better, drenched in the unfamiliar night. He stopped thinking of all the reasons he shouldn't be here and started thinking about tomorrow. He couldn't wait for Kitty to arrive. He knew it was right not showing her the manuscript in London. This would be much better. He imagined bumping into her on a beach in the late afternoon . . . a conversation among the sands . . . there was something about meeting people on holiday that erased all cultural and social barriers. In London, he would be nothing to her, another aspiring writer with a handful of loose pages, but here . . .

'Your first day?'

Jason looked up, startled. A man was hovering above him. Two glasses of clear white liquid in his hands. He didn't look like a waiter.

'A drink?' the man proffered, and Jason nodded. 'Name's Wynn. Glad to meet you.'

He didn't like people sitting next to him uninvited, but a warm aniseed glow had descended, and the sound of another Englishman dressed unlike the clubbers, in a smart brown top and khaki slacks, intrigued him.

'You staying or island-hopping?' Wynn asked. His black hair, curly and skewed, rested on top of his head like a coil of snakes, continually in motion. His face was long and thin as if it had been stretched and folded then put back into place. The creases under his eyes looked like canyons seen from the windows of a plane. Moving in jerky, staccato motion, as if he were living in stop-frame time, he sat down. He passed Jason the impossibly tall glass. 'A Long Island cocktail. Can't spend your first night without trying one of these.'

They sat and talked for the next couple of hours. The drink had obliterated all sense of time and passage. Jason slipped into the kind of easy familiarity that one does on holiday when finding someone so similar to you that it almost obviated the purpose of going away.

He didn't tell him about Kitty at first. He kept her to himself. He said he was burnt out from the city and here for a rest. Sun thirsty and beach crazy. Wynn laughed and ordered another round.

'You made a good choice,' Wynn replied, swatting at the cicadas nose-diving the table. 'Don't let what happened put you off.'

Jason wasn't sure he'd heard him right. 'What did you say?'

'If you don't know then that's better. It makes no difference anyway. Would spoil your holiday. What happened, happened, and there's no reason to think it'll happen again.'

Before Jason could ask him to elaborate, a snow-white Scandinavian approached their table. She had long perfect hair and even longer, more perfect legs. 'Hi. The bartender sent me over.' Her accent sounded like something out of *Beowulf*.

Wynn smiled at her. He had such a disarming smile. A movie-star smile. The girl's shoulders immediately relaxed.

'Round the back, ask for Panos.'

She thanked him and disappeared.

Jason looked Wynn a question, but he either didn't notice or was purposefully avoiding it. Three times this happened in the next forty minutes, and he began to understand how it worked.

'Pills?'

Wynn laughed. 'I thought you'd see,' he replied while lighting a cigarette. It was unfiltered and elliptical in shape like someone had sat on it. 'Pills . . . powders . . . whatever you want.'

They sat there, table between them, sky and stars above, the smell of the Greek night drifting through Jason's senses: the thick swirls of cigarette smoke and warm spicy wind, aniseed, slowly roasting pork, mint, parsley and the wild bitter tang of burnt diesel.

It was then the idea came to him.

Or at least that's how it seemed. It could have always been there, in some form or other, a shapeless, shifting tremor which seemed to magnify and coalesce in the sharp Aegean light.

'Would you consider doing me a favour?' Jason leant forward, holding himself so he wouldn't fall, the alcohol and night burning through his veins.

Wynn smiled. 'I don't even know you.'

'That's why it's perfect.'

'You're starting to sound like that guy in *Strangers on a Train*.'

Jason laughed, nervous and drunk. 'It's nothing like that. I promise.'

Wynn moved forward, his breath sweet with aniseed and smoke. 'Well, what is it then? I'm intrigued now.'

Jason had the story ready. He'd spun it through his head these past few minutes. It seemed perfect. He downed his ouzo. His face filled with blood, and for a few seconds the world teetered and almost collapsed. 'It's nothing really. I just want to impress this woman who's arriving tomorrow night.'

Wynn looked almost disappointed. 'What, you want me to book you a romantic meal?'

Jason shook his head. 'She's not that easily impressed. I had something a little different in mind.'

'Go on. I'm listening.'

'I want you to stop her in the street. A dark, empty street. She's arriving on the evening boat.' He pulled out the copy of her latest novel. Showed him the photo on the back.

'Try and sell her some weed. Nothing physical. Nothing too threatening, please. I don't want to scare her . . . what are you laughing at?'

'You don't want to scare her?' Wynn seemed inordinately amused. Jason wondered whether it was the drink or something else.

'No. I mean it. Just hassle her for long enough that she's pissed off.'

'Then you come along and save her? Fucking knight and all that shit?' Wynn grinned. Understanding flashed through his face.

'Something like that,' Jason admitted.

'Something like that. OK. Shouldn't be too hard. She something special, this woman?'

He didn't want to tell him the truth. He could hardly voice it to himself. It sounded pitiful but he couldn't think of any other way.

Wynn lit a cigarette, pulled hard. The smell of his cigarettes made Jason want to gag. Wynn stared at him in silence. There was something mischievous about his face. 'Buy me drinks for the rest of the night and you're on.'

The music changed. The lights spun and swirled and tried to outdo the stars. Jason pulled on a fresh ouzo. 'It's a deal,' he said. 'But please, just you, Wynn. No one else. I don't want her freaked out.'

Wynn lifted his glass. The thick murky liquid looked like phosphorescent milk. He swallowed. 'No problem,' he said, his eyes unaffected by the alcohol, focused and alert.

Later, Jason stumbled back dazed to his hotel taking the long way around. The streets seemed to close in around him, and he got lost several times but didn't care because the night air was so soft and a pleasant breeze was blowing for the first time since he'd reached the island. He felt giddy and alive, his days bristling with possibilities; so different from only a couple of nights ago. It was a strange sensation, not quite unfamiliar, more like something you find in an attic, a long forgotten part of your life. He sat and stared at the sea, the black roiling silkiness, the distance, the invisible horizon.

But something was bugging him.

As the alcohol wore off, he realised what a thoughtless and stupid plan it was. This was no way to start. No way at all.

He walked back to the club. Found Wynn. Told him he'd changed his mind. He'd just approach her on the beach. Wynn shrugged. He didn't seem disappointed or relieved. No problem, he replied. They laughed at how stupid the idea had been and drank another ouzo together.

The next day he sat and sipped his frappé as the heat swirled around him like a cloud of locusts, bringing the dark with it, the horizon sealing in the sun. From where he sat in the taverna, he could see the docks; people standing, herding their suitcases, waiting for the night boat to Athens. There were men holding up name cards, and he was tempted to sneak a look, see which one was hers and pay him to take over. But something failed him. He didn't want to face her yet. He had other plans.

The night came down slow and easy, and from far off Jason could hear the distinctive sound of the hydrofoil cutting through the water. He wondered whether he'd have time to

47

order another drink before the boat docked. He'd already learned that sounds were deceptive out here on the island.

She looked both radiant and hassled as she stepped up to the gangplank. Something in his body shook. She looked like starlight and magazines. The captain put his hand around her waist, and it was so sleazy, so practised, but she brushed past it defiant.

He almost felt bad for what he was going to do.

It was strange no one had picked her up. Surely she was staying at a good hotel? But maybe she'd wanted to walk, not realising how dark it got, how treacherous the streets became as they disappeared into pools of blackness once out of the harbour.

He paid for his coffee and followed her. Just to find out where she was staying, nothing more, he told himself. He stayed behind a group of tourists and watched the wheels of her suitcase and turned when they turned, onwards, upwards, towards the grand hotels in the mountains.

He'd stopped to light a cigarette, drop back a bit now the streets were emptier. He walked slowly up the cobbled steps. He couldn't hear the drag and scrape of her suitcase anymore. Had he lost her?

He rounded the corner.

She was standing with her back up against the wall. Her face was white and drawn and full of fear. Her eyes wide and angry. Two men held her up against the wall.

Neither one of them was Wynn.

Jason heard the blood pounding in his head. He saw the men, their expressions grim and bitter. He wanted to turn and run but instead he took a deep breath and stepped forward.

SIX

They had her up against the wall. The taller man ripped her shirt open. Buttons crackled on the cobblestones. Her bra blazed blue. She shivered at the touch of his hand. The sea wind on her skin. He looked up at her and smiled. His breath stunk of fish. She wanted to cry but knew it would be the worst thing she could do and even though the impulse was strong, she held back, made her stomach rigid and waited for what was to come.

But the man was only after her money belt.

He ripped it from her body. The rough straps burned her skin.

Then she saw the other man. Walking towards them, anxious eyes, hands deep in pockets. She wondered whether he was their leader, whether they were finished or had plans to take her somewhere else.

'Hey!' The man shouted as he walked up to her assailants. She couldn't quite make out the look on their faces. They didn't seem surprised, only perhaps pissed off that their evening's entertainment was being curtailed. She couldn't move. The tall man was still holding her up against the wall. Breathing into her face. Dark and swampy, he leered and grunted, tongue flicking out of his mouth, his jaw wide and solid as a piece of ancient rock.

'Leave her alone.' The stranger said, and she felt a wave of relief pass through her when she heard his accent, knew that he was English too.

The two Greeks looked at the Englishman.

'I think you should let her go!'

She was surprised and encouraged by the command in his voice, the calm clamour of his threat.

The taller of the two assailants glared at the Englishman. He put his hand in his pocket. She was expecting the half-moon glint of a knife, but nothing came. They eyeballed each other in the dry, stuck air. The man was still holding her money belt. She thought about what had nearly happened. And how stupid she'd been trying to get to the hotel by herself.

The taller youth spat on the ground in front of the Englishman, bunched up the money belt and shoved it down the front of his trousers. The man with the jaw stuck his hand out and grabbed her jeans. She jerked back but he held tight. He winked and then, as quickly as they'd appeared, the men were gone, rounding the corner and disappearing into the black night.

'Are you OK?' The Englishman asked her. He looked relieved, but there was also something nervous and hesitant about him as if he'd been caught doing something wrong.

'You saved my life,' she replied, only realising how stupid it sounded after it was too late.

He shrugged. 'I don't know about that.' Smiling now. 'You lost your belt.'

'It's only money.' She stared at him as he lit a cigarette. His hands shook.

'Where were you going?' His voice was soft and comforting.

'I was heading to my hotel. Couldn't find a taxi.'

He reached down and picked up her suitcase. 'I'll help you get there if you want.'

She smiled. 'Thank you. Thank you for getting involved, for not walking past.'

'I thought they were going to . . .'

'I thought so too.' She began to cry. It was totally unexpected, like going down a lazy river only to find yourself suddenly careening down a waterfall.

He passed her a tissue. She wiped her eyes, feeling embarrassed and pathetic.

'I'm sorry,' she said.

'Don't be.'

He took her to the hotel at the top of the hill. They didn't speak on the way up. There seemed nothing to say in the aftermath of such an event. They climbed past the silent houses and sloped roofs. The blue doors and white walls like something from a fable. They took paths that led nowhere and backtracked, passing cafés hidden in the shadows of buildings, men sitting in the street playing backgammon, skinny cats and all-night butcher shops. There seemed no way to navigate these streets but at random as if they had been built just for the purpose of confounding outsiders. She watched the strange man who walked by her side and let the effort of climbing burn off the adrenaline which was buzzing behind her eyes.

He stood by the lobby while she checked in and got her key. He fidgeted and tried to get his nerve up.

'Would you like a drink?' he finally stammered.

'No. I'm fine, thank you,' she replied, a little too fast.

He couldn't catch her eye. He turned away.

'I just need to be alone after that,' she added, feeling his embarrassment. 'It's a small island. Let's bump into each other. We'll have that drink then.' She extended her hand. The fingers were long and perfect. 'Kitty,' she said.

He shook her hand, felt his heart shudder when flesh pressed into flesh, felt everything that was slipping away from him. 'Jason,' he replied, then turned and walked out of the hotel.

She sat on the bed shaking. A hard, soul-shuddering shake. She'd been so scared and only now did it manifest itself, twitching muscles and making her tremble. She walked over to the minibar and took out a couple of miniature bottles of

Glenfiddich. She poured them into a small plastic glass and swallowed. The whiskey was harsh, like liquid fire burning down her throat, but she welcomed it and tried not to clench her muscles when the spasms came.

After she was sick in the toilet, she brushed her teeth and poured herself another tiny bottle. She was glad to be alone. She wouldn't have wanted Jason to see that.

She opened the glass doors which led to her balcony and sat there for a while watching the lights of town twinkle and burn beneath her, the sea a great dark splurge that seemed to lap at the beach. It calmed her and reminded her what she'd come here for.

She knew she should call the police. Report the whole business and claim her insurance. She looked out to sea. A string of lights quietly crawled on the black velvet ripples. A ship heading somewhere in the night. It filled her with something she couldn't describe. She would do it tomorrow. Go to the station and report the mugging.

She felt better having made the decision not to go tonight, not realising until now how much it had weighed on her.

She had another few miniatures and felt pleasantly drunk, the evening a fast receding blur. It was so strange to be alone in a hotel room. Something about it. The bare essentials of life. The empty walls. Space enough to be yourself. Something she liked.

She stumbled back into the room when the cicadas started dive-bombing her light, and she reached for the phone and began punching in her home number.

Don would understand. She could tell him all about it, receive his commiserations and forget the whole damn incident, but, before she punched in the last number, she placed the phone back on the hook.

Don would try and convince her to come back. He would use the incident as proof she shouldn't have gone alone.

He would be sorry, yes, but he would also be secretly pleased, pleased things hadn't gone smoothly, safe in the knowledge that if he'd been there, none of it would have happened.

She realised that for once this was something she didn't want to share, and it was a new feeling, one which felt instantly right.

She'd always told Don everything that happened to her. It had become as natural as breathing. She supposed it was one of the reasons they were still together. They knew the worst about each other. They'd shared so many years that to have split up would have somehow erased those years from her life. Without him she would feel historyless, a book left unread halfway through.

And then she thought about the fair-haired Englishman, Jason, who'd saved her earlier that night. There was something incredibly romantic about it, she couldn't deny. Saving her from those men who would have done God knows what, stolen more than just her belongings. Of course, she understood how on holiday everyone seemed dark and mysterious, a possibility to explore, a new life to take, but there was also something so sad about him, like a dog lost after the rains, something in the way he moved and spoke and in the way his eyes had held hers for just a moment too long.

SEVEN

Nikos watches the mirror ball spin. Reflected in it are the faces of the dancers. Muscles rigid, they gyrate with a seriousness and determination which belies their activity. This is supposed to be fun. Or at least that's how it's sold. Watching them, nursing a whiskey and a deck of cigarettes, he's not so sure. Their faces are flabby and detached, their clothes shapeless, their eyes misty and far away. He's glad he's not a teenager in this new century. Times are harder, and fun comes at a price. Yet, they seem oblivious of all around them. The sun-smacked sea and sand, the local beauty spots, the murder of one of their own.

This is the third bar he's been to tonight. It could be the first. There's no difference between them, just the colour of the neon and the name. There are shelves stocked with cheap alcohol. A dance floor big enough to get lost in, a sound system loud and distorted, a man with pills standing in the corner.

They have it down well. He notices how one person takes the money and another handles the drugs. The chain is broken, making it harder to make a case. But he's not here to make a case. Not here to take one drug dealer off the island just so another can take his place a few hours later. The men behind the drugs are always far away. Sipping good wine in cliff-top villas or scudding through the waves on their yachts. This is the bottom of the food chain. The handshakes and loose powders, sudden smiles and frequent trips to the bathroom.

This is what he came back to the island for. This is everything he hasn't achieved.

He's been back for a little over six months. He's been watching and making notes. He remembers standing on a hill last year, overlooking Athens, Spiros, his boss, laying it out. 'You know the island. They know you. It'll be much easier than bringing in a mainlander.'

'I'm retiring in five years,' he'd replied, wondering where this was leading.

'How about two?' Spiros had shot back. 'Full pension. Two years and you're out. I need you there, Nikos.'

'Why Palassos?' He'd said, thinking back to the green hills, the blue harbour, the place he swore he'd never return to.

'We have information that Palassos is a major supply drop for neighbouring islands. Whether the stuff is being made there or it's being used as a clearing house, we don't know. The current Chief of Police is under house arrest. Too many white envelopes. He was caught taking a bribe over some land deal. I need someone I can trust and someone the islanders won't be suspicious of.'

He'd sucked on a cigarette, watched the lights of the city explode as darkness fell, and agreed. Two years on Palassos. Chief of Police. A promotion and a mission. Find out where the drugs come from. Find the source and report back.

But he'd got nowhere near the source. He'd followed mules and dealers, sweated them in the cells, but they didn't know who they were working for. The chain always seemed to dead-end. He fudged his reports to Spiros. And then, two months ago, the boy's murder – the second summer in a row now – and Nikos began to understand what it was he'd really come back to Palassos for.

* * *

He spots them just as he's about to leave and try another club. He checks the photos he's laid out on the table – there's no doubt.

He watches them dance, hold hands, swoop into kisses, and there's something that makes him want to leave them alone. Maybe they're happy. Maybe this is only the way old men see things.

But he has a job to do. Questions to ask. A killer to catch.

He orders another drink though he's already lost count. They'll be more responsive later on, he knows. Just wait for the night to drag, for the pills to crest that peak and nosedive down into the valley. He remembers reading that the KGB would always knock on doors at four in the morning, the hour of least resistance, and he suspects it applies to these clubbers just as well.

As he waits for them, he scrolls through the past few days since his meeting with the coroner, looking for something he's missed.

They identified the girl easily enough. They sent out a memo to hotel and hostel managers. Two days later they got confirmation.

They were in her room three days after the discovery of the body. They found her passport hidden under the sheets. The naivety of it broke his heart. They come here so guileless, thinking only about sun and sand, and end up on a slab under halogen lights.

Caroline McGowan. Twenty years old. There was a student card from Manchester University and an open plane ticket. They went through her things. There wasn't much to go through. There were three paperbacks. Lurid romances with pastel-shaded covers, thumbed, spines cracked, recent print-ings. A CD Walkman which felt like an ancient relic in his hand compared to the slim iPods most of the young people carried. There was a letter from home. A short handwritten note from her father, hoping she was having fun, telling her to forget everything that had happened and enjoy herself. Some changes of clothes, toiletries and a small bag containing five wraps of crystal meth.

He spent the next week flashing photographs. Not the face-less mortuary ones but copies of her smiling passport face, pig-tails and rosy cheeks. The passport had been issued in January. The photograph was probably only a few months old.

He got headshakes and bemused expressions. He got brush-offs and denials. She'd been on the island for two months but the population changed so frequently no one remembered her.

Then he'd got lucky. Two Italian boys, about to leave the island, said they recognised her. The boys giggled to each other, and it was obvious to Nikos they'd slept with the girl.

He took them in. Placed them in separate cells. Left them overnight. In the morning they were ready to talk. The sound of rats and steel doors had flushed their bravado. They told him everything. How they'd met her on the beach one night, how they'd talked. They even confessed to the drugs they'd offered her and told him how she slept with one then the other in return for a handful of pills. They were good-looking young men, and Nikos couldn't fault her taste. But the night of the murder they'd been at the *Blackout Bar and Hotel*'s monthly wet T-shirt contest. They'd got drunk and loud, and people noticed them. They were alibied by five different clubbers and two bartenders. They were shocked and sick and scared when he showed them the photos, the faceless ones, trying to pry anything loose.

Before he let them go, he made them flick through fuzzy stills, grabbed from club CCTV videos. They said they didn't see who she was with most of the time, the club was too dark and the alcohol too plentiful. And then he caught it. A short blinking movement, a tightening of facial muscles. He pressed them and threatened them, and they admitted, yes, they'd seen the girl with this other couple. They seemed to be friendly. She often sat at their table.

He looks at the photos in front of him again. Three nights dredging through the clubs and he was certain the couple had left the island. But there they were, fifty yards away from him, at the edge of the dance floor, a redhead crashed in the arms of her boyfriend.

He caught up with them outside their hotel. The sun was a sliver of orange in the Eastern sky. The air finally cool and fresh. He badged them, and they giggled, still high, still drunk, thinking this was some local's idea of a game. When he showed them Caroline's passport photo, their faces dropped as if a plug had been pulled.

He watches them now as they wait for their drinks. It's an amazing thing, seeing the drugs and alcohol drain from their faces, leaving them white and scared and young again. It was easy to forget they were only kids.

'We just thought she'd split.' The girl says. Her hair is dreadlocked, red and dirty, looks like rope hanging off a fishing boat. Her accent's slurred, East Coast American. Nikos wonders if Daddy's a lawyer or a doctor back home. He thinks of the letter he found in the dead girl's room, the spidery handwriting of an old man who'd never see his daughter again.

'How did you meet her?'

The girl cocks her head from side to side as if shaking her brain into action. 'Oh, you know,' she slurs. Her lips are chapped and cracked from too much sun, and her teeth small like a rodent's. 'You hang around long enough you meet every-one here. It's not exactly Cincinnati.'

The boy laughs. He has a straggly ginger beard clinging like moss to his cheeks and a silver hoop pierced through his bot-tom lip. His fingernails are bitten and encrusted with dirt.

'Where did you meet her?'

The boy starts to say something. The girl cuts him off. 'It was a few weeks ago. At *The Wooden Horse*. She was sitting alone. Looked kind of sad. I thought maybe she'd broken up with a boyfriend or something, so I went over and introduced myself. We had a few drinks, and then Brad said let's go back to the room and party. Caroline's eyes lit up. I remember she nodded her head rapidly. We went back to our room and . . .'

'That's enough.' The boy puts his arm on hers, a small but nonetheless effective show of who's boss. Nikos stares at him. Stares until the boy looks away.

'Listen. I don't care what you were doing up there. I don't care about drugs or sex or anything like that.'

Brad shakes his head up and down, 'Yeah, sure.'

Nikos grabs the boy's wrist, feels him struggle, clamps tight. The boy's face drains of blood. 'I don't give a fuck about that. I only want to find out who did this to her, understand?'

The American couple nod.

'But if you won't tell me everything you know then maybe I will start being interested in, for instance, what you've got in your pockets right now.'

He sees the boy shift, uneasily flicking his eyes towards his girlfriend and knows she's holding for both of them. Fucking coward.

The girl leans forward. Her eyes meet Nikos's, and, though they're dilated and dreamy, he can tell they're beautiful eyes, turquoise green and intelligent.

'We did, you know, some stuff.' Her head turns towards her boyfriend to see if he's going to stop her but he doesn't. 'There was nothing weird. I mean, we did some crank and talked all night. There was no sex, nothing like that.'

'I'm sure.' Nikos says non-committally. 'You became friends?'

'Sort of,' the girl replies, and he can hear the tiredness in her voice, the way the words scrape through her mouth. He knows he hasn't got long. In another half an hour the drugs will have worn off and the couple will be useless to him until they wake up again.

'Explain *sort of.*'

'Well, it's not like at home, you know. You become friends on holiday because you keep seeing the same people in the same places. We had nothing much in common, really. Except clubbing.'

'She was a geek,' the boy interrupts.

'A what?' Nikos says, unfamiliar with the expression.

'You know, man, a square. The kind of girl who likes to get fucked up but not too fucked up. And then when she's fucked up all she can talk about is her father back home in England. How much she loved him. How she misses her mother. A real drag, if you know what I mean.'

Nikos bites down on his tongue. He focuses on the morning he found Caroline up by the ruins. Makes that flicker on the cinema screen of his mind.

'How often did you see her?' His words squeeze out through clenched teeth and distant eyes.

'After that?' the boy replies, 'Maybe two, three times.'

'I need to know everything you know about her, and you need to know that until I know this you're not going to bed.'

Brad sighs melodramatically. 'I told you not to get involved with that skank,' he says, turning to his girlfriend.

Before he knows what he's doing, Nikos slams his open hand across the boy's mouth. He inhales as the pain rips through his knuckles. The boy's head snaps back like a cheap doll's. The lip ring hangs half off, drops of blood staining the boy's cheeks and shirt.

'Fuck,' the boy cries, but his voice is weak and broken.

'Sit down and tell me what you know,' Nikos snarls. He knows the boy's a coward. He's not going to call the manager or make a fuss. He just sits there, shaking slightly, his fingers playing with the broken lip ring.

'You cut me, man.'

Nikos smiles. 'I'm doing you a favour. You still have that lip ring on in gaol and they'll think you're a faggot. First they'll give you what they think a faggot wants, and then they'll beat you for making them do such a thing.'

The boy's eyes are wider than a stuffed toy's. 'Gaol?'

'Or you can tell me everything you know about Caroline.' Nikos picks up one of the cocktail napkins and passes it to the boy, still surprised by his own outburst of anger. Brad takes it and wipes his chin, grimacing from the pain. 'Thank you,' he mumbles, and Nikos smiles because he knows this boy isn't going to hold anything back now.

'She screwed us, man, she fucking took us.'

'It was our own fault,' The girl interrupts.

'Tell me,' Nikos whispers.

'She said she knew where to get good prices on crank. But she needed to get a decent amount together,' the girl says.

'When was this?'

'A couple of days later. I liked her. Despite what Brad says, I thought she was sweet. That's why I was a little shocked when she made the offer. We were sitting on the beach. It was still too early to hit the clubs. Brad was complaining about how much they charged for shit on the island. I said we're not in Cincinnati now. That's when she told us. Said she knew someone who was willing to lay off a quantity at a great price.'

'How much?'

'Fifty wraps. I laughed and said man, that was way too much, what would we do with all that? She was so logical, so calm and sweet. She just laid it out for us. Keep a third and sell the rest. There were always people looking to buy at the clubs. Even if we sold them at rock bottom we'd still make a profit. I didn't like the sound of it. The hassle, you know? Hanging around waiting for people to buy rather than dancing and having fun. I told her so.'

'What did she say?'

'She became quiet, sullen, like we'd just spoiled her party. Called us cowards and fakes. Eventually Brad gave her a hundred euro. After all, it was so cheap, but she never got back to us.'

'You know who she was getting the drugs off?'

The girl shakes her head.

Nikos sits back, eyes staring straight ahead, his brain fizzing and popping with this new information. That feeling of disparate ends coming together. She'd seemed so sweet, the murdered girl, but he supposed everyone did to those who didn't really know them. He would now have to dig back into the other victims' lives, unearth their secrets and shadowed hours. Learn the steps they took to their fateful rendezvous. And maybe . . . just maybe it would mean he didn't have to delve into his own past, the things he's spent his whole life running away from.

'I think he was English.'

'What?' Nikos feels the blood flow back to his skull. 'Who?'

'The guy with the drugs. I was hanging out at the *Horse* one night. I was just sitting at a table, drinking. I saw her. About a week before . . . before she went missing. She was talking to this corkscrew-haired guy. They were laughing and drinking together. He gave her a piece of paper, and they shook hands. That's all I saw, man.'

'How do you know he was English?'

Brad laughed, 'Looked like a faggot, you know? Kind of floppy. I stood next to him at the bar later on. He ordered some drinks. Had the same accent as the girl.'

EIGHT

The next day, Jason found out about the murders.

He was sitting over coffee in the bar when the owner came over and introduced himself. He sat down next to Jason as if they were old friends reunited after many missing years. His name was George, and when Jason complimented his English, he explained that he'd lived in London for many years, ran an estate agency, was pushed out of business by the dirty tricks of the brand-name competitors and came back here to set up the *Blackout Bar and Hotel*. His hooded eyes looked serious and beautiful, and his black beard made him seem more like a priest than a bartender. He wore turquoise jewelled cowboy boots and a western styled shirt. There were photos of American Indians decorating the walls of the bar, and country music played steadily throughout the afternoon.

By lunch, Jason was drunk on free ouzo, and the day seemed slightly brighter, the memories of the past further away, like islands left in the wake of one's travel. He thought about last night, how Kitty's hand felt on his, the way things had gone so smoothly and how he'd fucked it up by asking her out for a drink.

He remembered his first sight of her up against the wall. Who were those men? Was it coincidence they were there at that particular moment? Or was it Wynn?

He told George he was a writer. The word felt strange in his mouth. Not quite a lie but not really the truth either. They talked about books they both liked, Cormac McCarthy and

Larry McMurtry, George's favourites. Jason told him how, after he'd given up on the gallery, he lost himself in books, finding between their covers everything that was lacking in his own life.

'Yes, it can be like that. Writing fills the holes that life creates. Plots plug the gaps in the world.' George stared down into his drink as if the past still swirled there. When he began to speak again, his voice was clouded by hesitation and the faint trace of a long-suppressed stammer.

'I lost someone when I was very young. Someone close. I was only ten, and suddenly childhood disappeared for me. The rest of the kids, they had a few more years before the world revealed itself to them. For me, there was no going back from that moment. You sit in church and pray to God like everyone else but you're only mouthing the words. You're really cursing God. Asking him why. And then you don't even mouth the words any more. You look up at the sky, and it is only the sky.' He crushed the cigarette out as if it were to blame. He didn't even flinch when the fire burned his thumb. 'Do you think there's one moment that changes your life? That sets it off on a totally different path, like taking the wrong turn in a labyrinth?' His eyes bored into Jason's. 'Or do you think it happens incrementally, a little here and there until you no longer recognise yourself?' The cigarette disappeared into the black tangle of his beard. Merle Haggard sang about being a branded man.

They sat in silence, listening to songs about leaving women, impossible distances, devotion and doubt. Later, George bought out a tray full of small meze dishes: pink pastes and olives crinkled like the skin of old men, little green vine leaves, beans in blood-red juices and fried seafood.

'This was a good island once,' he said. It came between the dolmades and souvlaki, while he was sucking on a cigarette. 'Everyone says it about everywhere, but here it's the truth.' George shrugged, scratched his beard. 'Who knows? Maybe it's like that everywhere. I only know it was once good here.

Tourists came and enjoyed their holidays, told their friends. Then the developers started building. Put up the big hotels, the cookie-cutter clubs. Changed the face of things. Changed deeper stuff too.'

They ate slowly; the conversation followed suit. There was no way Jason could rush him, but the food was good and the coming blackness of night, better.

'When they found the body . . .' George was saying; Jason wasn't really listening.

'What?'

'Oh,' he waved his hand like he was dispersing a fly. 'Not things to talk about over a good meal.'

'I will fucking die of indigestion if you don't tell me.'

George let out a deep breath, sighed. 'Last year, they found the body of a girl out by the ruins. A Swede. Backpacker. She'd been mutilated. Then, two months later, another one, a local boy. Now it's happening all over again.'

Though the heat still blazed, Jason felt a sharp shiver of goosebumps explode under his skin, his breath turn short and sharp.

'There's a serial killer *here?*'

George stared at him as if deciding whether to go on. He looked over Jason's shoulder, then back down at the table. 'They're saying it's the work of a cult,' he whispered.

'A cult?' Jason wasn't sure he'd heard him right. 'How do they know it's a cult?'

George shrugged as if the answer to all such questions was obvious. 'They looked at the evidence, put it together and that's what it spelled out. Ritual murder. Take the Swedish girl. All her major organs were missing. They'd been precisely removed, and then she'd been stitched back up with centipedes in place of her organs. Then there was her face.'

'What about it?'

'It was gone. Not her head but only the face. Expertly peeled off as if it were nothing more than a balaclava. Exactly the same with the others. But don't look so surprised. These islands attract this kind of thing. People come. They gather and find like-minded others. This is the way it's always been here. A refuge for the crazy. For those who want to invent the world out of their own heads.'

'What kind of cult?' Jason's mouth had gone dry. He knew nothing about cults apart from what he'd read in newspaper headlines. Big splashed scare stories. YOUR CHILDREN ARE AT RISK. THE WORLD WILL END TODAY.

'A centipede cult. They found markings near the bodies. Carcasses inside the girl.'

'A centipede cult?' It sounded ridiculous. Jason smiled. 'This is a joke, right? This is what you tell all newly arrived tourists?'

George waved his arm, sweeping it across the still air. 'Centipedes. Beetles. Ach, it's all the same. The name means nothing. It's the nature of the cult that draws them. Secrecy. Dark deeds under the stars. A sense of awe. Of God. That's what they're trying to recapture.' George paused, scratching hard at his beard, the sound like a thousand cicadas vibrating. 'They arrested someone last year, but, two months ago, it started again.'

'The same MO?' Jason was surprised by his own curiosity. That quiver of fascination you get when you're driving down a road and up ahead you see black smoke billowing from the tarmac, the cherry flash and pulse of emergency lights. He thought about cloud-streaked nights and human sacrifices upon rock formations, in circles and oracles. Sea and endless sky. Goat men and the drinking of blood under the open-eyed Mediterranean sun.

'A local boy a couple of months ago and an English girl last week,' George continued, 'They'd been mutilated too. There are things in the deep interior no one talks about. Shadows and darkness.' His voice disappeared as the music roared above them, some man singing about his lost and lovely girl.

NINE

The directions she'd got from the hotel were useless. But she found it anyway. Followed the blue uniformed cops until she arrived at a small, one-storey building with a sign in Greek and English and a broken cross on top. Cops stood smoking outside, talking amongst each other, flicking their butts into an alley already overflowing with them.

Police stations reassured her. Made her feel back in control. But not this one.

She walked past the murmuring policemen and into a hallway thick with smoke and unintelligible chatter. She'd spent long hours in London, hanging out at police stations, talking to detectives, asking questions, aware they deferred to her more for her long hair than her short sentences.

But this was unlike any police station she'd ever visited. Everything looked temporary as if they were in the process of moving in or moving out. The room smelled of sweat and unwashed clothes. The walls had cracks like knife scars running across them. Faded blue angels clung to the high corners. Even with all the lights flaring, the room seemed steeped in some kind of ecclesiastical gloom as if the detectives were but figures in a faded lithograph.

She'd almost gone to the beach. Almost forgot the whole thing. It was only money, she'd told Jason last night. But it was more than that, she knew. And perhaps it was just that she wanted the comfort of known surroundings, the clatter and hum of law enforcement going about its business. Some measure that this island had rules and people who enforced them. Or maybe all she wanted was to hear the concern in someone's voice when they told her how sorry they were and how they would deal with the incident as soon as they could.

But, as she stood waiting for the desk man to ask her what she was doing there, she knew it would be none of these things.

Policemen hurried in and out, their faces pale and harried, their speech clipped and breathless. She could see that most of them were from somewhere else, their uniforms bluer and shinier than the locals'.

She told the desk man she was there to report a mugging. She wanted to speak to a detective. After an interminable moment where the man just nodded and she was certain he couldn't understand a word of English, he finally sighed, coughed something up into a folded grey handkerchief and pointed towards a row of tables where men sat hunched over phones which were like extensions of their own bodies, cradled tight against reddening ears.

She stood in the centre of this scene and took in the room around her. The walls flecked and stained with coffee. The piles of papers lying on the floor, unboxed and unlabelled. The dark whisperings of the detectives. The map on the far wall. The photo of a group of ruins, the broken columns like bones in the moonlight.

'Yes, can I help you?'

She jumped at the sound of his voice, the touch of his hand on her shoulder. She snapped away from him, remembering why she was here.

'I've come to report a mugging,' she said in her best accent. The voice she used for hotel managers and recalcitrant salespeople.

The detective towered over her, tall and thin and stooped. His cheeks were mottled by a three-day beard, his clothes rumpled and stained, the shirt hanging out. He stood there staring at her, stroking a moustache she was certain had gone out of fashion in 1977. His stare made her feel guilty in its unblinking intensity. She'd often written about policemen's stares and

68

how they affected the innocent. This was the first time she'd felt it. She was about to repeat what she'd said, wondering if the man had understood her, when he spoke.

'A mugging.' His voice was slightly accented but flat and uninflected like the speaking clock.

She'd never felt like this in front of a policeman before, guilty, unsure of herself, feeling all the words in her head racing to her defence. 'I was mugged,' she began, her tone laced with uncertainty and apprehension. 'My wallet . . .' she continued, but the policeman lifted his hand to silence her.

'Costas,' he called, and a young man put down his phone and walked over towards them.

She looked at the young man as he stood to attention. He was barely in his twenties, his eyes misaligned so that it seemed he was looking in two directions at once. His head was nodding rapidly as the older policeman said something to him in Greek. They both grinned, the young man sneaking a glance at Kitty. The detective turned and disappeared into the smoky bowels of the station.

The young policeman stared at her, still grinning. His head nodding up and down like one of those plastic dogs people put in the backs of their cars. He pointed to a desk filled with stacks of scattered papers. How could anyone work like this?

'Yes?' the young man asked, his voice sliding the words through his mouth as if they were sweets he'd just got tired of.

'I was walking up from the ferry last night. I had my suitcase . . .' she began, thinking now that she was here she may as well get it over with, when the young man raised his finger to stop her.

'Suitcase?' he stuttered, and she realised she'd been given someone who spoke maybe five words of English.

'Do you understand anything at all?' She tried to keep her voice down, to suppress the anger and frustration crawling up her throat.

Costas nodded his head then shrugged his shoulders.

She searched her memory, but she didn't think classical Greek had a word for 'suitcase'. Her phrasebook was back at the hotel. 'Hopeless,' she said and got up, her knee hitting the underside of the table, causing the other detectives to look up from their phones.

'Thanks for all your help,' she said to the room, her tone new and unfamiliar like she'd just discovered it the way you discover a skirt you'd forgotten you'd bought. The detectives smiled, nodded their heads or lit cigarettes and then went back to what they were doing. She'd come here not for justice – she knew muggers were rarely caught – she'd just wanted someone to say, *it's all right, we'll deal with it*, and instead here she was in the middle of a police station shouting at the unimpressed detectives, letting all the frustration of the past two days explode through her.

She was suddenly so embarrassed. How could she have just snapped like that? She turned and saw the detective with the moustache talking to someone by the door. She walked up to him, her legs striding long and purposeful, each step grinding against the stone floor of the station house. She wanted to explain something to him, she didn't quite know what.

He turned to her, his eyes facing the other side of the room. Someone shouted, and everyone stopped what they were doing. She was about to say something when the detective abruptly turned, ignoring her and headed into a small, dark office filled with serious-looking men in business suits.

She walked back from the station and sat in a small café. Under the marqueed darkness, the air still and solid as concrete, a futile fan spinning overhead. She kept looking up, hoping that Jason would be walking along, that they'd bump into each other like she'd predicted. The police station and moustachioed detective receded. The sun scraped them away. She began to feel different already. Not the person who'd boarded a plane twenty-four hours ago. She thought about how distance changes you. How unfamiliarity forces you to become yourself. It was strange and exhilarating to be free of encumbrances and responsibilities. Back home she always felt tethered to a leash of phone messages and emails. There was always someone to get back to, a launch, a birthday, a litany of small duties to distract you from your life.

She ate lunch quietly and without appetite and drank a bottle of mineral water. She stared at the misty humps of nearby islands, like whales breaking through the water, and wondered if she'd somehow alighted on the wrong island. To her left, two donkeys, tied to a lamppost, stood stoically in the heat, flies spotting their muzzles like black freckles. Their owner tried to entice passing tourists for a ride, hitting the donkeys with a switch for punctuation. The animals shied and staggered but they were hobbled, and there was nowhere for them to go. Their eyes were milky and tired. She couldn't stand their forbearance, their silent suffering, and she turned away.

Ahead of her she could see the yachts sloshing and swaying in their moorings. Great big Cadillacs of the sea, sealed and air-conditioned with all the accessories: satellite TV, Cycladian sculptures and running stock reports. She watched the servants, dressed up in white suits in the forty-degree heat, pouring drinks, emptying ashtrays, washing the bow. She couldn't think of anything worse. Even looking at the boats made her feel seasick.

She sat there and thought about Don. She'd married him a month after she'd got the deal for *Crime Novel*. They'd known each other for years. They fell into marriage as if it were a lunch date, something they felt they ought to do. And then the accident. That awful day, the worst of her life, lying in the emergency-ward bed, Don on the other side of the country, she alone with only the white walls, the white smocks of the doctors and the white emptiness inside her.

The waiter startled her out of herself, asking if she wanted anything else. He kept asking her if she needed help. She'd forgotten how over-attentive men in the Mediterranean could be.

A part of her recoiled against this, and she sent him away with a shrug, but there was also something thrilling about it, something which promised a certain enchantment. And now that she was alone . . . she wasn't sure Don ever looked at her like that any more . . . she noticed something had changed, something subtle and yet surprisingly fundamental.

'On the house, madam.' The waiter hovered over her, blocking the air from the rickety fan. He put a slab of thick, crumbly cheesecake in front of her. A cat ran under the table, brushing her bare feet. 'I don't like cheesecake,' she said, pushing the plate away.

'A drink, perhaps?' She was about to shake her head, then stopped, looked up at the waiter, seeing his face for the first time, only a boy really, and asked for a cup of coffee.

She was on her second cup when he joined her. She hid behind her coffee cup as he sat down, her heart already racing from the caffeine, now kicked into overdrive. The man smiled at her across the table. There was a bright artificial buzz in his eyes.

'You're English, right?' He asked, his voice thin and nasal and Northern. 'Me too. Name's Wynn.' He pushed his hand forward but she was still holding the cup, and she just smiled and he retracted it. She could see something in his face change. She wanted to get up. Would he follow her, do what last night's pair had only threatened to? She wondered if she'd been transported to an island of rapists and thugs.

'Don't mean to be rude or anything but least you could do is say something.'

'I'm sorry.'

'So, you do speak?'

She nodded. He kept staring at her breasts. It made her acutely aware of her own body. She felt it squirm under his heavy-lidded stare.

'I wanted to be alone.'

'Garbo, right?' Wynn smiled at her. His teeth were as yellow as the nicotine-stained fingers of her father.

'I wasn't quoting.' She needed to take control of the situation. She didn't know why he'd sat here. What did he want? She looked around. The waiters were nowhere to be seen. She was the only customer in the restaurant.

'Your first day here?'

She shrugged. She could sense things quickly spiralling out of control. She could feel the ground beneath her and the heat blasting her head. Where the hell were the waiters?

'Don't be scared.' Wynn leaned forward, and she could smell his breath, sweet and sickly like the flesh of a papaya. 'I was only trying to be friendly. In a strange land and all that.'

'This is Greece.'

Wynn shook his head. 'This is the islands, love, and there's a big difference.'

The word *love* felt like a hand crawling up her back.

'What is it you do?'

The question surprised her. She thought about lying, telling him she was an accountant, something that would stop conversation dead.

'I'm a writer.'

Wynn smiled, but he didn't seem surprised like people normally were. 'What kind?'

'Crime fiction.'

Wynn lit a cigarette, leaned towards her. 'Wow. You must have trouble with stalkers and crazy fans, right?'

Despite the heat, she shivered. 'No more than anyone.'

Wynn stared at her. Shook his head. 'Must make you really paranoid when people like me approach you.'

'It's not the first thing I think of.'

Wynn smiled. 'Maybe you should. Not everyone's who they appear to be. Things that at first sight seem accidental can prove to be quite the opposite if you take a closer look.'

She grabbed her notes, put them in her bag, upset by Wynn's overfamiliarity. 'Thank you for the advice.'

'I suppose you're here to write about the cult?' Wynn continued, startling her. 'The island's glorious history and all that?'

She looked up at him bemused, but, for the first time that day, also a little intrigued.

'You don't know what I'm talking about, do you?' Wynn laughed. 'They don't put that in your guidebooks, and thirty-three years . . . guess that's still a bit too close to be called history.' He crushed his cigarette. 'You have wonderful legs.'

She blushed.

Wynn smiled. 'Sorry, if I'm intruding. Don't mean to be. Just you looked very sad sitting out here and I thought . . . maybe . . . well, never mind. Really, that was all. Just wanted to see if you were OK.'

His smile disarmed her. What could she say?

'No problem,' Wynn said, getting up. 'And you really do have gorgeous legs. You ever need any help, come and see me,' he added. 'There's some strange people on this island.'

Who did he mean? Was he talking about the men from last night or just trying to freak her out? She hated the way she thought, always through the dark glass of suspicion. 'Thank you,' she replied and watched Wynn smile his dazzling smile as he turned and disappeared into the glare of the sun.

She got up from the table and walked in a daze through town. There seemed to be nothing more than tavernas trying to be English cafés and souvenir shops selling the same tacky items. It depressed her. The white buildings reflected the heat. The uneven pavements made her stumble. Everything was old and cracked, patched and mended but yet scarred with memories of past violences and upheavals. As if the whole island itself was a ruin, battered by wind and time.

She noticed photos of young men and women pinned to the side of shops and curled around lamp-posts. The images faded and ghostly from the endless sun. She couldn't read the words any more, but she knew what they said. The last refuge and hope of families. The human equivalent of lost-dog posters.

Soon the small tavernas and grocery shops thinned out, and she passed a row of boarded-up businesses and hotels, failure writ in their very stones and broken windows. She continued to the beach and took off her flip-flops and walked barefoot on the hot sand. She liked the friction the sand caused as it rushed between her toes, and the sea smelled the way the sea was supposed to smell. Kelp and old plastic bags washed up on the shore and stuck to small rocks, strange fish darted in the green shallows. The beach was deserted, no one crazy enough to be out here in the full heat of the sun. The island had become a ghost town, and it felt as if she were the only person left.

She was walking back into town when she saw them.

She stopped and held her breath. The man who'd introduced himself as Wynn was standing outside a restaurant. But it was the other man who caught her interest.

The two of them were talking as if old friends. Then there was a quick shuffle of hands, and they parted. She stood there unable to move. Then she followed Jason.

TEN

He heard someone coming up behind him. He was carrying a small amount of weed in his pocket. Listening and watching for cops. He jumped when he heard footsteps.

He smiled, but Kitty didn't smile back.

'What were you doing with Wynn?' She stopped in front of him, her mouth pursed tightly, her eyes cold as blue ice.

How did she know who Wynn was? His name? A thousand questions flashed through Jason's head. Had Wynn talked to her, and, if he had, did he mention the little favour he did or didn't do? Was she going to have him arrested? Tell him she never wanted to see him again? Jason decided to go with the truth. Well, part if it anyway.

'He sold me some weed.' His voice was almost unrecognisable to him.

'You smoke that stuff?'

'It's not exactly crack.'

Her face was unreadable. Something flickered behind her eyes. Was this the last time he'd see her? The mention of drugs hadn't gone down well. He was about to apologise, make up some excuse, when she said, 'I don't suppose you'd be up for that coffee now?'

They sat under the shade of a huge tarp. The sun kept at bay for a while. Jason's head throbbed and screamed. He couldn't look Kitty in the eye. He thought about how different this scene would be if he hadn't met Wynn that first night. How easy and innocent and full of promise. But it was inside him, gnawing away like a parasite, casting a dark stain on everything.

He watched the tourists crowded around the surrounding tables. Their beer bottles reflecting green light. They complained about the food and locals. They laughed loudly and spat on the floor. They wore their tattoos and football shirts like primitives from another era, their women quiet and acquiescent behind them. They had no secrets to tear them from this moment.

Kitty told Jason about Wynn sitting at her table, harassing her. She didn't mention him saying anything about that first night.

'Probably just seeing if you were a customer,' Jason said, which seemed to relieve her. While Kitty ordered, he wondered what Wynn had really wanted.

'So, did you go to the police?'

She looked up over her coffee. There was a certain apprehension in her face, something he couldn't quite read. 'It was a waste of time,' she replied curtly. 'Wouldn't sully their hands with something as inconsequential as a mugging.'

Her voice was tinged with bitterness. A hardness he hadn't seen before curled her lip. He wondered what had happened.

They didn't say anything for a long time. Their chairs faced the sea, and they stared at it, silent and slick, as they drank their coffee. The ferry boats sliced through the waves, trailing foam and gulls. Jason couldn't stop thinking about Wynn. What he wanted and why. There were already too many coincidences. The men appearing the night before, Wynn sitting down at Kitty's table today. Was he watching them right now?

He'd made a huge mistake. He should have sent her the manuscript. Even at the bottom of a rabbit cage would be better than this.

He looked away. Afraid of catching her eye. He kept expecting to hear Wynn's voice at any moment, see him approaching their table, the mocking tone and snide innuendos.

'Are you here on holiday?'

Her question took him by surprise. He turned towards her and almost blurted out the truth. He almost said: *I followed you. I wanted so much to meet you, I didn't think there was any other way.* 'I came to do some work; to write. I wanted to get away from London. I thought it would be a quiet island or perhaps I thought it wouldn't bother me. I'm not so sure any more.'

He caught the change in her expression, brief as it was, when he mentioned writing.

In the silence which followed, it came to him. He remembered what George had said and knew he had to tell her. She wrote about it all the time, but here it was – real and unsolved. He wondered how she would react. A part of him wanted to shock her. To see her feel such utter hopelessness in the face of death she wouldn't write another happy ending ever again.

'What murders?' she replied, and something in her perked up, blood rushed to her cheeks, blushing them. She leaned forward. Her eyes lit up. The coldness of a few minutes before completely forgotten.

'Last year, a girl was found by the ruins, mutilated, her internal organs missing, her face peeled off. Two months later, the same thing, except a boy this time. They arrested someone and the case was closed.' She was nodding, her hair falling in and out of her face. Jason continued, snared by her stare. 'Last month, a local boy was found dead in the ruins near the monastery. No face. Another girl last week. Same MO. They believe it's a cult. The bodies had centipedes sealed inside them.'

He thought she would look horrified. He thought she would be shocked, but a strange kind of smile cut across her face. '*Now?* This, what you're talking about, happened now?'

'That's what I was told. Why?'

'I heard something happened here with a cult in the early seventies. Maybe they got it wrong. Maybe they meant this.'

And that's when he began to invent. He told her about the state of the bodies. The orange tinge to the skin. The altar. The things painted on it. The nights of terror and supplication. Finding it easy. Rolling off the tongue. Watching her draw in. The language of pain and disposal. The wonder of horror and death.

'I saw missing posters around town. You think . . . ?'

He looked up at her. He understood his time with her now relied on this. 'Yes.'

She took it all in, the sun dazzling her face. A smile formed. 'Where did you say the murders happened?'

He could see she was hooked. He wasn't sure where this story, this plot he was spinning, would lead them. 'There's an old monastery up on the mountain. Somewhere on its grounds, by some ruins.'

'There was a photo of ruins on the incident board at the police station. They looked really creepy.' She took a sip of her drink. Her eyes blazed. 'It would be kind of fun to go up there, don't you think?'

ELEVEN

It's one of the smaller clubs on the island. The dance floor only holds a hundred twirling bodies. The bar is badly stocked and overpriced. The space-age motif is at least twenty years out of date.

Nikos stands at the counter, waiting for the owner. He cracks open a bottle of Thai beer. It's only ten in the morning. He never used to drink this early. But the heat is already unbearable. The thought of having to go from club to club, asking his questions, flashing his photos. He tells himself the bartenders and managers will be more likely to talk to him if they see him breaking the rules.

He wipes the foam from his moustache and looks out across the dance floor. The cleaning squad hasn't arrived yet. There's the smell of stale beer, unwashed bodies, salt and vomit. There are crushed cans of lager dotting the floor and empty bottles standing sentry on tables. He rings the buzzer again and heads towards the booths. The soles of his shoes squelch and stick to the black and white chequered floor. He navigates around the broken bottles, lost earrings and cigarette butts. It looks more like a battlefield the morning after than a place where people came to have fun. He remembers the sole nightclub that was around when he was a teenager. People came to sit and sip wine. To dance the local and national dances. There was often a live band playing, *bouzoukis* and fiddles vying with the cicadas and wind.

He approaches the booths, and the smell of cheap leatherette floods his senses. It's the only thing that's the same as forty years ago.

He finds the fine sprinkle of granules along most of the tables. Snowflakes of coke and meth lodged in the cracks and folds of the wood. People get careless as the night goes on. He takes out his penknife, inserts the blade into one such crack. He puts his finger to the fine powder that emerges and dabs his tongue. Not coke but meth. The bitter taste burns and mixes badly with the beer.

'Hey! What you think you're doing?'

The owner's crossing the dance floor, swinging a baseball bat. His face is twisted with rage and incredulity. He stops in front of Nikos, feet placed wide apart, muscles tensed. 'I said what the hell you think . . .' and then he sees the badge.

Nikos watches the owner sway behind the bar. It's still early in the morning, and there's no music, just the intermittent buzzing of a broken fluorescent. The owner, Milos, cracks open a bottle of beer, pours it for Nikos. 'On the house,' he smiles, his teeth gold and capped and crooked. Nikos takes the beer, sips, watches the owner. He's not nervous, that's for sure. He's propped up against the bar smoking a cigar, nodding his head, making small talk. His gold medallion hangs flat on his chest. His white suit is crumpled and torn. There's the red swirl of lipstick decorating the collar. An almost-closed door leading to an office behind him. The bronzed legs of a young girl under a huge poster trumpeting the club's recent residencies. Nikos doesn't recognise any of the DJs' names. He watches as the owner tries to surreptitiously close the door with his foot, but Nikos can see the girl's painted toenails, the gold ankle bracelet, the impatient tapping of her foot.

This is his fifth bar in a row. So far there's been nothing. Blank-faced stares and rebuttals. Amnesia and total blindness. Being Chief of Police doesn't seem to impress the owners. The fact that the previous chief was currently sitting at home, wearing an electronic bracelet, doesn't help things.

The owner slides a dirty white envelope across the table. The seal is broken, and Nikos can see the red and green plumed euros nestled within. He places his hand flat on the envelope. The owner smiles.

'Last time I checked,' Nikos says, 'it was a minimum of five years for trying to bribe a police officer.'

Milos stares at Nikos. His face hardens and then cracks into laughter. 'Very funny,' he slaps the surface of the bar with his hand. 'Your predecessor had no sense of humour. I like a man who can laugh.'

Nikos reaches for the photos in his jacket pocket. He takes them out and lays each one flat on the bar. The owner looks down at the faces of the teenagers. He looks back up at Nikos waiting for the punch line.

'What is this?'

'This is what you're going to tell me about. I want to know how often these kids were in your bar. Whether they hung out together. Who they associated with and what they sold.'

'This isn't that kind of place.'

'Yeah, I can see that by the state of your booths.'

Milos looks uneasily over Nikos's shoulder. 'I never seen them before,' he says.

'Look again.'

The American couple's revelation about Caroline had opened things up. When they'd found her body, they'd thought she was another tourist, her long legs and blonde hair enough to snare her in the sights of some psycho. But the fact she was involved in the drugs trade. This was something that had to be checked out. All he needs is one connection and the pattern will begin to reveal itself.

'Maybe I see them. Maybe not. The young people all look the same to me these days.'

The flickering fluorescent makes Nikos dizzy. The beer in his hand is empty before he realises it. The teenage girl in the other room is tapping her feet to an imagined beat.

Nikos points towards the back room. 'Maybe she saw them.'

Milos looks back towards the door. 'She knows nothing. What's your problem? You have nothing better to do than

82

harass innocent businessmen? It's us who pay your salary. We never had a problem before, why you want to make trouble?'

'Things have changed. You better get used to that.'

The owner spits onto the floor. 'Nothing changes. You'll find out soon enough. You're just a hiccup. The world goes on the way it always did.'

He walks to the docks. The first boats are coming in from Athens. Disgorging more pleasure-seeking tourists, their smiles and tans luminous in the early morning light. They walk past the churches and local stalls and head straight for the faux pubs, the English breakfasts and watered-down beers. He wishes he was still in Athens. Wishes he'd never come back to Palassos, never accepted Spiros's invitation . . . but it's too late. There's nothing he can do to make the island what it once was.

He talks to stewards and old men sitting in booths selling tickets for the ferries. He flashes photos of the dead teenagers. Most of the old men shake their heads, foreigners all look the same to them, or comment on the beauty of the two girls, their blonde hair and dazzling smiles. And then he gets lucky.

It's the last of the booths selling ferry tickets. The youth behind the counter sits reading a lurid mystery, cigarette clamped between yellow fingers.

'These two I see a lot.' He points to the photos of the two local boys, nodding his head.

'What do you mean a lot?' Nikos keeps the tremble out of his voice.

'Once a week, twice a week, they bought tickets.'

'Where to?'

'Different islands. Angelos' – he points to the boy found by the ruins two months earlier – 'I kind of knew from school. That's why I remember. We always had a catch-up chat.'

'And you never saw the girls?'

The ticket-taker shakes his head, 'No, that I would remem-ber, no doubt. Very pretty. You see this?' He points to a small black hole at the top of the ticket stall. Nikos looks up. 'I take photos. I put a camera there. Every time a beautiful girl comes up, I take a snap. Something to look at when I get home.' He gives Nikos a smile that's all teeth and tongue. 'Those two I would remember.'

'You don't take pictures of the boys?'

The man shakes his hand, 'Of course not. What do you think I am?'

'And the boys, how often did you say they bought tickets?'

'Twice a week maybe. Every week.'

'Did you see them get on board the ferries or were the tickets for someone else?'

The man shrugs. 'Why buy tickets for someone else?'

Nikos thanks him and begins walking back towards the station. He'd questioned the ticket offices on the off-chance. It still didn't mean anything but the fact that the two murdered boys travelled regularly between islands is interesting.

He looks out towards the neighbouring islands, rising sleepily from the mist. The view is the same as it always was. Everything else has changed. When Spiros offered him the post he'd thought he'd come back to the island he knew. He thought thirty-three years was long enough to forget what happened.

'Hey there!'

Nikos turns around. A raven-haired girl is waving at him. She's wearing a tight T-shirt that ends just above her midriff. Denim cut-offs the size of a handkerchief. It's when he notices her painted toenails that he recognises her.

'You were eavesdropping on us in the bar?'

She smiles sweetly. 'Milos doesn't let me come out, talk to other men. He can be very possessive like that. I had to sneak out.'

'You wanted to see me?'

She nods. 'Those photos you left with Milos? I recognise them.'

Suddenly all of Nikos's attention is on this small improbable girl. 'Which ones?'

'All four. The two girls used to spend a lot of time at the bar.'

'Are you sure?'

The girl nods. 'Milos likes me to stay inside during club hours. There's nothing much to do so I watch the CCTV. It's like our own reality show.'

'They were selling drugs?'

'No, not seriously. Only to pay for their own stuff, I think. They were more like go-betweens.'

'Explain.'

'They would sit down at a table full of newly arrived tourists. Start to chat to them. As you can imagine, the boys loved them. Then they'd ask if they needed anything for the night. You see, the tourists might have been scared of getting it off a local but when a young girl like that offered them some, they stopped worrying about being busted.'

'And the two boys?'

'They were in and out. They used to go to other clubs too. I think they resupplied the dealers.'

Nikos lets this information wash through him. 'Why are you telling me this?'

The girl clicks her tongue. 'Caroline. She was nice. We talked some when Milos wasn't around. What happened to her . . . I still can't believe it. People like that, it scares me. I don't want to be scared every night I have to walk home alone.'

Nikos takes out the last photo, playing a hunch. He shows it to the girl. She immediately nods. 'The English guy, right?' she says.

Nikos takes back the photo of Wynn. 'You ever see him with any of the others?'

'Definitely the two girls. They seemed friendly. I think he was fucking them.'

TWELVE

They caught the bus to Talos. They sat in the heat-drenched atmosphere, the only two passengers, struggling to get air in the close and cramped seats. They passed ruined yards and scorched fields. Farmers who looked plucked from another century. The terrain constantly puckered and folded, a landscape made for hiding. They climbed narrow roads away from the shoreline and into the mountains, the deep interior, the heart of the island.

She'd read about it in her guidebook. A large, densely forested centre. Locals lived there. Tourists never visited. The guidebook mentioned that the deep islanders were suspicious of tourists and sometimes hostile. It warned against going without a local guide. It was easy to get lost, and help might not be forthcoming. But of the cult and what had happened on the island thirty-three years ago, there was no mention. Of course not, Kitty thought, it was a guidebook: they didn't want to put people off.

She stared at the map. The island was divided into two by a mountain. At its summit sat the monastery and ruins. The north side of the island was undeveloped, unreachable except by foot.

They climbed steadily for half an hour, the open windows bringing no relief in the stifling air. The roads were narrow and looked only recently cut from the mountain. The forest swarmed around them, the trees green and unbelievably lush, rock breaking through the brown earth like a network of scars. Darkness eclipsed them many times as the overhangs of cliff blotted out the sun.

* * *

Jason had no idea where the girl was found, but he didn't tell Kitty that. He'd been encouraged by her excitement and didn't want to disappoint her. Besides, there would be nothing to see. Just a monastery. A picture-postcard view of the sea. It would be as if they had bumped into each other by chance, two lone tourists in the middle of nowhere.

They passed no one on the way up, and the driver stopped where the road did. They were still some way from the monastery, but the rest had to be done by foot.

They followed the path through the dense forest, lost from the light, canopied by trees. They climbed in silence until they found the trees clearing, the sun and sky suddenly spilling down on them. At the head of an outcrop of rock they could see the square stone monastery which perched like a vulture on the island's shoulders.

Kitty looked up at the massive granite cross. But she felt nothing. She wanted so much to believe in something greater than the world in front of her. A mystery beyond the numinous. The way her parents had. The way they tried to teach her. She yearned for it. But it was not enough, this yearning. And belief was so far away, like love when you've never felt it.

'It's not . . .'

'Black?' she finished his thought. 'You expected it to actually be black?'

The Black Monastery. She'd read about it in her guidebook. The phrase chilled her. The way certain words took on specific resonances. She loved reading about old places, spaces of devotion and faith. Rooms which held more than their occupants. The way architecture mirrored desire.

The first monks had settled here five hundred years ago. She'd read about the sanctity which was so well preserved that trespassers were summarily executed. Then it had been sacked, like all monasteries had, and the bodies of the monks hung from the eaves. There was confusion over when it had next been anointed. There were legends of Satanic and pagan worship in the ruins of the old monastery. Demons and witchcraft. Her guidebook had laughed at that. Said these islands were full of superstition and dread. Isolation bred it. A changing world fed it.

Eventually, the new structure had been built over the old one like a shroud. Monks came again, and the island blossomed as a trade centre. This lasted until the war. The Nazis took over the building and used it as an interrogation centre. Only in the sixties did it revert to a place where monks could once again prostrate themselves before God under the harsh sun. Then, abruptly, some ten years later, the monastery was desanctified and lay empty until it was redeveloped into a tourist attraction in the mid-nineties.

When she'd read all that, she'd intended to visit, but that was for history; now she knew they were going up there to see the scene of a crime, and, although she didn't expect to find anything – it had been cleared by the police, after all – she felt a snapcharge of excitement in this mission. Something which served as a salve from the slowly pulsating town below, finally waking up, going to the bars, preparing for another long night of dancing and drugging.

A path ran up to a gate swinging lazily open. As Jason lit a cigarette, and she turned away to escape the smoke, something moved in the woods to her left. She saw a shadow, the size of a man, dart between two trees, and before she could get Jason to look, the shadow disappeared and the woods looked unmoved and untrampled as they had been for years.

'What was it?'

'Nothing,' she shrugged. 'An animal, I suppose.' She didn't want to tell him. She wasn't sure what she'd seen – it could have been anything – the heat, tiredness and stress all piling against her to produce this phantasmagorical movement, this break in the mundane which was what she so hoped to have gained from the monastery.

They walked up to the gate. The sign said, 'No Shorts, No Bare Flesh, No Photography.' They walked past it and up the paved path to the front of the monastery. They could see the twinkle of blue behind the stone wall and faraway islands across the illimitable span of sea.

A sign on the front door said the monastery was closed for the day. The door was locked. Jason stared at the padlock. Rust clung to it like scabs. It didn't look like it had been used for a long time.

They walked around the building's perimeter, trying to get a glimpse of inside, but the windows were all shut; old wooden slats where once there'd been stained glass.

He watched as she leant against the door, ear pressed up to the wood. Her face tightened in concentration. In profile, she looked like a different woman, as if there were two Kittys sharing the same body.

'Listen.' She grabbed his shoulder, pulled him closer. 'Did you hear it?' They'd circled back to the front again.

Jason leaned up against the door. At first, all he could hear was the rush of wind and roar of sea. Then . . . yes, there was something. Voices? Or just the wind again?

He knocked on the giant wooden door. Felt the sound echo through the interior. There was no reply. They looked at each other. Jason nodded. Thumped on the door again.

Nothing. He turned back. Kitty was gone. Only the sound of wind and far-off surf crashing against black rocks.

He looked down the hill. He could see her silhouette against the trees and distant mountains. He walked towards her.

'There's another path.' She was pointing to a scuffed dirt track that led from the back of the monastery.

Jason stared at the path, the way it led into the darkness and then the face of the mountain which cleaved the island in two.

'Let's follow it.'

He was about to say *No, that's stupid*, and then realised well, what the hell, it wasn't worth arguing about and the path would just tail off a couple of hundred yards into the trees anyway.

But it didn't. They followed it for a couple of minutes until they reached a large wrought-iron gate, eight foot tall, wedged into the rock of the mountain. The padlock was old and cracked but wouldn't budge.

'The footsteps disappear into a cave.' Kitty pointed past the reinforced entrance into the darkness beyond.

'It's not a cave.' He was reading the faded sign on the gate. 'It's the entrance to a labyrinth.' He tried the gate again but though it creaked and wavered, the lock held tight.

'Dead end,' she said, a smile parting her lips.

He nodded and stood in front of her.

He wanted to reach forward and kiss her. To hold her in his arms. To let the wind blow their hair into one another's until it was impossible to disentangle. Now was the moment. The suspense. The isolation. The view. The flirtatiousness of mystery. He moved a step towards her, expecting her to step back. She didn't. She looked into his eyes. He stared into hers. Took another step. One more and their lips would touch. He would only have to . . .

'Yes? Can I help you?'

They both jumped. Tore away from each other as if caught in some illicit act.

A tall man was striding towards them. Where had he come from? They hadn't heard his footsteps at all.

'You're trespassing. You shouldn't be here.'

'We came to see the monastery,' Kitty replied.

The man was dressed in black jeans and an old black shirt with a white collar. His beard dark and tangled. His body was stooped by his height as if ashamed to be closer to heaven than the rest of us. His hands were rough and dark around the nails where he'd cut himself many times. His eyes seemed lost in his face, like drowning stones.

'I'm sorry, it's closed. You will have to go back.' His voice seemed unused to speaking, as if he were still trying it out.

'Because of the murders?' Jason looked the priest in the eye. The priest didn't flinch. Didn't betray any emotion or reaction.

'Long time before that. No need for these things any more. Not enough believers to keep the place going.'

'Where does the path lead to?'

'Nowhere,' the priest replied, his words clipped and final. He crossed his arms, and his gaze became detached. 'I'm afraid the monastery is closed until further notice.'

'But we just wanted to look around.'

'Then go to a museum. This isn't a place for tourists. This isn't a place for you to snap photos and read guidebooks.' He uncrossed his arms and stared at Kitty.

'But I thought that's exactly what it was,' she replied, pointing to the signs in English.

The priest looked disgusted, as if he'd just taken a mouthful of something he didn't expect. 'You have no respect for God. I can see it in your eyes. This monastery is hereby given back to God. There will be no more tourists. Only worship and abstinence. These are the twin poles of life. Everything else is distraction.' He turned and walked off in the direction of the woods.

They sat on the stone wall which fenced the monastery from the great emptiness that stretched out to the sea below. The courtyard was built into the edge of the cliff, and a two-foot stone wall had been erected to mark the division between the place they stood and the yawning reach of the sea. Jason didn't want to think about the drop behind him. His stomach fluttered.

'They could have thrown her over.'

Jason looked around, startled. He almost lost his balance. 'What?'

'I said they could have thrown the girl's body over. Would have been a more efficient way of hiding it. It could have landed anywhere inside the canopy of trees. Or they could have buried her. There's something weird about just leaving her here. It's like they wanted her to be found.'

'Wow. You really do think like a crime writer.'

Kitty stared at him, then turned away. The silence loomed bigger than the sky. 'You know who I am?' Her voice was cold, lost on the breeze.

Jason couldn't believe he'd let it slip, cursed himself, looked away. And just when they had been so close to . . . he realised he had to say something quickly, and it had to be good. 'I recognise you from those Tube posters,' he stammered.

What could he do? Tell her the truth? That he'd stalked her, that he'd been following her all along? And what would she think then? Stranded here in the memory of another murder, lost and so far from the rest of the world. 'It took me time, I didn't think so at first, only when you started showing such an interest.'

'That obvious, is it?' She replied, and something changed in her look. He saw her muscles relax and jaw unclench.

They didn't realise they were on the wrong path until they came across the trap.

There had been two paths leading back from the monastery. They'd argued over which was the one they'd originally taken. They walked through the dark forest, side by side, run out of words, both trying to allay the creeping dread.

'Oh my God!'

Something in her voice stopped him cold. He looked to where she was pointing and saw the trap.

He moved closer to it. It was an old-fashioned animal trap made of steel, rusted and flaking, its teeth clamped down hard. Inside the trap was a single shoe. He stopped and looked around. Thought he heard something. Shadows danced through the gaps in the trees.

It was an old trainer. A woman or a child's, caught in the jaws of the trap. There was still enough light to see the blood smearing the white canvas.

He bent down by the trap. The shoe was gripped by its middle, and there was a small pool of blood on the ground below. The earth around it was darker. He'd expected to find a foot, tatters of flesh, but what he saw was worse.

Centipedes were winding their way in and out of the shoe, through the eyeholes and openings like living spaghetti. He looked up at Kitty. She'd seen them too. Her face was white and drawn. 'We need to get out of here.'

'We're on the wrong path.'

He shook his head. 'I think this was here all along, we just didn't notice it coming up.'

'No way,' she said. 'We saw it now, we would have seen it on the way up. I knew it was the wrong path.'

'Well, why didn't you say so?' He was shouting now, quickly losing his composure, feeling the night weave its way into his bones.

'You were so sure.' Her voice raised too. 'You wouldn't have believed me. Men always think they know better about these things.'

'Bullshit. Don't bring that into it. We made a mistake. I made a mistake. But it doesn't matter now. We can either go back up and take the other trail or we can keep following this one. It's got to lead somewhere.'

She stared at him and didn't say anything. She was ashamed for screaming at him, blaming him. But she was spooked. The trainer caught in the trap had made her feel like running, and the reality that there was nowhere to run to made her feel worse. 'OK,' she finally consented. 'Let's follow it. It's going down. At least that's the right direction.'

He'd nearly lost Kitty when they heard the scream.

It came ripping out of the night, bursting it open, a cry of terror, somewhere to the west, the unexplored terrain, and they stopped dead in their tracks, and then it was gone like it had never existed.

'Jesus.'

Kitty turned to him. Her face white. 'Let's get out of here.'

'What if someone's in trouble?'

Kitty hung her head. Fright turned her face bone white.

'Kitty? Shouldn't we—'

'No.' Hard as a thunderclap. 'Let's just go back to town.'

She turned away and looked towards the dark stain of the sea. 'Let's go,' she repeated, and Jason nodded, his heart heavy with relief.

THIRTEEN

The laptop hummed. Its screen as blank as the hotel walls surrounding her. She felt bad about not having done any writing
yet, not even having thought about it. Life had suddenly
become more interesting than fiction. Certainly more so than
the book she was stuck on. A string of tea masters poisoned
in the middle of traditional Japanese tea ceremonies, all the
rage in West London, with Lily pretending to be a student,
unravelling the whole mystery. Pointless, she thought, so damn
pointless, and once again felt the urgent desire to trash the
manuscript, wipe the discs and start from scratch. Her finger
hovered over *Delete* as if by pressing a button she could
change her life.

She couldn't stay in her room. The silence felt like drowning.
The blank screen was everything she hadn't done. She checked
her guidebook. Flicked through photos of fishing boats
and churches. There was no mention of a cult living on the
island in the seventies. She scanned the text again, fingers
running through the pages, until she found what she was looking for. A small paragraph describing the island's historical
museum.

She packed her notebooks and sunscreen and strolled down
to the café. Sipping her tea, she watched groups of policemen
alighting from the ferry. Or were they soldiers? It was hard to
tell, even in countries like Greece. They were dressed in a dark
blue that seemed almost military, and their expressions were as
grim and sombre as any stranded soldier's. She wondered what
the murders did to an island this small, a community closed

onto itself like a fist. The tiny fractures and changes that would take years to fully surface.

In the café, only a small group of old men sat drinking cloudy ouzo and talking, their arms flapping, a conversation only intelligible through the shapes they cast in the still air. Kitty thought the waving of their arms was like the lapping of birds, as if they were desperately trying to regain the power of flight and were shocked to find they could no longer do so.

She finished her tea, but it left her unsatisfied. Surprised, she found herself wanting coffee and could almost smell the rich aroma, feel its bitter kiss on her tongue.

But no, she'd promised herself this morning, and, even though she wanted it, she would abstain. There was strength in that she knew, strength and a certain comfort in denying your desires.

She walked through town and disappeared behind its twisting streets and overhangs. The alleys seemed to close in around her, the brilliant white cliffs of houses rising out of the cracked earth. She continued climbing, past windowless houses, the hum of air-conditioners and buzz of cicadas. She was in a part of town she didn't recognise. No shops here, only houses, asleep, siesta time. White squares stacked up against each other like a textbook Cubist landscape. Anorexic cats trying to cool down under parked cars. The far-off click-clack of backgammon pieces. Unexpected groves and withered trees. Children playing in the dust. Down below, the pulse and beat of a hundred bar stereos collided and juddered with a mechanical voraciousness. Up above, in the deserted town, there was silence.

* * *

The doors were made of thick, cracked wood and devoid of signs. They were locked. The guidebook said the museum was open all day, but the guidebook was proving to be wrong about a lot of things. Normally, she would have given up, the old Kitty, but the gruelling climb and the thought of her empty hotel room made her bang her fist against the wood. She heard the sound reverberate inside and waited. Nothing. She banged again, and, just as she retracted her hand, she heard the soft fall of approaching footsteps.

A woman said something in Greek. Her voice was faint and warped as if by the wood of the door itself.

'I'm here to see the museum,' Kitty shouted.

She heard the slow creak of a lock, and the door opened, exuding a musty smell which immediately relaxed her; the smell of old books and manuscripts.

'Please come in.'

The woman was in her early fifties, beautiful but ageing badly, with long black and grey hair which seemed to collapse upon her neck. She wore dark framed glasses and had the serious, isolated look of someone who spends more time with books than people. The woman too had a faintly musty air, as if she slept with the books she took care of.

'So few people come these days, sometimes I forget to unlock the door.'

Kitty followed the librarian through fake Doric arches and into a cool, marbled foyer. She saw a desk and an ubiquitous computer monitor, sheaves of rumpled paper, a pack of Chesterfields and a fashion magazine.

'Please, look around.' The woman returned to her table and lit a cigarette. Kitty flinched. All those books and she was smoking in here! But telling the woman off wouldn't be a good way to start. She smiled, thanked her and turned towards the museum.

It was so nice to be away from the sun and cheap tacky delights of town. So nice to be in the cool dark spaces where books lived. She passed rows and rows of volumes, their spines crawling with weird hieroglyphs and unpronounceable names, and headed towards the far room where the exhibits lay.

She walked past bejewelled armour suits standing forlornly in glass cabinets; remnants of a different time. How useless those suits would be against modern ordnance. Past paintings displaying the island's history: a ship being sunk at sea, a galleon half submerged, men swarming like rats in its eddy. Proud and wrinkled faces, almost folded they looked, of men wearing traditional costumes and brandishing guns or axes. The heroes of the island, the little sign said, describing how firebrands would give up their lives swimming out to Ottoman ships and setting charges in them. Primitive pre-twentieth-century terrorism at its most effective. The other exhibits repeated this theme of sacrifice and surrender like a leitmotif winding through the displays.

She walked around and let history submerge her. The argument with Jason, the scream on the mountain – everything dissolved as the old scratched and flaked paintings took her into their frames, their contents suggesting that, despite outward appearances, the world hadn't changed all that much.

She walked past glass cases filled with scimitars, those strangely curved swords which looked like flashes of the moon; ancient one-loader guns, creaky and waterlogged; home-made daggers, some whose blades still evinced the dark stains of their usage.

She'd always loved how history could take her out of herself, and, in those days after the accident, when she couldn't bear to see children huddled around their mothers in the Kew sunshine, she would walk the silent dead halls of the British Museum as if in a trance, as if needing those rooms as someone might need drugs, a quick hurtling to oblivion. She felt the same sensation now. It made her realise how tense she'd been since arriving – tense about what she'd left behind as much as what had occurred here. Something about coming unanchored from Don had allowed her to realise it, as if he'd been a lid which had kept her pressed down. She had a sudden flash of realisation that it was only in un-Kitty-like acts that she would find herself.

She spent an hour as if in a dream, gliding from room to room and, having started backwards, she felt the weird slippage of time as she went from mass-produced clothes and weapons to handmade, from empire to rural enclave, from Christ to the Ram.

She stared at the massive map of the island which covered one wall. Almost a perfect triangle. The long strip of beach to the south, the tavernas and clubs, and rising from it, the old town, the weathered houses and creaking doors. Then the deep forest climbing up to the promontory at the top of the mountain. It looked like a map of some fabled land, something you would find in the fly leaves of a Tolkien book.

She read about the Occupation, the reign of the generals, the coming of the leisure age. There was a wall devoted to the labyrinth. She stared at the faded photos of dark, umbilical tunnels. The sign said the labyrinth had been built sometime in the era of the Minoans. That, over the centuries, walls and paths had been added. It had been used as a meeting place for islanders during the time of the Ottoman occupation. Then by Partisans in the early 1940s. Since then, the sign said, it had been closed. Floods and earthquakes had made it dangerous. So many paths had been added, no one knew any more which was the one that led out into the sunshine.

She didn't know a lot about labyrinths – the myth of Theseus and Ariadne, of course, but not much more. She learned how labyrinths were linked to early mystery religions; how, unlike mazes, there was only one choice and that was whether to enter or not; how they were seen as a metaphor for not running away from your fears but facing them. She re-read the minotaur myth she thought she knew: how King Minos of Crete hired Daedalus to construct a labyrinth which would hide the half-animal, half-human offspring of the King's wife; how, once built, the King shut Daedalus and his son, Icarus, in the labyrinth; how Icarus only escaped by making himself a pair of wings. She'd never known the two myths were connected. How many other liminal connections were there?

She read how Theseus, the King of Athens, had to send, every nine years, a tribute of seven boys and seven girls to feed the minotaur. She thought about the victims of the recent murders. She wondered if the cult was using the natural hiding places of the labyrinth. She remembered the fresh footprints they'd seen behind the locked gate. The scowl of the priest. She traced her fingers against the neat lines on the map wondering what was happening on this island and how it was linked to the past. She turned a corner, and some of her questions were answered.

It was the last room. She'd looped back on herself and stood just to the left of the library.

There was a photo of a clearing and uniformed policemen with long sideburns and longer hair standing around looking dazed. Another photograph of the ruins. A set of bone-white columns, broken and cracked, describing a circle around a small clearing. She squinted, put her face up against the photo, but couldn't make out what lay in the centre. She read the sign below, amazed the town would not only acknowledge but actually enshrine such an event.

She scanned the paragraph of text:

Site of cult suicide in 1974. An unnamed cult was found to have committed mass suicide on the morning of 23 June. They had been living for over a year in the interior of the island, in the vicinity of the ruins. No photos exist of them and their belongings were all that was left to show of their passage.

It was an oddly poetic and yet uninformative statement. It struck her as weird. It was almost as if they were proud such a tragedy had occurred on their island. Perhaps they thought it put them in the big leagues.

Arranged carefully around the photos and text were small boxes of amber containing dead centipedes. They circled the display like an orange halo ringing some Byzantine saint. Someone had put time and care into this.

She wound her way back through the library to the office. The librarian was staring intently into her monitor, a cigarette clamped between her teeth.

'Hi,' Kitty said, her voice soft and low as the lighting above.

The woman glanced up, reached for her cigarette and placed it in the ashtray. She didn't smile.

'It's a very nice museum,' Kitty continued, not sure what to say or how to lead into it. She noticed the woman's bitten fingernails, the cuticles red and cracked.

The woman shrugged. 'It is what it is.'

'I liked the room about the cult.'

The woman looked up, examining Kitty's face. 'What's there to like?'

'I guess we can't help being drawn to such events. It's like the firebranding of the Turkish fleet you had in the first room. Big violent events make chapters of history.'

'Ottoman, actually.'

'Pardon?'

'You said "Turkish", but back then it was Ottoman.'

Though her tone was friendly, Kitty could tell this was a woman who liked to correct others. She knew it because she herself had this trait, enumerated and recalled by Don, who would goad her, telling her stuff he knew was untrue just to see her correct him.

'Wasn't this the island that Leonard Cohen settled on?'

The woman looked up from her computer, frowning. 'Hydra,' she corrected, pronouncing it with the silent H. 'That's where he lived.'

'Oh, OK. I was wondering if there was a book on Palassos? Maybe something with more about the cult in it?'

The woman frowned. 'You didn't see enough in there?' She looked back down at her computer.

'It only made me more intrigued.'

The woman crushed her cigarette in the ashtray. 'Some things are better left untouched.'

The librarian's evasiveness frustrated Kitty. 'If that's so, why even have a display?' Then, without thinking, she added, 'I'm writing an article about these islands and I want to make sure I get my facts right.'

'Your facts?'

Kitty couldn't tell if the librarian was being sarcastic. The woman shifted her eyes, looked Kitty up and down as if measuring her for a dress. 'You a writer?'

Kitty nodded, mentioned the names of a couple of her novels.

The woman switched off her monitor and turned towards Kitty. She did this weird thing with her mouth, like she was sucking the insides of her cheeks. 'What exactly did you want to know?'

'I wanted to know more about this cult. It sounds fascinating. Why did they choose this island? What did they believe in? That kind of thing.' Kitty made sure her tone was laced with naivety. It seemed to be working. The woman was more engaged than she'd been all morning. 'I was wondering if there was anything written about it I could use?'

The librarian looked up. 'Yes. There is actually. A book written by a German who lived here during those years. It includes several chapters about the cult as well as the tourism boom that came in the late seventies. A terrible old book. Fussy and pedantic but with a startling lack of insight. You know how German ex-pats get so romantic about the old days before civilisation crawled in? He was one of those. Had the book published himself. It's not something you should use: most of it is wrong.'

'I want to get the story right,' Kitty repeated. 'I could use whatever help you can give me.'

The woman nodded, having made up her mind. 'It was before my time here. I only know from the book, which I don't particularly trust, and from talking to people on the island. You know what, there's a small café four streets down, you go and get me some coffee and I'll tell you what I know, save me having to lock everything up, OK?'

She came back with coffee. She lost her way again in the twisting alleys but followed the white conical point of the church steeple protruding like a finger into the sky. She cradled the two cups as she opened the door. Something caught her eye. A flicker of shadow to her left. She turned, spilling coffee, and saw him standing there, across the street, watching her. The man with the jaw. The man who'd mugged her. She remembered the malefic smell of his breath, spilling more coffee as she quickly closed the door behind her and fell into the dark silence of the museum.

She stood in the cool hallway. She stared at the door. Would the man follow her in here? She looked down at the cracked tiles, breathing slowly, trying to stop the thoughts in her head. It was just a coincidence, she told herself. It was a small island. She looked up, and the door was still closed. She turned around and headed back to the librarian's office.

'How long have you been working here?' She asked, passing the woman her coffee. Her voice was trembling. Seeing the man with the jaw again had affected her badly, but she wasn't going to let the librarian see how much. She took deep swallows of air and concentrated on the woman in front of her. She noticed her hands again as the librarian took the cup from Kitty, so raw and mangled as if the woman was punishing them for what her life had not delivered.

'Six months. My husband comes from here though we lived in Athens most of our lives. When he came back to the island, I followed him.' The librarian gave her a raised-eyebrow salute, the kind women give to other women to signify the demands of men.

'Thought I'd hate it. Coming from a big city. But I just fell in love with the place. With the landscape, you know. The peace and quiet. After a couple of weeks, though, I got bored. The island women tend to stay inside. I saw the sign one day saying they needed a new librarian. It was either that or sit home all day. My husband, he's not so happy about this but he's got used to it. Many women still don't work here on the island.'

No, Kitty thought, not unless you count cleaning the house, cooking and taking care of the children.

The librarian took two small sips of coffee. 'But you don't want to know about me, right, you want to know about the cult . . . our big headline story.' The woman laughed, more to herself than anything else. Kitty sipped her coffee as the story unfolded, listening to the woman's voice as it echoed through the long halls of the museum.

'I don't know when the first ones came. I think in 1970 or so. Certainly we saw them more and more in Athens back then. Wide-eyed blond kids, mainly from America but from England and Northern Europe too. They had long hair and colourful clothes so they stood out. They came here for many reasons, some political I'm sure, but mainly I think it was a thrill for them, a cheap way to live in the sea and sand and get away from their responsibilities back home.

'At first, they stayed on the mainland, but I guess that was too much like the cities they came from so, eventually, they began to spread out into the islands. Some islands got reputations as good places for them, tolerant, a lot of free land, and became big hippie communities during those years. Hydra for example. Cohen, Joni Mitchell, Crosby, the whole Malibu Canyon set. Well, Palassos was less so. But even here they eventually ended up.

'I think they started out in town but it was all farmers and fishermen then. They wouldn't have been very tolerant of outsiders, let alone Americans with garish clothes, the men with hair longer than most women's. So, while there was no outright violence, I think they made it clear the hippies weren't welcome. I think that's when they began to drift towards the interior' – the woman looked up at a yellow stain on the ceiling above her – 'or maybe it was the interior that called to them. Who knows? Many went back of course, back to their universities or wars or just the rest of their lives. They were happy to sit on a beach all day and smoke weed, but living in the interior required much greater self-sufficiency. It gets cold and windy in there, there's no obvious recreation, and you have to haul everything in yourself through those mountains.

Many came in those years, some stayed a few days, others until the end.'

The woman took a long drag off her cigarette and crushed it in the ashtray. She popped another Chesterfield from the pack, angled it towards Kitty. 'You smoke?'

Kitty shook her head.

'Good thing,' the woman said, putting the cigarette to her lips. 'This will kill me. I know this. But I still smoke. Funny, huh?'

Kitty saw nothing funny about it at all, but she nodded, eagerly waiting for the woman to get back to her story. Her accent was clear and precise but her voice betrayed a certain loneliness which Kitty recognised, the loneliness of living with someone and yet being alone. It came out in conversations with strangers, an eagerness to talk and a thankfulness for being listened to seriously.

'At some point, they stopped seeing the hippies in town. Before that, every week some would come and buy provisions, hang around drinking coffee and then go back, but around this time they became totally self-sufficient.'

'When was this?'

'Oh, maybe late '73 or so. The murders occurred about six months later.'

Kitty looked up from her coffee. 'Murders? I thought it was group suicide?'

'That was later. This is something not many people talk about on the island, like they do not talk about the years of occupation. It is too raw. Some pain never goes away.' The woman shook her head, sighed. 'It was June of 1974 when a local couple found the bodies of two schoolchildren, naked and mutilated. They'd been staked to the altar out by the old ruins.

'Police from Athens were called in, detectives and the like. The two boys were both seven and from local families. It was the first time something like this had ever happened on the island. Though the police took the bodies away, the couple who'd found them had already told all the taverna men about the mutilations and centipede bites. Stories and rumours whipped through town all day. Vigilante committees were set up, local police and some of the island men decided to go and pay the commune a little visit.

'But they were too late. When they got there, the entire cult was dead. That's the story everyone tells. That's the story that goes into the history books whether it makes sense or not. You believe in remorse? Well, maybe that was it. There were thirty-five people, and each lay in his or her sleeping bag, a single gunshot to the head,' she exhaled, the words wrapped in bitterness, broken off like shards of glass.

Kitty was about to mention the recent killings when there was a bang in the next room. She jumped. A door slammed. She'd been so ensnared in the tale she'd forgotten where she was. As the librarian looked towards the door, a man entered. He was wearing a string vest and looked like he hadn't washed in months. With him came the sea breeze and a faint smell of diesel. He looked at Kitty, and she had to turn away. His eyes penetrated her like needles. He began to talk to the librarian. His voice gruff and staccato. She picked up a few words but his tone was so slurred they seemed cut off from meaning. Kitty wondered if this was her husband or someone sent by the man with the jaw. The old man kept gesturing, his arms flaying the air. The librarian didn't say anything, just nodded once in a while and did that funny thing with her cheeks. The man stared at Kitty, shook his head and walked out.

'Are you OK?' She tried to take the librarian's hand, but the woman pulled it back.

'It's nothing,' she replied, leaning back into her chair. 'Nothing at all. But this is it. That's the story. That's all I know.'

'What about the book you mentioned?'

The woman looked towards the front door, then back at Kitty. 'It sees the cult as some kind of utopian society that went wrong. The writer actually praises them for setting themselves up as self-sufficient and then tries to grapple with how the idealism which set the whole thing off could have turned into such tragedy. Needless to say he doesn't have an answer. Who does?'

'Do you have a copy of this book?'

'Sure.' The woman got up, flicked ash which had settled on her blouse and led Kitty back into the library. She looked through one of the shelves, moving books and setting off miniature dust devils. 'That's strange.' She turned to Kitty but didn't explain herself. Kitty followed her back into the office where the woman was going through an old leather-bound book.

The librarian then checked something on her computer, shook her head and frowned. 'This can't be right. It says some-one from the monastery took it out and never returned it. One of the priests.' She seemed to be talking to herself more than Kitty. 'Why on earth would they do that?'

FOURTEEN

He looks across at his wife. She's sitting at the table, shelling peas. Her fingers slide in under the flesh and peel back the skin. A scowl sits on her face but it is not a recent visitor.

'Who was she?' Nikos says, feeling the words fall through his tongue like razor blades.

Alexia looks up, acknowledges the depth of pain in her husband's eyes. Wishes their lives had begun differently, wonders where they would be if they hadn't met that day. How much easier his life would have been. The past now seems to her like something carved out of stone: you can't change it, the best you can do is turn it into rubble.

'She was English,' she replies, dropping more peas into the plate. The sound they make reminds her of the hospital monitor's constant pulse, the rhythm of living.

Nikos takes a deep breath. There are days which wait for you all your life. You know they are coming but not when. You try and prepare yourself for them but, really, you know there is no preparation and that, each year, as the lies get more deeply embedded, there is less and less chance of reprieve.

'What kind of questions was she asking?' He tries to keep his voice down, but there it is, rolling under his sentences, and, in her eyes, he can tell she's heard it too.

Alexia looks up. 'She wanted to know about the cult,' she replies, broaching the topic, the words cold and flat as a sudden slap.

Nikos exhales. This is what he's been dreading. What he spends most nights waking up from. Sometimes he feels as if he's stranded in deep water, constantly paddling to keep afloat from the rip tide of the past. 'She doesn't *know*, does she?'

His voice is almost a whisper, Alexia has to lean forward to catch it. In the silence between this and her reply she can see the past thirty-three years collapse in her husband's eyes. She shakes her head quickly. 'She said she was writing about the island.'

She watches the lines deepen in Nikos's face, the way the years have taken everything from him: his looks, his humour, his certainty in the rightness of what he was doing. 'You know what this could mean,' she says, and it's no longer a question.

'Maybe it's time.' He doesn't know he's going to say this until he does, but, as soon as it leaves his mouth, he knows it is right.

The plate with the shelled peas goes flying to the floor. The ceramic shatters, sounding like a gunshot, and peas scatter across the tiles. 'No!'

He looks at his wife and can see fear make her small and gnarled like an old root. He remembers her as a young woman, the fullness of her smile, the carefree glitter of her laugh.

He takes her hand. Kisses it and keeps it clamped in his. 'We should never have come back to Palassos,' he says, because he can't say all the other things, the things he wants to say.

She nods. 'I know, Nikki, I know . . . but it's too late. We made our choices. We have to stick to them.'

'Even if they damn us?'

She takes her hand out of his and places it on the table. 'Yes,' she replies, and there's nothing he can say to that, so he only nods. It's the unspoken agreement that's held them together but also apart these past thirty-odd years.

He looks down at the fragments of plate surrounding his feet. He's about to bend down and pick them up, but he doesn't.

She gets up and disappears into the bedroom. She'll sit there, propped on the bed, and read, this he knows, and while normally he would try and coax her out, use sweet words and sweeter promises, today, now, he lets her be, glad for the space it affords him. Space to think about things he doesn't want to think about.

Christ, he can hardly remember the man he'd been back then, just out of the academy, a rookie cop on an island where nothing ever happened.

Until it did.

And while he never quite understood what happened that night, he knows it was bad, knew it back then, and now that these things have materialised again, here in the middle of their lives, he knows he was right – something terrible had happened, and they only thought they'd got away with it.

He leaves without telling her. He slips out the back door like a thief or an unfaithful husband. He waits outside the police station until he sees Elias lock up. He waits a few minutes more, then he goes in.

At times like this, it's easy to be reminded it was once a church. With the men gone, the phones mute, the computers sleeping, it could almost be the church Nikos took his mother to on Sundays and holidays. He remembers her hand in his, so much smaller, as if she were the child and he the parent. The sense of peace and surrender upon entering. The smell of incense. The sonorous tones of the priest. But now it has a different function, and these are just memories in an old man's head. He stares at the walls, the ceiling, the dark smudges where crucifixes used to hang, but it's no use. He can't bring that time back.

He takes the key out of the secretary's desk. The island being small, the ground floor is all they need. They store files and old furniture in the basement. Since coming back to the island, Nikos hasn't seen anyone go down there. He's never had a reason to until now.

The key turns in the old lock. It sticks and scrapes against the edges but finally gives.

Nikos takes a deep breath of the musty air. He's always liked the smell of damp, can't explain it, something reassuring in its very earthiness, but today he thinks it smells of death. Which is no surprise as the basement is the old church crypt. The only part that wasn't renovated. He slips the key out of the lock and hesitantly closes the door behind him. He's plunged into darkness. Into the smell of wet earth and cold stones. He feels along the rough wall until he locates the switch. The light, when it comes on, is barely enough to illuminate the underground room.

He walks slowly down the creaking steps, testing each before putting his weight on it. The light flicks and flutters, fades and returns. He can see carvings on the walls, primitive graffiti, markings from another time.

He reaches the bottom of the staircase and takes in the crypt. To his left, there are empty niches; once holding the relics of island martyrs, they now lie empty, the stones crumbled and collapsed upon the ground. To his right is an area of broken furniture. Chairs missing legs, tables that don't stand up, rotary phones and cracked file cabinets. It's like a graveyard, he thinks, the ruins of a desk-bound civilisation.

He sees the file cabinets and boxes at the other end of the room. This is what he's here for. The island's police records, stretching back to before his time and Petrakis's time, boxed and forgotten down here. He takes the torch out of his pocket and begins to scan the writing on the boxes. It's immediately apparent they're in no kind of order. Some have only dates scrawled on their rodent-bitten fronts, others names now lost to history, others yet with only a string of numbers to mark them out. He lights a cigarette, gets on his knees and begins going through the boxes.

The dust spumes around him. The files, some of them, fall apart in his hands, the paper thin now like the skin of old people, transparent and brittle.

Above him is a fresco, the colours undistinguishable from each other. There are angels in the corners, their faces like cherubic babies, their hands small and plump. In the centre, Jesus lies crucified on a black cross. His hands are mangled and twisted in pain. His face contorted beyond recognition. The spear in his side seems to twist in the flickering light, the drops of blood trickling into a grey-earthed Golgotha.

Nikos puts the checked boxes to one side. He quickly realises the names and dates scrawled on the fronts have little or nothing to do with the contents as if all history becomes one once consigned here.

He flicks through reams of reports, badly aged photos whose subjects are no longer apparent or thin as ghosts. He hears rats scampering in the corners, the dead sound of the underground world. He can feel his heartbeat like the ticking of a clock. His hands turn black with dust as he opens more boxes but there's nothing relating to the cult or the murders of the two boys.

He gets to his feet, his legs gone dead and buckling under him, and scans the room again. He hears creaking above him. The floorboards? Or Elias returned to pick up something he'd forgotten? He stands still but there's only silence. A rat scampers across the floor in front of him, its tail obscenely white in the cloistered gloom.

He crosses the graveyard of furniture and finds an annex previously occluded filled with broken stone saints and ruined Magdalenes.

He stares at this strange gathering, the saints missing arms or legs like crash victims, their beatific expressions covered by a thick layer of dust. The Marys stare open-eyed into the blackness. Three of them, different sizes, all missing hands or feet. There's a broken cross with nails still protruding from its points, a St Nikodemos hobbled like a leper, his white face staring up from the floor. And beyond all that, more boxes.

He winds his way through the statues and past faded icons and opens the first box. In it are back issues of *Playboy*, some forty or fifty of them. They date from the eighties, and the women on the covers look strange and unappealing. He wonders whether he would have found them attractive twenty-odd years ago in their garish hair and ridiculous make-up. The next box contains receipts for coffee and stationery. He reaches for the third box and stumbles. He curses as he cuts his hand on the sheared-off face of an icon of St Cyril. Thin droplets of blood spot the saint's face.

Inside the box is what he's been looking for. Transcripts and records from 1974. The case of the murdered boys. The suicide of the cult. He's shocked to see himself in one of the photos, almost doesn't recognise his younger face, plumed by sideburns and fear. This is not who he thought he was.

There are many photos of the police entering the hippy camp. There's a younger Petrakis, muscles and moustache, a grim look to his face, his lips thin and bloodless. Photos of the ruins. Photos of the boys. The camp. The tent. The sleeping bags. The bodies. He puts them back into the box and drags it across the dusty floor. He's about to do the same with the other two boxes when he hears the door above him snap shut.

Sweat pops out across his face and neck. His heart feels lodged in his mouth. He reaches for his gun then remembers he left it back at home. He waits for footsteps, the sound of someone coming down the stairs, but there's nothing. He remembers closing the door on his way in, wonders whether it's possible it swung open. He squats there for ten minutes, breathing slowly, trying to pick up any change in sound or light. Maybe it *was* Elias coming back for something he'd forgotten, noticing the door to the basement was open, closing it. He tells himself this and stands up.

He takes the two boxes into the light. He sits on the floor and sorts the files into one box. He almost twists his ankle on St Erasmus' neck but manages to right himself. He takes the box back up the stairs with him, placing it at the top of the staircase as he slowly puts the key back into the lock and opens the door. He waits for the shot, the scream, but there's only the rushing silence of the crypt below him and the cold, damp air.

He locks the door, checks the other rooms but there's no one there.

He takes the back way out, the box nestled in his hands. He checks the street but it's empty. As he walks back to his house he's certain he's being followed. It's not something he sees but rather senses, an instinct bred from being a policeman all these years. He's been wrong before; still, it's with a feeling of relief that he unlocks his back door and takes the box into the storeroom.

He makes himself coffee, brushes the dust off his jeans and goes back to the storeroom. He unearths the old crumbling folders that contain all the case files and notes. He finds the one marked *June 1974*, lights a cigarette, and begins.

FIFTEEN

Her voice snaked through the black telephone, all whisper and stuttered breath. 'I need to see you.'

'I know. We need to talk,' Jason replied.

'That sounds very mysterious.'

He could almost hear her smiling on the other end of the line.

'It's about what we heard last night.'

The restaurants and tavernas were all closed. The main street was packed with drunken revellers bellowing football chants. For a split second, Jason thought he was back in England on a Saturday night and everything that happened on the island only a dream. But the sight of Kitty, in black dress and yellow flip-flops, brought him back into this night with its caterwauling soundtrack and Bacchanalian roar.

'Shall we risk one of the clubs?'

Her suggestion surprised him, but there was nowhere else to go at this time of night.

The Wooden Horse was built around a mirrored dance floor. Men sat at tables staring at the ground, watching the bronzed legs of miniskirted girls reflected in the dazzle of the dance floor. The music was deafening, pounding beats and piano riffs, repeating over and over. They ordered hot dogs and wine and found an alcove to sit in, sheltered from the worst of the noise.

'I'm dying to tell you what I discovered.' Kitty took a sip of wine, made a slight gesture of distaste and then decided what the hell and drank the rest of the glass. 'I went to the museum—' she began but was interrupted by a girl crashing against their table. The girl's eyes were milky and unfocused, and when she tried to apologise, the words came out slurred and broken.

Jason looked away and poured some wine, thinking this is better, hold it back, keep what he'd discovered for later. He raised his glass, 'Go ahead.'

She told him about her visit to the museum. As she described the dusty shelves and strange displays, he could tell she was pleased to have someone to narrate this to; that it was something she needed and yet never got enough of. She described the librarian even though just telling the story would have been enough, but she wanted to place him there, so he closed his eyes and listened to her voice glide effortlessly over the detonating bass and screaming dancers.

Jason thought his news would be unexpected, but it was not as unexpected as what Kitty had to say. The cult wasn't something new. There had been precedent and history, and now, thirty-three years later, it had come back, like a bad dream can sometimes come back to haunt you long after you've woken up from it.

When she told him about the dead children, he thought about the dead child in the opening chapter of her first book, and her voice stumbled a bit as she got through this part, and then she told him about the mass suicide, using details as shorelines on a map that delineated this peninsula of death. Jason wondered how much she was embellishing, certain that some particulars were far too complicated and perhaps, literary, to have been passed on to her by a woman whose first language wasn't English. But he never questioned or doubted her, for he knew the truth of the story lay not in the details but only in its resonance.

'Jesus,' he said when she'd finished.

She poured some more wine, nodded, acknowledging the strangeness of the story, the way it opened up these last few murders into a whole realm of history, imbuing them with meanings and timelines previously occluded.

'Do you think the cult's still active?' She paused as if to think, but he knew she'd already thought about this and had worked out a theory since leaving the museum.

'It's been bugging me,' she replied. 'The librarian told me all the members had killed themselves, but I'm not sure how anyone could know.'

'Know what?'

'Hippies had been coming to the island for two years, looking for the cult. Some stayed, and some left, either to another island or back home. I don't know how anyone could have kept track of how many members the cult had, so how could they know they'd *all* killed themselves?'

'And if they hadn't, then maybe they're still out there committing these current murders?'

Her teeth sparkled in the strobe light. 'Yes.'

There was a crash on the other side of the dance floor. A couple lay on the ground giggling. Dancers navigated around them, none offering a helping hand. Kitty and Jason watched as the skinny girl tried getting up, but her legs crumpled like a cheap camping chair. The boy just laughed, his eyes popping like pinballs. Two bouncers, squat unshaven men with yellow vests and black boots strode towards the fallen bodies. The bouncers said something unintelligible and began kicking the couple until finally they got up. The girl started to say something then crunched down and puked. The dancers were drugged in the sway of the beat and didn't notice. The bouncers grabbed the girl and took her off into the darkness beyond the dance floor. The boy stood there limply, his face a cartoon of incomprehension, shouting silently in the drum-and-bass drenched air.

'The whole island's so tense,' Kitty said, turning towards him, but Jason thought it was she who seemed so.

'Four murders in two years. It's not surprising. Their livelihood depends on the tourist trade. The island's getting a bad reputation. George told me only half the number of tourists booked this year compared to previous years.' He poured some more wine. The story she'd told, and what they'd seen, had sobered him up, and the wine was far better than she allowed. 'Must be worse this year,' he continued. 'They see their revenues falling, and then the murders start up again, two summers in a row. They realise they've put away the wrong man and that the killer's still on the loose. That it could be anyone.'

'You'd think after what happened to those children they wouldn't want tourists on the island again.'

'Money can be very persuasive.' This was a bad time to be a tourist on Palassos, and yet it was partly because there weren't enough tourists that the situation was like this.

'You know, you'd make a good crime novelist.' She smiled and tilted her head.

He tried to keep his face steady and his eyes neutral. He tried to forget the reason he'd originally followed her all the way to Palassos.

'So, what was it you found out?' Her voice was soft and heavy with wine.

Jason stared at the roiling tablecloth, the sashaying dancers, the silver-starred night. He moved his chair closer to Kitty's. He took a sip of wine to steady his voice.

'They killed another tourist?' Kitty leaned forward, almost toppling her glass in the rush to get to the story's punch line.

Jason shook his head. Waited a beat. 'The priest.'

'The priest? From last night?' She put the glass down. It sloshed and spilled. She didn't notice. 'But we were just talking to him,' she said, as if there was a rule somewhere that people didn't get killed after you'd just talked to them.

'George said some kids found him this morning by the sandy bay on the north side.'

Kitty looked puzzled for a second, her fingers tapping out a silent beat on the table. 'I wonder if it's the same priest.' She sat back and let the information sink through her as the light flickered blue and steady on the tablecloth, looking not so much like a rippling ocean any more but like police lights flashing behind you in the night. 'The priest just doesn't make sense.'

He didn't know what she was referring to. He looked at her blankly, hypnotised by the bare-chested dancers, the gleam of their medallions and shine of their white shoes.

'All the others were young. The priest, if that's who he was, was old. It doesn't fit the pattern at all.' There was a slightly miffed quality to her tone he hadn't noticed before.

'You're assuming there is a pattern.'

'There's always a pattern.' Her voice was filled with the authority of someone who'd published five books ascertaining this fact. 'Even if those patterns do at first seem random and meaningless to us, they're still patterns, and all patterns eventually reveal themselves.'

He knew not to argue with her. He believed in coincidence and random acts of the world. In the mystery of not knowing and our need to see patterns and read the world in paradigms whether they existed or not. But he didn't tell her this. Last night had made him realise how quickly she could flare into argument, how under that polite exterior there bubbled another Kitty. This sharing of information had drawn them together; he didn't want to ruin that.

'So, what's the pattern?'

She smiled, her eyes met his then looked away. 'Over the past two years, four people have been murdered on the island. All were under thirty. A tourist, then a local, then another local and finally, a tourist. It's too symmetrical. One of each, last year and this year.'

'Doesn't mean it couldn't be random.'

She shook her head, 'Let's leave that for the moment. Concentrate on what we know. All the crime scenes point to ritual murder: displaying centipede bodies, centipede poison and markings relating to centipede mythology. Not to mention their faces had been peeled off, which, to me, suggests a personal, intimate crime. Someone patient enough to do it properly. All four were found in the same area, by the ruins. That's a pattern, no doubt about it.'

'You seem very sure of yourself.'

His voice startled them. Jason almost dropped his glass.

Wynn leant down over their table. His breath stinking of cigarettes. One wedged in the corner of his smile. 'I didn't realise you'd talked to the priest,' he said, placing two drinks on their table. 'Compliments of the club,' he added, still standing, blocking the light from the dance floor. His eyes went from Kitty to Jason; in the artificial light they looked wild and feral like something you'd glimpse in a dark wood.

'So, I see you two met after all.'

Jason froze. It felt like every muscle in his body had been siphoned out.

Kitty stared up at Wynn's corkscrew hair and white-toothed smile. 'What did you say?' Her voice was hesitant, unsure.

'Two English people on a small island. I guess things happen the way they do.'

Jason couldn't speak. Couldn't move his lips. His hand stayed glued to the glass. Was this the last moment he'd spend with Kitty?

'What are you talking about?' She'd regained some of her confidence, her voice rising high over the programmed beats.

Wynn shrugged. 'Oh nothing, just passing the time,' he replied, grinning at Jason. 'Enjoy your drinks.' He turned and walked off into the dark.

Jason tried to get his breathing back under control. The dance floor swirled around him. The sky seemed closer and the ground further away. If only he hadn't got drunk that first night, had gone to another club, had said no . . . if only they'd met some other way . . .

'Oh my God.' Kitty grabbed Jason's wrist. Her fingers clamped tight. She was staring off into the far corner, into another booth where an older man sat, his fingers stroking a salt and pepper moustache. The man nodded at Kitty and smiled. Even in the dark Jason could see her face drain of colour, hear her breath stutter and stop.

'Who's that?' He had a sudden flash that her husband had arrived unannounced and their time together was over, but Kitty just shook her head, took a large swallow of wine and turned so that her back was facing the man with the moustache. She looked up at the stars. Then back down at the table.

He took her hand and held it gently. She stared into her glass, lost in thought. It was getting late. Jason felt drained. Wynn's sudden interruption had left him unable to connect to this moment but, as he felt Kitty's hand on his, he realised it had somehow brought them closer together.

SIXTEEN

Wynn glances down at the table, the scarred palimpsest of previous interrogations. Half-moon valleys from nails dug in tight. Stains that could be spit, coffee or blood. Names carved and scratched out.

'I asked you a question.'

Nikos looms over him. There's a cigarette in his hand and a bemused expression on his face. His fingers reach up to his moustache, then back down to his pockets as if unable to control them.

'A question you know I can't answer.' Wynn smiles, notes the way Nikos's mouth tightens and purses. He's getting to him, and that's good.

'I know you sell drugs for someone. I need to know who.'

'What would make you think that? You seen me collect payslips?'

'I see you and that's all I need to see. A piece of shit drifter like you wouldn't be doing this by himself.'

Wynn notes the detective's anger, the red rising thread within him. If he can only play this right.

'Even if I was working for someone, you think I would tell you?'

Nikos shakes his head. Side to side. Slow and easy. 'No,' he replies, 'I guess you wouldn't. I guess you're too stupid to see the big picture here. After all, if you were working for someone you could tell me who they were and get yourself out of this mess.' He waits a beat, then turns his back to Wynn.

The silence fills the room like smoke. It's all in the waiting, Nikos knows. In what you don't say. The gaps you leave.

He'd been watching the drug dealer these past few days. The American couple had confirmed his link to Caroline. The two murdered boys had bought ferry tickets every week, doing the rounds of the islands. The girl from the bar had said they'd often come in with Wynn. Every other lead has dead-ended. The past is a room he doesn't want to enter. Not yet, though he knows, deep down in that place where you keep secrets from yourself, that soon he'll have to unlock that door. And that once a door is open, everything springs out. All the lies and secrets and things hidden so well. All the years too. But maybe this has nothing to do with that. Maybe these current murders only look the same. Maybe that's the point.

Wynn had come along easy. Professionals always did. They knew the score. Knew there was no point running or ducking. Knew too that they were protected. He thinks of the phone call, Petrakis's dry and bitter tirade. The feeling swells in him, he has to grip the table, but maybe, just maybe the two things are one. Maybe he can do what he was sent to this island to do and solve the murders at the same time.

He turns and faces the table. Wynn stares at him wide-eyed and unguarded. There's a ten by eight manilla envelope on the table. Wynn hasn't looked at it once.

'Open it,' Nikos says.

'Uh-uh,' Wynn shakes his head, 'No disrespect, detective, but I'm not getting my fingerprints on that.'

Careful. Another sign of a professional. Nikos leans over, takes the photos out of the envelope. Four of them. He lays them face up on the table in front of Wynn.

Wynn looks down, flinches, kicks his chair back. 'Jesus Christ!'

'It's not him,' Nikos deadpans.

'What the fuck are you showing me these for?' Wynn moves his chair back as far as it will go. Suddenly this is real. Suddenly this is no longer about a handful of pills. The realisation hits Wynn like a blow to the head. Is he being set up? He begins spooling back through conversations that meant one thing and now mean something else. His hands start to shake. He shoves them into his pockets so the detective won't notice.

'Don't recognise your handiwork?'

Wynn snaps his head up. His cheeks are flushed and his eyes wild, trying to rest anywhere but on the table.

The photos stare up at him. Four head shots. No faces. Just teeth and gums, muscle and sinew. Eyes boring out of hollow sockets. Hair hanging limp, thick with blood.

'You think I did this?'

Nikos admits, it's a good performance. Good as any he's seen. 'The one on the left,' he says, 'we found her last week. Pretty girl. Or was. Second-year student. Father waiting for her at home.'

'Why are you telling me this?'

'Maybe you don't recognise her without her face. She worked for you, Wynn.'

Wynn's shaking his head so furiously, Nikos thinks it might snap off like a doll that's been played with too much.

'I've talked to her friends. I've talked to bartenders and DJs. They all saw her with you the night she was killed. Her friends told me she wanted them to go in with her. Buy some drugs and sell them on. This beginning to sound familiar?'

Nikos takes out another photo. The before portrait blown up from her passport. 'Recognise her now?'

Wynn's nodding. Sweat pouring down his face. 'I didn't kill her,' is all he says. He's trying to think of a way out of this. He wonders who knows he's in here talking to the police. Whether they'll believe he kept his mouth shut.

'You think that really matters? We just want a peaceful island. A prosperous island.' The words come rolling off Nikos's tongue so easily it scares him. 'We need an arrest. A conviction. People to feel safe again.' He watches Wynn take it all in, sees the composure slip from his face, the gradual realisation that the rules he plays by are not the rules here.

'I didn't do it,' Wynn repeats, his voice laced with doubt and hesitation.

'I told you. We don't really care about that little detail. You were seen with her the night she went up to the monastery. We have witnesses who'll testify to this. What did you tell her, Wynn? To meet you up by the ruins so she could take delivery of a package?'

'No.'

'We have witnesses, remember.'

Wynn's body is as taut as an athlete's before the start of a race. 'If, as you say, she was working for me then why the hell would I want to kill her?'

Nikos smiles. The hard part's over with. 'You didn't want competition. Isn't that how drug dealers work? You agreed to let her sell but you were never going to let her go through with it. You set up a meeting place, and then you wiped out a future competitor making it look like the work of a serial killer.'

Nikos picks up the other photos, spreads them out. Places his hand on the back of Wynn's head and forces it down. Wynn fights, but sitting down, physics is against him. Nikos pushes until Wynn's face is two inches from the surface of the photos.

'What about them? Did you know them too? Did they also work for you? Did they also possess entrepreneurial desires? Look at them, you fuck!'

Nikos takes his hand away. Wynn's head snaps back. His breath comes in short staccato bursts.

'Tell me who you work for, and all this goes away. I know you're not working for yourself. You're not Greek. I know how these things work. No one's going to allow a foreigner control of the island trade. You're an errand boy. A butler in chinos and sweatshirt. They give you the drugs, they set the price. You go out there and sell, recruit others.'

Wynn's shaking his head. 'That's not the way it is.'

'Bullshit.'

'You're looking in the wrong place.'

Nikos backs up from the table.

'You should be looking at who was up there at the monastery when the priest got killed.'

Nikos stops pacing the room. He turns around and stares at Wynn. 'What the hell are you talking about?'

'When that girl was killed. When the priest was killed. I was at the club. I'm always at the club. Fuck, at least forty people can vouch for me.'

'I'm not asking for your alibi, I'm asking what you meant just then.'

Wynn leans back into his seat. Flash-toothed grin returning to his face. 'This has nothing to do with drugs, detective. This isn't the fucking wild west or south central LA. You're asking all the wrong questions.'

'What should I be asking?'

'Maybe your first question should be what were the two English tourists doing up at the monastery the night the priest was killed.'

Nikos stops. He takes a deep breath. Holds it in. 'Which English tourists?'

'The writer, Kitty and her boyfriend, Jason.'

'You know this for sure?' He can't work out if Wynn is telling the truth or trying to sidetrack the investigation. His gut tells him the first, his head the latter.

'They were up there, detective. You should be talking to them.'

SEVENTEEN

She walked back to her hotel in the deep swell of the night. Jason had offered to accompany her, but she wanted to do it alone. She braced the gauntlet of waiters and post-club revellers packing the streets, bare-chested, like animals crowding a slaughterhouse. She watched their bodies twist, twirl and sweat under the artificial lights. Did they even know people were being murdered on the island? Did they care?

The hotel was cool and quiet. At the price she was paying, she wasn't surprised. Built when people still came here for ruins and history, it now stood atop the hill like a post-revolutionary palace. They didn't serve English breakfasts, there was no club, and the restaurant required shirt and tie.

She made it to the lift and then changed her mind. She was still buzzing from the conversation with Jason. The feeling they were getting somewhere. She swiped her key card and entered. The business room was just a room like her own except it had an internet connection. There were two tables, two computers and a printer.

She sat down and stared at the keyboard. She'd never liked the Internet. This chaos of unregulated and self-propelling information like an infinite labyrinth with no escape. The way it drained you of time.

The priest was dead. Jason's news had been unexpected. She'd been seeing a pattern, tracing its outlines, and now the pattern was gone. It had only existed in her imagining. Was this the same priest who'd borrowed the book on the cult? Why would a priest want a book on the cult?

She began typing.

Pages of script flashed in front of her. Greek headlines and hieroglyphs. She struggled through the words, her phrasebook by her side, the language coming slowly back to her like a dream you never really forgot.

She found two references to a missing priest. She read them slowly, trying to squeeze as much information from the four scant paragraphs which appeared, three weeks apart, on the website of a local newspaper. The first was a guide to monasteries of the islands. Dated over a year ago. The Black Monastery was listed alongside others. It praised the fine location and great views but said the building had been rebuilt so many times it was not considered a good example of island architecture. Two priests were mentioned: Theo Karelis and Laszlo Vondas. She re-read it and closed the link.

The second piece was about the missing priest.

It was dated from a year ago, 11 June. The day after he disappeared.

She read the terse paragraph. A priest from Palassos had disappeared. Theo Karelis, sixty-eight, long-time resident of the island and former abbot, had not appeared at a funeral he was supposed to preside over. A search of his flat found everything as it should be, passport, wallet and ID card all accounted for. But no priest. The matter was being treated as suspicious.

The photos were old and grainy, but the man in them was at least twenty years older than the one they'd encountered at the monastery.

She banged keys, loving the feel of pressure on her fingertips. Waited for pages to download. But there was nothing more. She pulled away from the screen and thought about what she'd read. One priest missing and the other dead. Both originally working out of the Black Monastery. Within a stone's throw of the ruins.

* * *

She took the lift up to her room. Feeling her body pulse and twitch. Paths and suppositions flooding her head like electricity. She wanted to call Jason and tell him what she'd found. She knew it was too soon. They'd just said goodbye. She didn't want to alienate him, become the constant whining presence on the other end of the phone. She would leave it until they met again.

Her room was cool, the air conditioner going full blast. She took a bottle out of the minibar, poured it into a small plastic cup, added ice and sat down at the table. She sipped her drink, was about to open her laptop, when she noticed the flashing red light of the answering machine.

Jason. Her first thought. He'd called, left a message. She felt light-headed but was sure it was the whisky. She pressed the button. Heard the tape rewind, whir and click.

But it wasn't Jason's voice.

'Hey, babe.' Don's voice sounded warmer on tape than in person; something she'd never got used to.

'Just calling to say the gig went fine. And, hey, thanks for asking.'

The long tone sounded like a spike punched into her head. The tape stopped, but she could still hear it, a thin insect whine. She rewound the tape, listened again, thinking maybe she'd misunderstood him but no, the biting tone was even more evident the second time around. It was only when she was apart from him that she could see the deliberateness of his actions, how he'd probably spent hours getting the words sharpened just right. She wanted to pick up the phone and tell him what was happening here, the mugging, the murders . . . but he would just shrug, say *Well, you were stupid to go alone.* She got up and wiped the tape. She pressed the button so hard it snapped and sprung to the floor.

She turned her thoughts to the priest. This was safer territory. She kept thinking about Don, hearing his voice, but she tuned it out, pretended he was a TV blaring from the next room. She thought about what she'd read and what it meant. She didn't believe in coincidence, and the disappearance of one priest and murder of the other was, she was certain, somehow tied to the recent killings.

She turned on the radio. A classical station. Put it down low. Took off her shoes. Her feet felt tired and old, the skin dry and cracked. She stared at her laptop. She wanted to get things down. The sequence of murders. The clues. The timelines and history. She always thought better when she had things written down. Lying there in front of her. Statistics and facts, hemmed into columns, trapped under the buzzing screen.

She swallowed another sip of whisky. She looked around the room, rubbed the circulation back into her feet and opened her laptop.

She felt it immediately. Something warm and sticky covered her fingers. She looked down. The tips of her fingers had turned black. She shook them vigorously, sending black spatters flying. She put a finger up to her nose. It smelled deep and rich. She stared at the stuccoed wall in front of her, the spatters of oil like dead flies. She looked back down and pressed the reboot button. Nothing happened. No noise. No blinking lights.

She picked up the laptop. It left behind a black puddle spreading like a tear across the table. Shiny and viscous, slowly oozing. She looked at her hands, black and sticky. She bit down on the scream coming from her throat. She got up, went to the bathroom, letting the hot water course over her hands, blackening the soap, watching the grey residue swirl down the sink.

Someone had been in her room. Were they still there? She'd checked the main bedroom and the bathroom was clear. But there was still the balcony. A cold tremor rippled across her spine. She stood, staring at herself in the mirror, willing her heart to slow down. The phone rang in the other room. She left the hot water running. By the time she got to it, the answering machine had clicked on. She stood over it, not wanting to pick up, not knowing why. The message played and then beeped. There was silence and then, faintly, she could hear breathing – soft, almost like the wind. She stared at the machine as if this would make it give up its secrets. The breathing continued for a minute and then clicked off.

Was it Don calling back? Was he on the island unbeknownst to her? She quickly deleted the message and walked over towards the balcony. She pulled the net curtain across and felt something brush against her arm. A small centipede landed on her wrist. It felt cold and wet. She shook her arm, and the centipede fell to the floor. Dazed, it swivelled its head and looked towards her, its antennae flicking wildly. She crushed it with her shoe, feeling the soft sticky explosion between her feet, the shrill whine and cracking of the exoskeleton. She went back into the bathroom and put her trainers in the tub. Let hot water run over them.

Back in the room she stared at her computer but the black pool had only widened. She needed her notebooks. She reached under the bed for her bag and pulled it out. Inside were her papers and the Lily manuscript. The bag felt light in her hands. She unzipped it, the teeth of the zip glinting like centipede legs.

The bag was empty. She stared down into it as if it were her vision and not reality that was amiss. There was something green in the side pocket. She carefully pulled it out, shook it on the floor, but no centipedes fell out. Only two printed tickets. She picked one up off the tiles and stared at the small print. It was a ticket for tomorrow's boat to Athens. In the space for passenger details, neatly printed, was her name.

II

EIGHTEEN

He stares down at the priest's body stretched out flat before him. He feels awkward, seeing the priest in this way. Wonders how many people ever saw him nude. He's used to viewing naked corpses, but, after all, this is a man of God.

They're alone now. Together. It is almost like confession except there is no screen between them. Nikos leans down and angles his head. He wants the priest to whisper secrets into his ear.

He reads the body like a topographic map. Lines and signs are hidden in the deep folds of skin and tissue. Words from the dead. Messages and pleas.

The last year he'll be doing this. Reading the dead. Making them talk again. Forcing them to reveal all the things they were too ashamed to in life. He stands back for a moment and wonders what the connection is to the missing priest, Karelis.

He leans down towards the mouth. It is puckered and shut like the coin slot on a broken vending machine. The blood is dried to the colour of ripe plums. The priest's hair comes off in his hands like candy floss. These things no longer make him sick, only tired.

He starts at the head. Notes the man's face is still there. The cuts and scars across the priest's back are old, part of his flesh. The wounds in the priest's stomach and groin are recent. They gape like open mouths. They grin and leer and say you will never know the answer. They are the residue of hatred. Something so intense that the priest was stabbed twenty-one times before the killer felt sated. The wounds are deep and furrowed. They suggest anger and history, a personal crime. The unleashing of pent-up animosity and bottled rage.

But underneath all the blood and tissue there's something far more interesting. Or rather, it's what's missing that draws Nikos closer, bending down, his chin almost touching the cold hard flesh. He gently lifts the priest's penis and peers underneath. There is scar tissue, old and wrinkled like papyrus. There is nothing else.

Nikos moves away, disgust and dread lodged like a stone in his throat. Did the priest castrate himself? Or did someone do this to him? He checks through the coroner's report, the cramped handwriting and old-fashioned script. The castration is at least twenty years old. Nikos remembers reading about Origen and other holy men who castrated themselves to become purer for God. Who cut the source of their temptation as one would cut a balloon string, watching desire float away into the blue and endless sky.

He smells the skin, the tang of departure, and then its sourness too. He envies the dead their stillness. Their detachment from the world. This is only the first stage. As the skin falls away and the fat melts, they will shed even this, their corporeality.

He leans back and thinks about all the bodies he's encountered. How he feels more comfortable with them than with the living. How they can never lie or betray you.

He makes one last circuit, looking for anything he's missed, but there's only the flesh, hair and sightless eyes.

He leans back down into the priest's face. 'Tell me,' he whispers to the dead man.

He puts his ear to the priest's mouth, and, for a second, he's certain he can hear the old man's breath like one can hear the ghost of the sea trapped in a shell, but it is only his own body making the sound, and he leaves the morgue, unsatisfied as always.

* * *

The room was bare as a monk's cell. Which was no surprise. Vondas may have been ousted from the monastery, but his habits hadn't changed in the least. Nikos stands there, unable as yet to enter, taking in this scene, the smell of the dead priest still on his hands. He knew Vondas slightly, as a policeman, not a friend or parishioner. He feels he knows him better now after having seen the priest's body, the secret folds and hidden ravines of his life.

He takes a deep breath, pulls the notebook out of his pocket and switches on the one bare bulb dangling off-centre in a corner of the room. There's a single bed. The sheets white and tidied, no pillow or blanket. The bed looks like an army cot, steel snakes and broken springs hanging from its underside like stalactites. The mattress sags, describing the imprint of a man no longer there.

On the wall, next to the pillow, about two inches up, he sees something strange. He gets on the bed so he can take a closer look. The cement in this one small corner has been chipped away. The wall is pitted and caved, and there are dark smears surrounding it. The indentation is only a couple of inches deep. There is grey dust on the floor under the bed and two broken fingernails, white ellipsoids torn and cracked. Nikos scrapes some of the dried blood off the wall into an evidence bag.

Next to the bed is a small plain table with no drawers. On it lies a bible and a half-filled cup of water. There are no crucifixes anywhere.

There's a desk on the other side of the room and a small, scrappy bookshelf filled with leather-bound volumes, their spines faded and torn. A wastebasket. An air-conditioning unit. No telephone. No computer. Nothing else. The room feels like a cell, and the fact it had been a deliberate choice makes it even worse.

He stands in the silent room and asks the priest all the questions he's too scared to ask himself. The walls don't reply. The ceiling says nothing.

He stares out the window at the rippled sea below. He can smell the priest's sweat in the bed sheets and curtains. It's sour and musty and the last thing left of him.

He begins to examine the bookcase. The tattered covers and bent pages evince a lifetime of study and perusal; thumbprints stained black are visible on some of the pages while others hold dead ash from long-extinguished cigarettes. They are all apocrypha. The testaments that never made it to the finish line. Odd books for a priest to have, Nikos thinks, but not as odd as the things he saw in the mortuary this morning. He flicks through the books, but there's only dense text, footnotes and printed commentary. Nothing in the priest's hand, no secret photo of a long lost love or saint to ease the dread of night.

His head feels heavy and tight as if he's been up all night drinking. He moves to the window. The harbour is devoid of boats this morning and still and perfect as a postcard. He tries to imagine what it was like to live in such a room, to be encased by the heat and white walls, the emptiness of space. A prison made by the prisoner who then voluntarily served his life sentence in it.

He gets on his hands and knees, checks the floor, under the bed, by the table. There's nothing, not even dust. How can a man who lived so simply attract so much hatred, so much violence?

He gets up and peers under the mattress, between the sheets. Runs his fingers along the wall looking for other indentations, secret hiding places, but he doesn't find anything until he turns on the air conditioner.

The switch breaks off in his hand. He looks at it lying in his palm. Sweat trickles down the back of his neck. The wires dangle like loose tongues, their colour faded to a dull grey. He lights a cigarette, hoping to cover the smell of his own sweat, and picks up the broken switch. He tries fitting it back on but pushes too hard. The plastic cracks, and the unit's face shears off and lands clattering to the tiles.

His heart hammers in his chest. He can hear it like a drumbeat from the next room. His hands are shiny and wet, and he wipes them on his trousers before reaching in. The hole is about one foot deep and a few inches high. He extracts two cloth bound books and a green paper file. He searches carefully in the hole but there's nothing else, and he feels a little disappointed. No guns or drugs or centipede carcasses.

He sits down on the bed, lays the items in front of him. He picks up one of the books. It is much newer than the ones on the shelf and far less handled.

He opens it to the title page, but he already knows what it will say. His hands shake and the pages flutter. It's the book about the cult. He feels blood rush through his head and blackness take hold of him as he flicks through it.

The word 'NO' has been scrawled on each page. Slowly, methodically, in the margins and above the text. Between the lines and under them. Through and across the letters and over the images like a black rain.

Every page has been defaced. Even the photos of the island, of the labyrinth and the ruins, have been etched out in a series of calligraphic strokes, black and spiky as whips.

It is impossible to read the underlying text any more. He flicks through pages, each one covered in spidery NOs, like a cancer spreading across the text, becoming more dense and intertwined as the book progresses. The last pages are a cross-hatched nightmare of black on black, the original text no longer even visible.

He puts the book to one side and reaches for the second volume.

It is another, newer edition of the first. A library copy due back nearly a year ago. Only the first fifty pages have been filled with the scribbled NOs.

It reminds him of the penance books the nuns at his school made them keep. A place to record all the bad things they'd done. They would be forced to look at it every day before going home, to meditate on their sins in black and white and fill the rest of the pages with what they were going to do to make up for them. A kind of karmic account book.

The knock on the door makes him jump. The book falls to the floor. The sound of it hitting the tiles fills the room. He stares up at the face of Elias, his deputy. Nikos beckons him in, picks up the book and shows it to Elias.

'You think he scribbled out the words because, somehow, *they* were to blame – the words themselves? Now that the actions and events were gone, the words came to stand for the things which had happened, and Vondas, by negating this history, felt he was negating the reality too?'

Nikos looks up surprised. Since when is Elias given to abstract theorising? It's strange, like seeing someone you know well in a set of clothes you could never imagine them in. But maybe he's been reading up, getting prepared for his promotion.

'I don't think we'll ever know that,' Nikos replies. He tells Elias about the morning in the morgue. The stab marks around Vondas's groin. The castration scars from many years ago. The scratch marks on the wall.

'You'd think God would fill their lives with light and meaning.'

Nikos looks up. Elias's face is like a puzzle missing the last piece. 'I think God takes away as much as he gives.'

They put the books to one side. Nikos picks up the green file. He carefully opens it and takes out the worn and folded clippings inside.

'It's a piece about the disappearance of Karelis. Some follow-up articles.' Nikos picks out the last of these, stares at it, shaking his head and then hands it over to Elias.

In the photo, Karelis's face is totally covered by more NOs as if he were wearing a black mask of angry mosquitoes.

NINETEEN

'Seems you've managed to make some unsavoury friends.'
George stubbed his cigarette and snorted. He poured himself
an ouzo. It was barely ten, and the sun bright as a sky full of
burning angels. Jason sat slouched and hung-over across the
table. He'd come down here for breakfast not bad news.

'Who are you talking about?'

'Long hair. Northern accent. You know who I mean.'
George bolted down his drink.

What the hell was Wynn doing here, looking for him? Jason
tried to keep his face steady and blank but George was too
blasted to care. He sat in jeans and flannel shirt, looking like a
faded version of the air-brushed John Wayne which glared
down at them from the wall. He kept picking at his food, leaving cigarettes to smoulder in the ashtray. Hank Snow sang
about losing his baby in a fire.

'I very much hope you haven't got yourself involved with
him.' George swallowed a piece of octopus. It looked like
rubber alien spines. It smelled worse. Jason felt a swelling
nausea lodge in his chest.

'He's a piece of shit.'

'What do you mean?' He wasn't sure he wanted to know.
Not with what Wynn already knew about him. George swallowed another tentacle. Jason looked away, taking deep
breaths.

'They say he came here to take over the drug trafficking.
That he killed and tortured his rivals. Made a show of
force. Ruthless and devastating. The old faces that used to sell

pills – we don't see them any more. Either he scared them off, or they're lying at the bottom of the sea. Either way, he got what he wanted. Money.' George raised his hands in the air, a gesture of exasperation offered up to the heavens. 'That's all it's about these days, and human life is just another expense to chalk up, another loss to be put against future gains. Stay away from him, Jason.'

'If that's what you think then why do you let him sell drugs at your club?'

George looked at him, tired and weary, his eyes like slit figs. 'What do you expect me to do? Let this business collapse as well?'

'I don't understand.'

'I'm too old to fight. I came here to get away from all that. And who's forcing anyone to buy anything? It's what people come here for, and if they don't find it at my bar, they'll go to another bar and find it there. It's their business not mine.'

Jason swallowed his drink. He couldn't see anything wrong with what George was saying but then again he couldn't see anything right with it either.

'No one used to care about these things. There were no problems until that new police chief came in this year. You'd think with the murders the police would have better ways to spend their time.'

'The girl who was found last week, did you know her?' He wanted to get George off the subject. There were only three hotels on the island, and George's was the cheapest. A one in three chance.

George nodded. 'I saw her a bit. Here and there. She used to come to the club.'

'Was she here on holiday?' He didn't know where he was going with this but he wanted more information, more facts he could tell Kitty when he saw her again.

'They come here on holiday. This is how it begins.' George's hands made the universal expression for *What can you do about it?* 'Then, they realise their money's running out. That there are easy ways to replenish it.' He swallowed an octopus eye. Liquid spurted out and landed on Jason's hand.

'You mean she was dealing?'

'I only saw what I saw.'

'Working for Wynn?'

George looked at him and shrugged. 'Or against him. I don't know. All I know is she disappeared. Then they found her. Poor fucking girl. Her family . . .'

George got up and excused himself. Jason watched him leave and thought about what he'd inferred. The dead girl had been selling drugs. It could have been a coincidence. But how many coincidences did it take before you started calling it a pattern? Was she working for Wynn or trying to undercut him? He remembered George's comment about rival dealers kissing the sea floor. The other victims were also young. Had they been selling drugs too?

The sun smoked and snarled above him. Police marched along the boardwalk as if on parade, stiff and blue, and so unlike the sea. But Jason could only think about Wynn. How he'd eavesdropped on them last night at the club. His leering smile and insinuating tone. Was he planning on telling Kitty? Or using it as a way to blackmail him? He'd thought Wynn an annoyance, someone who enjoyed playing mind games with other people, but he was wrong. Wynn was something much worse.

TWENTY

She sat by the bed and waited for the phone to ring. On the floor lay empty Glenfiddich miniatures, their caps like frozen insects pock-marking the white tiles. She hadn't slept. She'd called the police and was told to come in the next day and make an official report.

She'd checked the room again, on hands and knees, making sure, and then Don had phoned.

Thinking it might be Jason, she'd answered. A momentary dizziness when she hadn't recognised his voice.

'You get my message?'

She'd said she had. Despite herself, she apologised for not having called back. Then she told him. Everything. From the mugging to the murders to the theft of her manuscript. The silence on the other end seemed to suck her words into space. Then, finally: 'What do you think you're doing, Kitty?'

She had no answer for that.

'Don, last night you didn't call twice did you?'

'Of course not.'

'I think someone's following me.'

'Kit, you're sounding a tad paranoid.' His voice was snarled and tangled as if the telephone line itself had made it so. 'You should come back. You're no good on your own, you should know that by now.'

She slammed the phone down and walked across the room as if the mere act could give her the distance she needed to flee from her life.

* * *

The police station was busier than last time. It was not something she wanted to do, but the quicker she could get it done, the sooner she would see Jason.

She remembered the feeling of humiliation and anger when she was here before, but no one seemed to recognise her when she gave her name at the desk. Don's phone call had unsettled her. When was it he stopped caring? When was it she started realising? Perhaps after the accident, but it was hard to tell. A slow, spinning away that was only measurable once it was too late. She bit down on her memories and asked to speak to someone regarding a burglary. The desk sergeant looked up, bored and tired, his eyes small shrivelled things. 'Someone who can speak English,' she added.

'You're back again.'

She turned and saw the policeman with the moustache. He was smiling, but it was not a friendly smile. There was too much teeth and too little eyes.

'My room was broken into,' she said, trying not to be unnerved by his gaze. 'I want to report it to someone who can speak English.'

To her surprise, the policeman held out his hand. 'Come,' he said, 'we can talk in my office.'

After last week's treatment, she was too astonished to say anything. She followed him, noticing how everyone else in the station room stopped and watched her, mumbling among themselves, voices thick with smoke and speculation.

'I'm sorry it's so noisy at the moment,' the policeman said, pointing to a chair behind the table. 'I've been wanting to speak to you,' he added, watching her sit down before taking his own place.

'You found out who mugged me?' She was unable to contain her surprise.

The policeman smiled. 'I'm afraid not. As you can see,' he pointed to the frenzy of movement in the main room, 'we're working hard on it.' His laugh was like dry wood crackling under fire.

'It's not funny.'

'No, of course not, I'm sorry.' And he genuinely did seem so, Kitty thought, warming to him despite herself. 'Now, please tell me why you're here.'

She told him. About the missing files. The damage to her computer. The tickets in her bag. While she was running through all this, the policeman just kept nodding and stroking his moustache.

'Are you going to write any of this down?'

The policeman shrugged his shoulders. 'I'll remember,' he said, 'I have a long memory.'

He was insinuating something, she knew. She was about to reply, then closed her mouth, thinking better of it.

'Actually, I had some questions for you,' he leant forward, his elbows covering the table. 'It's good you came in. Saved me the trouble of trying to find you.'

She nodded, not knowing what to say. She'd written scenes like this a hundred times before, but she'd never felt the dread she was now feeling. A thick, dark coating filling her heart and mouth.

'You were at the monastery a few nights ago. The night the priest was killed.'

It wasn't a question, so she just nodded, wondering how he knew.

'What were you doing there?'

'Sightseeing.'

The detective laughed. His hand slapping the table. 'Yes. Very good. Of course. Except that the monastery was closed. Has been for a while.'

'Tell that to my guidebook.' They'd done nothing wrong, she knew, and she wasn't going to let this morose policeman make her feel like they had.

He seemed to be contemplating this, nodding to himself. 'It was you or your boyfriend's decision to go up there?'

Kitty felt the blood fill her face. She didn't know why, the policeman was just doing his job, but her reactions were becoming unpredictable to her like a character in a bad soap opera. She wondered if it was the island or if it was just being alone. 'He's not my boyfriend.'

'So you say. But that doesn't answer my question.'

'We were bored. We read about the monastery in the guidebook. Is it illegal to go up there?'

The policeman shook his head. 'No. It isn't. I'm sorry if I sounded hostile. Comes with the job, I'm afraid. I just wanted to know if you saw anything strange, anything unusual?'

The priest, the trap, the scream. 'No, nothing out of the ordinary. A closed monastery and a lot of trees. Am I a suspect?'

Nikos shook his head, 'No, of course not. I'm sorry.' He took her hand. She almost pulled back but there was something in his eyes. 'Things have got . . . how can I say? . . . very difficult around here. I didn't meant to suggest you had anything to do with the priest's death. I was hoping someone might have seen something. I just need to eliminate all the loose ends.'

Kitty let her hand rest in his. It was strangely familiar. 'And whatever's left is the solution?'

The policeman smiled. 'We've obviously been reading the same books.'

They stared at each other. She'd thought he seemed cold and inscrutable but as she looked at him she could see he was hiding something deeper, a sadness at the very core of him, a man lost in the middle of his life. She smiled, wondering how alike they really were despite culture and continents. 'I hope you find the killer,' she said.

He nodded slowly, 'I really hope so too,' but she could see he believed in it less than she did.

TWENTY-ONE

They met at a taverna by the harbour. The sea splashed and eddied, the boats rocked and twisted in their moorings. The sun scorched and sizzled.

'There were two tickets. You know what that means?' Her voice sounded thin and brittle like something made out of ice.

Jason nodded. A thick swelling in his throat prevented him from saying anything. What was there left to say? Someone had placed two tickets for today's boat to Athens in Kitty's suitcase. The message was clear. He looked up. She seemed smaller now, and he felt angry for the way they'd reduced her.

'All of this is my fault. I'm so sorry.' It was the closest he could come to admitting the thing which loomed over him like a second sky. The constant pebble in his shoe. If only . . . a cinema queue in central London . . . an adjacent seat on a long flight . . .

'Why do you say that?' Her face was unreadable. For a moment, he thought she knew. That, maybe, Wynn had told her.

Jason paused. Sensing this was not the time for confessions. Maybe he could have told her at the beginning, but now he was the only person she could trust on the island. He looked at Kitty and knew he couldn't take that away from her. The first lie can be forgiven, but the ones that pile up to buttress it?

'How much did you lose?'

She shrugged. 'Everything on the computer's backed up. The notes and pages . . . I'm not sure I would have gone back to them anyway. Perhaps it's better this way. Perhaps you need to have your bridges burned for you.'

He wasn't sure what she meant.

'Any idea what they were after?'

Their legs touched under the table; there was no awkwardness nor quick movement away.

'It's obvious, isn't it? I go to the museum, ask about the cult, say I'm writing an article, and a few days later all my notes and work disappears. That old man who interrupted the librarian and me. It's got to be him. I think the man with the jaw sent him. The librarian closed up after talking to him. The ridiculous thing is that all they got was Lily stuff.'

He didn't remind her that Wynn had overheard their conversation in the club that night, their theories and speculations. That Wynn might have reasons of his own.

'The police say anything useful?'

She shook her head. 'I mentioned the man at the museum. The detective didn't even make a note of it. He was far more interested in what we were doing at the monastery that night.'

'How did he know we were up there?'

She shrugged.

'Did you tell him we talked to the priest?'

'No.'

Jason stared at her. Thrilled but also a little bit scared by her deception. 'No?'

'There was nothing to tell. The detective treated me like a suspect. He was waiting for me to slip up, I could see it in his eyes, the way he twiddled his moustache every time I answered a question like it was some kind of lie detector. If I'd told him we'd seen the priest, I don't think he would have let me go. I think we're getting close. I see it in the way people react. In the way things are starting to come together. We've put coincidence behind us. I don't think we should use those tickets. I don't think we should give up.'

Her fingers wound in and out of the coffee cup in front of her. The nails clicking a tattoo against the porcelain.

Jason took her hand. She let it rest in his, then moved it away, as if suddenly aware of a breach in her defences. 'Those people ordered after us.' She pointed to a couple of locals whose food was being delivered. Jason looked around for their waiter but he was gone. The food they'd ordered, forgotten. He was about to suggest they leave, the atmosphere unfriendly and turning more so, when he heard Kitty call out to someone then stop mid-sentence. He saw the fine contour of goosebumps explode across her neck. A woman, silver-haired and stooped, holding the hand of a man with a Tom of Finland moustache, looked at their table uncomprehendingly. Then something in the woman's expression changed as the man leaned into her, whispering in her ear.

Kitty looked as if she'd seen a ghost. Her body tried to disappear into the chair but it was too late. Jason heard her take two massive gulps of air. Watched blood rush back into her cheeks as she sat up to greet the mismatched couple.

'Jason. This is the curator of the museum . . . the one I told you about.'

'Alexia,' the woman said.

He stood up to shake her hand but she didn't proffer it.

Kitty turned to him, 'That's the detective who questioned me.' Her words were like rapid expulsions of air, atmospheric bullets that pierced right through Jason's skin.

'My husband,' was all Alexia said, pointing to the man. He looked towards them, neither friendly nor unfriendly, nodding his head slightly.

'Sit down. Have a drink with us,' Kitty said, surprising Jason as much as it did the woman who began to make her excuses but was abruptly cut off by her husband. 'Yes. Thank you, we will,' he said, pulling out a chair for his wife.

'How's your holiday?' the woman asked, but Jason could see she was just saying it to be polite. She seemed distracted and uncomfortable sitting there.

Kitty smiled. 'Oh, you know. Can't fault it for excitement. Your husband knows the details.' The way she said the word *husband*, it was like she was squeezing the syllables through the gaps in her teeth.

The detective nodded. 'I thought we would bump into each other again but not quite so soon. I'm sorry about this morning. The situation is very tense and sometimes I lose sight of things.'

Alexia took her husband's hand. 'Nikos still pines for the days when he was a real street detective, don't you?'

'How long have you been a policeman?' Something had thawed in Kitty's tone.

'Thirty years, more or less,' he replied, an amused smile upturning the corners of his mouth.

Jason saw Kitty shift, her whole body taut like a spring. 'In Athens or here?'

Nikos looked at his wife. His expression seemed neutral but Alexia understood it and nodded back. 'Mainly in Athens. I served for a couple of years here back in the early days.'

Kitty and Jason exchanged glances. 'Were you here during the first cult murders?' Kitty said, her elbows white and sculpted spreading across the table, trying to bridge the distance between her and the policeman.

'Yes and no.'

Nikos sipped his coffee and lit a cigarette. That their positions had changed and Kitty was now doing the questioning didn't seem to bother him. He sighed, and smoke curled out of his mouth like the tendrils of a fairy-tale serpent.

'It was my first month on the job. Everyone at the academy laughed at me when I said I wanted to be stationed on my home island. Said there was nothing to do there but catch animal rapists. All the fun was in Athens. But I didn't think Athens was that much fun. These were the last days of the dictatorship, and the police, while nominally independent, weren't really at all. Here on the island no one bothered us. Also, it was the place I grew up. My mother was still alive, though barely, and I wanted to take care of her. But something happened to the island afterwards. Things changed.'

'How so?'

'It's hard to say. Things got a little darker for a while. The life of the village seemed stained by what had happened. The two children, of course. In a big city maybe it's different, but when something like this happens in a small community it changes everyone, affects everyone, not just family and friends. I think locals became more suspicious of foreigners and tourists for a while. There were beatings, I'm afraid. But then I guess, like everything else, it became part of the past, something to be forgotten. The developers moved in. The dictatorship finally crumbled, and tourism became the main focus. The only thing to save a lot of these islands from destitution. It's a double-edged sword. On the one hand, the island's transformed, new buildings go up, the quality of life changes.' He pointed towards the harbour where men sat bare-chested swigging cans of lager. 'You know how it is though, money eventually out-weighs everything else. You put up with it. The fake restaurants, the discos and noise and puking. Why? Because it means you can buy your mother a refrigerator or air conditioning. It's a decision everyone has to make for themselves.'

Kitty sat absorbed in the words Nikos was saying. Jason could see the little vein at the left side of her forehead twitch as she assimilated the information.

'Do you think the cult's resurfaced?' Jason asked, watching as Kitty turned and looked at him, a faint smile visible on her lower lip.

Nikos shook his head. 'No. That's not it at all.'

'What do you mean? You don't think 1974 and the recent murders are connected?'

'This has nothing to do with that,' Nikos replied bluntly, 'though perhaps whoever is behind this wants these connections to be made.' There was a look between husband and wife which Jason caught but could not interpret. He wondered why the policeman was so adamant.

'You think it's a copycat crime?' Kitty asked.

'Yes. There's no way it can be connected to what happened thirty-three years ago.'

'How can you be so sure?'

Nikos suddenly got up, looked at his wife. 'Believe me, I'm sure. It's my job to be sure. It was very nice to meet you but we have to go now.'

Jason caught the look of surprise – and was it annoyance? – in Alexia's face even though she tried to hide it.

The abruptness of the man's goodbye stayed with them as they sipped their drinks. When they tried to pay, the waiter explained that Nikos had settled it. They were finishing their coffee when Kitty jerked away from Jason. 'Over there.' She pointed to the side of the café, to an old man getting up. 'That's him,' she said, breathless and sharp. 'The man I told you about. The one who interrupted Alexia and me in the library. I think he's the one who broke into my room. He must have been watching us.'

Jason looked at the old man, his string vest and drunken walk, all crab-like and stuttering. He didn't look like any sort of burglar.

Kitty got up, grabbed her bag.

'What are you doing?'

But, of course, he already knew.

TWENTY-TWO

They've been here before. The things he doesn't want to talk about. The past. The years before he met her. Impossible to explain his reluctance to talk about these things without telling her everything. And, despite all the years, the shared breakfasts and late-night conversations, he still doesn't know how she'd take it, whether she'd hold his head and say forget it, that's all past and gone and you're not that man any more, or whether she'd look at him, her face turning stony as a statue and the next morning she would be gone, unable to continue living with a man such as he'd revealed himself to be.

'You told them it wasn't connected but I know that's not what you think.' Her voice is like wind, laden with jasmine and distance.

'How can it be connected?' The terseness of his reply causes her to withdraw her hand.

Explosions of emotion scare her, make her fold back into herself. He's never asked her about her parents but senses that a deep wounding and flattening resides there, and it is more for himself than for her that he never pries or tries to understand. He likes her just the way she is and doesn't want to reassess her according to a long-buried pattern. He knows it's what made her so. But that knowledge is enough.

He begins drinking on the boat to Athens, and he doesn't stop for twenty-four hours. The sea is grey and roiling. The boat lurches and buckles. The drinks spill from his hand. The memories tumble and fold like waves.

His life seems marked by boat trips: the one thirty-three years ago going to meet the detectives, bringing them back to a scene of mass slaughter; then a year later, him and Alexia sitting on deck with all their belongings, moving back to Athens, away from the island, away from the nightmares. But, of course, they never really stopped. Even in their new flat in Athens they scrolled like a film across the backs of his eyelids, the hard meat of his guilt. He'd thought that geography and space could change the past. He'd thought distance could make him a different man.

And then, six months ago, the long ride back to the island, their belongings at their side again, their hair grey and their eyes bleary and bored. His life a long string of personal failures mitigated only by the comfort of his wife's arms, her stillness and forgiveness.

He steps off the boat in Piraeus and into the nearest bar. It is dark and smoky and full of longshoremen and ferry stewards. There is no day or night here, no clocks or windows, only the measure of drink in the glass and the length of the cigarette burning between his fingers. He has an appointment tomorrow at the university with a man who lectures on cults. The strange death of Vondas. The scrawled-out cult book. Wynn's seeming innocence. He realises he needs to know more about how cults operate if he has any hope of disentangling this case. He knows it's knowledge he's avoided and that this case is like punishment for the years of denial and fear.

It must be night-time, but he's not sleepy. He has a hotel booked somewhere near the university but he can't bear the thought of entering an empty room. Here people shove and press up against him and their warmth and bulk hide everything he doesn't want to face.

He pukes in the street. Two girls dressed up for the night cross the road, pointing and giggling at him. The alcohol comes rushing up out of the dark pit of his stomach and, with it, the secrets, the lies, the pain and memory. He thinks this will never stop. His stomach tightens and twists in agony. His throat bleeds and chokes. The vomit covers his chin and clothes but even after it turns from yellow to green to red, it won't stop.

He wakes up in the middle of the night, the curb his pillow, his own puke the bed he lies on. He stares up at the sky, wanting to see the splatter of stars, but there's only the dim light reflected from high shuttered windows.

They wake him with a kick to the stomach. He looks up and sees two young uniformed policemen. Their mouths are moving, but there's no sound coming out. He reaches inside his jacket for his badge but one of the policemen kicks his hand away.

When they find out he's one of them, they take him back to the station, feed him bad coffee and force him under a shower. His clothes are ruined and torn. They find what they can in the squad room, and he thanks them through a head pounding with needles and the sound of blood vessels bursting. He sits in an interview room and stares at the wall. His back feels like elephants have walked over it. The numbness in his left arm is still holding strong, refusing the rush of blood and lymph.

The policemen give him a lift to the university. The sun is dazzling, the sky a scream that goes on for ever. He walks up the granite steps in clothes that are two sizes too small and ill matched. He desperately tries to remember the Professor's name, but it's gone. He knows what he's here for, but it all seems like another grand folly now. He's never been as good a cop as he thought he'd be. Never been as good a husband or lover as he'd have liked. This case is just the ribbon, the crowning failure in a life full of them.

* * *

'Glad you could make it.' Professor Pappageorgiou smiles and extends his hand. Nikos stares down at the gold chain around the wrist, the light reflecting off it, and excuses himself.

He doesn't make the cubicle but at least manages to puke in the sink and not all over his clothes. He rinses his face with scalding water, watches the blood bloom in his cheeks.

'Sorry about that,' he says when he returns.

The Professor nods, smiles sadly, and pulls out a chair. 'It's perfectly OK, just tell me what you wanted to know.'

TWENTY-THREE

They walked in the scorching harbour sun, the light illuminating every fold and curve of Kitty's skin. Despite being in the sun for several days, it was still white as a newly discovered statue. She put her hand in Jason's. 'This way we look more like tourists,' she said. The warmth of her hand smothered him. He tried not to press too hard. He could feel her heartbeat in the swell and surrender of her palm.

The old man stumbled a hundred feet up ahead, too drunk for them to be concerned about being spotted. For a moment, as they walked along the beachfront, he told himself they were on their honeymoon and strolling under unfamiliar stars. He looked at Kitty, nodded as she talked about what she thought the old man was hiding, but really he was looking at her eyes, the way they seemed to change colour every time she turned her head.

'I want to find out where he lives. To ask him why he trashed my room,' Kitty explained, her voice breathless and angry. 'What he was looking for. What he said to Alexia to make her shut up. He's drunk and alone, it's as good a chance as any.' Jason noticed how the violation of her work had affected her more deeply than the violation of her body that first night.

They walked in silence up towards the poor part of town. As they ascended, the houses got shabbier, less looked after, the yards messier, the hum of air conditioners disappeared. They passed by small, badly constructed shacks and wind-flapping lean-tos. Goats, drunk on too much sun, lolling around debris-strewn dirt yards as if they were zombies. Statues of local heroes, Christ-like in their suffering and martyrdom. Walls pocked with bullet holes, history writ on every stone and turn.

Finally, the old man came to a stop outside a squat one-storey house. He fumbled for his keys, dropped them, picked them back up and let himself in.

They waited. Jason hoped she'd had enough. That she would turn back now. But he caught her smile as she approached the door. He was beginning to understand how she only seemed truly happy when in pursuit of this mystery. He watched as she pressed the dirty white buzzer perched like a full stop on the side wall.

The old man opened the door, looked Kitty up and down. There was something military in his demeanour despite his obvious inebriation. A sickly yellow light spilled from inside and covered him like a sepia halo.

'What you want?' he growled. His breath dark and rotten with alcohol.

'I wanted to talk to you.' Kitty said and perhaps, for the first time, the old man connected her with the museum. He ignored Jason and stared at her. 'Talk to me?'

'I want my papers back. The stuff you took from my room.'

The man's face was as blank as the façade of the white stone wall behind him.

'You know what I'm talking about,' Kitty continued. 'What did you say to the librarian when I was in there?'

This time it registered on his face. Memory, shock and a flicker of fear. 'I told her not to talk about such things, OK? It brings bad memories.'

'They're not memories any more,' she replied. 'If you haven't noticed, it's happening again.'

The old man's face seemed to collapse before their eyes. It was a disconcerting thing to see. As if all the years had suddenly caught up to him. 'Leave me alone,' he shouted, and they both flinched from the force of his words rushing out like a shower of hailstones.

'Get away from here.' He grabbed the lapel of Kitty's dress, pulled her towards him. 'What do you know? Come like this to disturb me? What the fuck you know what it's like to lose a child?' The old man sneered into Kitty's face, but something he saw made him step back and let go.

Kitty had turned white. Jason had never seen her like this before. He wondered if it was the old man's assault, no less disturbing for his age. She raised her hand to her dress and neatly straightened her lapel. 'You think you're the only one who's ever lost a child? What about the families of the murdered teenagers?' Her words were flat and hard, like pebbles sanded by the sea.

The old man looked at her silently. As if measuring for truth in her face. He finally nodded and stepped away from the door, gesturing them to come inside. 'I'm sorry,' he said, as they walked past him into the hot, dark flat. His accent was heavy and broken but his English fluent. 'You are right.' He addressed Kitty. 'When something bad happens, it is easy to think you are the only person on earth it's happened to. That is perhaps one of the worst things that come from tragedy. We lose sense of our commonness. Pain separates us and tells us we are special. My wife . . .' He looked down at the dirty floor, the peeled linoleum cracked and reaching into the air like tiny fingers. 'She used to say that. She tried to believe this happens to everybody.'

The smell of stale cigarettes and alcohol hung like mist in the air. Dust covered everything as if preserving it for better days. The furniture was old and much-used, faded and functional, made out of cheap, garish material.

'Your son died in 1974 at the hands of the cult.'

It hadn't occurred to Jason, but Kitty had understood immediately.

The old man nodded, sat down and picked up a bottle of brandy. 'Yes. His name was Constantine. I'm Yanni.' He disappeared into the kitchen before they could introduce themselves.

The couch he'd sat on seemed older than the man, patched and repatched with different materials so that it looked like a psychedelic swirl, something you were more likely to see in a VW camper van. There were photos of a smiling boy, framed and positioned in every corner of the room. None of his wife.

The heat was terrible. Where once there had been an air-conditioning unit there was now just a hole in the wall opening up to a sliver of blue sky streaked with cotton clouds.

The old man came back holding three glasses. He staggered slightly and sat down. He smelled of fish and diesel, a strange, repellent smell which also seemed to emanate from the furniture and floor of the flat as if it had taken on his scent after all these years.

A small dog, silent until now, limped into the room. His eyes dropped, and he sat at the old man's feet. The old man reached down and absently stroked the dog then poured himself a glass of brandy.

'Yes, yes,' he said, putting the glass down, coughing, downing what was left before pouring them some.

'For many years no one wanted to know, and now that it's all happening again suddenly it's a thing of interest.' He seemed to be less rebuking them than meditating on the fickleness of time and fate. There was no hostility in his eyes, only a faraway look, as if a part of him had never left the summer of 1974.

Kitty took a sip of the brandy. Jason saw her lips curl, but she hid it well. 'You think the two are connected?'

Yanni's shoulders lifted and seemed to hump up around his neck as he shrugged. 'Of course they are. Any fool can see that. This island. The way the bodies were found. The centipedes. Anyone who tells you different is either a liar or an idiot.'

Kitty and Jason looked at each other. Was he making a direct reference to what Nikos had said? Had he overheard their conversation at the café? Or were they starting to see connections and lines where they only wanted them to be?

They didn't reply, and Yanni didn't elaborate. He stared at his glass, refilled it and drank it down. Wiped his mouth with his sleeve. He then filled the bottle cap, carefully trickling the liquid into it. He held it above the dog's mouth. The dog opened his jaw, and Yanni poured it in.

'It was your son they found out by the ruins?' Kitty's voice was softer, modulated, as if speaking to the victim of a recent crime.

Yanni nodded slowly. 'Him and his best friend. This is how it all started.'

He began to tell them about the village back in the early seventies, his wife Rosa and Constantine, his seven-year-old son. It didn't feel like he was talking to them, he didn't make eye contact, and the story seemed rehearsed as if he'd told it to himself a thousand times over the intervening years both as solace and reminder of the life he'd once had.

'The island was not like it is now. It was almost as if the events which occurred that summer changed things for good. It was a small fishing community before and then, it became this.' He stretched his hand towards the door, and it was almost as if he liked living within these walls to hide, not himself, but the village and the outside world.

'I had quit college when Rosa got pregnant and we moved back to the island. Once I'd wanted to be an architect, even studied for a couple of years, but as soon as the baby was on the way we knew food was more important than dreams and so we moved back. I began helping my father in his fishing boat. But things were bad. The fish were dying out, and every morning we would come back from sea with less and less, the fish all small and no good for selling. But we made out as we could and, when Constantine was born, I thought there would never be a happier day in my life. I was right.'

He stopped to stir the ice cubes by shaking the glass. He stared down at the swirling liquid, his eyes heavy and hooded.

'For my son I wanted better. I cursed myself for having taken the easy route, for coming back here, becoming what my father was. I was determined that Constantine would have a better life.'

He stopped abruptly and looked at the hole in the wall. The sky had darkened and the clouds had disappeared.

'What happened the day he went missing?' Kitty had taken the old man's hand in hers and held its trembling. It engulfed her palm.

'He'd been on a church retreat for the weekend. He was always going on them. I guess it was the only place for kids to get away from their families. He was with his best friend, Yorgi. They were always together those two, but, you know, unlike other kids of their age they didn't get into trouble. I never knew what they talked about but you could tell they were good friends from the unspoken sentences which always hovered between them. As if they knew each other too well to have to say anything.

'So they were away for the weekend, and me and Rosa came down to the harbour to pick them up on Sunday morning but they weren't there. The school coach disgorged all these smiling kids, sunburnt and full of stories they couldn't wait to tell their parents, and we watched them get off the bus one by one, but Constantine wasn't among them and neither was Yorgi.

'We were disappointed but not alarmed. You see, once or twice before they'd decided to hike down from the mountain after the camping trip rather than catch the bus. I was always proud of him for that little measure of independence. The labyrinth was still open back then, and you know how kids love the mystery of dark places, the stories they tell each other about the ghosts which roam them? So we went back and prepared the Sunday dinner, knowing the two boys would be back by nightfall . . . kids are scared of the dark, no?

'When darkness fell and they still hadn't arrived, I went over to Yorgi's mother's house. She was distraught, and I calmed her down which somehow managed to calm me down, repeating those soothing phrases, they must have got lost . . . you know how kids are . . . we'll check the labyrinth . . . repeating it until somehow I started to believe them too.

'They found them a couple of days later.

'I never thought a day would come when I would curse God and my own life so much. But it did. And the fact I survived it, managed to make it here to this century, well that was the worst insult. How could I live so long and my boy so little?'

The old man buried his face in his hands, crying, then, abruptly, as if caught in some shameful act, he looked back up, and when he continued his voice was hard and lifeless.

'God disappeared for me that day in 1974, and he never came back. I had to make the identification. To see him like that. Lying on a stretcher, a white sheet around him. He was smiling, can you believe that? Even dead he was still smiling. But what they did to him . . . that was when I felt God leave this world for good. The scars and mutilations. These are things I will never forget. They are as fresh to me as' – he looked down at his glass – 'as this . . .' The glass shattered in his grip. Kitty jumped as it crashed and sparkled all over the floor. 'Fuck you, God!' The old man screamed. 'Fuck you and your angels and your mercy which doesn't exist.' He began to tremble, a slight movement at first, which welled up in him like an earthquake until his whole body shook so much it looked as if there were two of him.

Kitty moved across from the sofa and took his bleeding hand, put her arms around him and held him as he shook and cried and cursed the God he no longer believed in.

'It's OK. I understand.' Her whispered words sounded so full of warmth and sympathy. 'I'm sorry we made you bring it all back up. I'm really sorry.'

'No. It's not you.' Yanni shook his head. Kitty poured him another brandy using her glass. 'It's all this happening again. When you said that thing at the door, I thought about them. These poor boys and girls. They have families too, no? They are going to spend the rest of their lives in the same place I have. I grew up with all these images of hell, of fire and perdition, but this is really hell, to outlive your own child, to never see them grow into what your dreams have laid out for them, to not see them make mistakes, grow up, become enchanted with the world . . . what could be worse than this?'

The ensuing silence was answer enough. After a little while, he continued, 'they locked me in jail that night. They didn't want me out there when they went to arrest the cult. Thought I might do something crazy. See these?' He held out his hands, crumpled into fists. The knuckles were misaligned as if they'd slipped or had never been properly formed in the first place. 'I spent that night punching the walls of the cell until the broken bones and pain made me pass out.'

'How did you feel about the killers of your son never being brought to justice?' Jason asked. He couldn't begin to imagine what it would be like to live with the unresolved hanging over you, the never-to-be-resolved.

'Huh? I didn't feel anything. I was in no state to feel. Later when I went back home and talked to my wife, it all came rushing up. Justice, the police had told me, self-administered justice – but what good is justice when you can't see your son play football, fall in love, hold the hand of his own little baby? What fucking good is thirty-five dead people against that?'

He stared at them, but they had no answers. There was nothing to be said. Kitty looked away, through the hole in the wall and up at the sky. Her lips trembled like waves.

'After that, things turned bad. Rosa slept most of the day and the night too. She wouldn't let me touch her. She would read the bible in bed, silently mouthing the words to herself and touching her crucifix. She found God in the same instant that I lost Him.

'She stopped washing and going out. I had to cook every-thing and clean the house when I came back from fishing. But I was happy with that. I needed things to distract me.

'We separated a year later. We reminded each other of the thing which had been taken from us. We saw Constantine in each other's movements and tone of voice. In the way an eyebrow curved or a dimple on a chin changed shape. She said God had cursed us, though what for she never made clear. She wanted to make amends to God, she said, and could only do that if she began again. She said she couldn't bear to look into my eyes any more because they were Constantine's eyes.'

Kitty let Yanni's arm drop back onto his lap. He seemed calmed or benumbed by the story he'd told. His hand gently stroked the dog.

'Did you ever hear from her again?' Jason asked.

The old man shook his head.

'Her mother sent me a letter a couple of years later, perhaps late '77. Rosa had hung herself in her mother's flat. The funeral had already been and gone. I had not been invited. I went a few years later to her grave, but it was broken and lying in unconsecrated ground.'

'What about your son's friend?'

'I never saw the body, but I heard he'd been killed in the same way. His mother and older brother were in the room next door when we were viewing the bodies, and I heard her scream and moan so much it almost drove me crazy. Crazy because I couldn't scream any more, because the night in the cell had drained me of all that, and I felt guilty that she could express her grief and I couldn't.'

'What happened to her? Does she still live here?'

'No, very soon after that she took her remaining son and left the island for good. I could understand that. But I could never leave. Who would visit his grave if I was somewhere else? But she had another son and didn't want him to grow up in the shadow of what had happened to his little brother. I can understand that, and maybe, if we'd had another child, Rosa and I would have done the same too. Maybe we would have started again somewhere else and she wouldn't have ended up . . . funny how life just never turns out the way you think it will.'

The streets were empty and cold. Litter blew against their feet. Jason walked Kitty to her hotel. They didn't talk. They held hands. Yanni's story had somehow brought them into the reality of this thing, the pain and left-behindness. The town seemed darker, occluded, as they climbed the hill. The wind came roaring down from the mountains. The streets they thought they knew disappeared or led into blind alleys filled with rubbish bags and feral cats. The buzzing of cicadas electrified the night.

Jason stopped. He put his hand on Kitty's arm, squeezed gently. Their faces were only a few inches apart. 'When did you lose the child?'

'How did you know?' Her voice sounded warped and disfigured. There was no expression on her face.

'What you said tonight. The first chapter of *Crime Novel*.' He stopped, shook his head, 'I'm sorry for bringing it up.'

For some reason this made her smile. '*Crime Novel* was written over a year *before* it happened.'

'I didn't mean to upset you.'

She took his hand. 'I'm fine. It's history. Bad times better forgotten.' She turned and looked at him. 'Thanks for coming with me tonight. I really appreciate it.' Her voice was smoky and whispered, conspiratorial in the dark heat. He saw her as an outline in the night, a serpentine silhouette framed in black. She leaned forward and they kissed. Her lips on his. The touch of warm flesh. A Hitchcock kiss. Jason didn't know if she'd intended it or if they'd just missed each other's cheeks. He didn't care. He wanted the kiss to last a thousand years.

TWENTY-FOUR

The coffee is bitter and black. The Professor apologises for not having sugar. The room is white and too brightly lit. Nikos feels his hands shake and places the cup back on the Professor's table. He takes two deep breaths to keep his stomach from lurching, but all it does is remind him of how many cigarettes he smoked last night.

'Thanks for seeing me at such short notice.' His voice sounds unrecognisable to him, slurred and cracked, punctuated by shallow breaths.

'It's not often I get a detective coming to visit me,' the Professor grins. It's meant to be a joke, but Nikos is beyond that. He stares at the table stacked deep with manuscripts, black and white pages slashed with red ink. There are old coffee cups and at least three full ashtrays. Alex Pappageorgiou sits across from Nikos, his hands placed neatly on the table in front of him.

'You know why I'm here, I assume?'

The Professor smiles. 'Remind me which cult murders we're talking about?' His laugh is full and throaty, a man used to laughing at his own jokes.

He'd been recommended by a friend in Athens. Nikos had called someone he knew on the special task force. Pappageorgiou had been mentioned. A professor of Ancient Greek, he'd spent the past twenty years studying cults. He'd written two books on the subject and lectured across the world. 'Lucky you found me,' the Professor had said over the phone. 'Next semester I'm teaching a course on desecrated utopias at Berkeley.'

He's not at all what Nikos expected. He's not some bearded crazy or stentorian pedagogue. He looks too ordinary, Nikos thinks, watching him across the table. A short man in a perfect navy suit, he looks more like a financier than a cult expert. His shaved head and baby face belie his age. His constant grinning jocularity and nervous energy are almost too much to take. He has a habit of rolling a pencil through his fingers like a string of worry beads.

Behind him is the map. It takes up three walls of the office. There are no bookshelves or paintings, only this map. It is a map of the world. North America to his left, Japan yawning across the wall to his right. Behind the Professor lies Europe, Asia and Africa. Black and red pins sprouting feathers are impaled at various points of the map and, next to these, on a sheet of plastic which covers the whole atlas, are dates and numbers, strings of integers like scratches pitting the surface. Nikos sits hypnotised by the map, the swirling ocean, his thoughts and the pounding presence in his head.

'I'm stuck,' Nikos says, the first time he's voiced this to anyone but himself. 'I don't know if the recent killings are the work of a cult or someone trying to make it look like a cult. I don't know what connection these killings have to the 1974 cult apart from the surface appearances.'

The Professor leans forward, his teeth flash white, and his gums seem bloodless and grey. 'What do you know about cults?'

'Not enough, obviously,' Nikos answers. He points to the map surrounding them. 'What's the map for?'

The Professor sits up straight, enthusiasm bubbling under his eyes. 'It pinpoints areas of cult activity throughout history. Timelines and deaths. There are lines you cannot see which connect each to each. This is the purpose of the map. To map out the connections we can't apprehend.'

'How does it work?' Nikos leans forward, takes a sip of his coffee. The map draws him in, its dense assemblage of colour and form.

'Look.' The Professor points to a small outcrop of land in South America. 'Jonestown. Perhaps the most famous cult suicide of all. November 1978. Jim Jones and a pitcher of Kool-Aid laced with Valium and Cyanide. Nine hundred and thirteen dead. This is one point of the compass. A thousand years before, give or take, another cult suicide, the same location as Jonestown. Thousand-year-old skeletons all with the same fractures in their skulls. Holes in their ribcages where the hearts were plucked out. Did Jim Jones know about this? Did he set up camp at this location because of it? Or was it something more liminal which called out to him and made him place it there? We don't know. We can only make these comparisons once we start tracking the dates. Setting up points of intersection. Lines of death and belief.'

'Are all the markers related to places of mass suicide?' Nikos stares at the Professor's hand arcing across the blue ocean. His stomach reels. This whole trip was a mistake, he thinks, there's nothing to learn here. This is only another way to avoid the things he really needs to do. But the blue of the ocean is calming. The Professor's mellifluous tones soothe him, make him loathe to leave.

The Professor nods. He smiles and fans his hand across the map. 'Tenerife, December 1970.' He points to the little dot of an island awash in blue sea. 'Police are called to a house where the neighbours have reported hearing screaming and chanting. They discover three women. A mother and her two daughters. Killed with a coat hanger. Their genitals mutilated. In the centre of the room, a stake with the mother's heart impaled on it. Looked like an ordinary serial murder, horrible in the extreme, right? But nowhere near as bad as the truth.'

Now that he was on a roll, the Professor barely stopped for breath. 'Killed by their son/brother on command of the family patriarch, a man enchanted and possessed by the teachings of Jakob Lorber's *New Revelation* which taught that all women outside the family were evil. The son was given his sisters and, later, his mother to have sex with. He sang hymns while his father played the organ, and he cut them apart and removed their sex and nailed it up on the walls.'

The Professor's hand, like a knife, slices down towards the heart of the African continent. 'March 2000. Five hundred and thirty disciples of the Movement for the Restoration of the Ten Commandments of God lock themselves into a church in south-west Uganda and set themselves on fire. They believe the apocalypse is coming and that only through fire will they be saved.' The hand sweeps again. 'March 1995. Tokyo. The subway gas attacks of Aum Shinrikyo. They believed the apocalypse was coming too.'

Nikos watches silently as the Professor's hands sweep over the tableau of death, detailing numbers and figures with the dry authority of a tax auditor.

'March 1997. Heaven's Gate. Thirty-nine dead. You know about this, you've read it in the papers, but did you know the majority of the men had castrated themselves?'

He follows a red line which spans across the ocean to the Middle East. 'Modern-day Syria. The temple of Astarte at Hieropolis. Thousands of years ago, a castration cult flowered there. The cult of Attis, also a castration cult, started in what is now Turkey.'

His hand traces a thin blue line across the Mediterranean. 'Exported to Rome and Greece where it flourished. Then back up into the Russian steppes, mid-nineteenth century, the Skoptsy, an ecstatic castration cult. Hugely popular for a hundred years. Blunt rocks their favoured method.'

Nikos takes this in, makes notes in shaky handwriting. He flashes back to the priest's body as the Professor begins to speed up, his hand tracing lines which were so faint that only in their tracing does Nikos spot them, reeling off dates and numbers dead as if the figures would correspond in some eschatological account book where everything would make sense.

'Centipede cults in Ecuador, Peru and the Greek archipelago. Satanic torture and ritual slaughter in Matamoros, Mexico, where kidnapped American students were strung up above a cauldron so that their blood could drip into the pot. Everywhere. At every time in our history. Always the same lines and points intersect if you know how to look at them.'

Nikos stands up and stares at the map. The brightly coloured feathers and tiny handwriting makes his head spin. What he'd thought were creases from a distance were actually more connecting lines, some dotted, some ellipsoid, stretching across the globe like a cat's cradle holding everything together. He turns to the Professor, who's straightening out a yellow feathered pin. Nikos looks down towards the Balkans. He has no trouble finding Palassos. Red and black pins sprout from the small island like Christmas decorations.

'Why centipedes? Does your map tell you that?'

The Professor turns to him, smiling. He's happy to have an audience.

'All these islands attracted this sort of thing. They had more freedom there. The mainland was often under occupation by this or that army. Each had its own religion to impose. These islands were shelters. That's why there's so many monasteries there. Also look at it . . . the land . . . the way it curves up towards the heavens. You must feel it. The nature of ascent. Of reaching up. The high places. The spikes driven into the sky. Why do we believe in mountain gods? Jehovah, Mohammed, Christ? You see: deserts and mountains. These are places where people have always gone to find God.'

Nikos nods, not sure what help this can be but enthralled by the Professor's delivery, the way he makes every sentence sound like some profound nugget of truth. His students must love him.

'What about the centipedes?'

'The centipede has long been a mainstay of these islands and Christianity, politics – these are all ephemeral flashes of history, gone while the centipedes are deeper, have more foundation. They were there before men even settled those shores.'

'So the cult wasn't a new thing? Even in 1974?'

'Way before. And way before that too. Say a thousand years ago. It wasn't but say it was. Dates have no real meaning. We know it happened and so the when of it just becomes academic. So, say a thousand years ago this island was isolated and besieged. That's the meaning of the high sea walls and cannons. That's the meaning of a city built inside a tiny horseshoe harbour whose streets wind and backtrack to confuse marauders and pirates. But these are other stories.

'This particular story is set during a great famine. Ships from a neighbouring island had besieged the port for nine months. Nothing came in, and nothing went out. People began to believe the gods had abandoned them. Couple this with a few years of harsh sun, no rain, no crops, and this belief becomes a certainty. Why have we been abandoned so? This cry is familiar throughout history. Then there is a freak occurrence. One of those things.

'That year, the last year of the siege, there is suddenly a huge outburst of centipedes. We know this because it was written down. Centipedes came from the forest and flooded the town.

'Now we know this sort of thing is not too unusual – think of years when locusts descend like a black mist and blot out the African sky – we know that certain environmental circumstances lead to certain irregularities. But back then they didn't have science or weather or ecology to help them make sense of it. They had the sky, the sea and the angry gods who no longer believed in them. That was how the world worked.

'The island was besieged from within. Carpets of orange covered the streets. Young children died from bites. Houses and tavernas were infested. The horses all perished. This went on. A religion was born. A small, island religion. The centipedes were gods. Angry, hungry, evil gods who needed to be satiated. The local priests abandoned the gods who had left them to starve and adopted these new ones. They built altars and painted friezes. They worshipped the centipede and propitiated it.'

Nikos tries to corral this mass of information. His throat feels dry and unfamiliar: 'human sacrifice?'

173

'Yes,' the Professor nods as if Nikos is a particularly dim student who's finally got something right. 'Don't be so surprised. It's not the only island in the Greek archipelago where such things have occurred. We know about the Minoans. We know about Crete and Thira. We know that when there are several years of famine and drought the gods are assumed to be displeased and that only human blood will herald the restoration. It's happened everywhere, in all periods of history.'

The Professor's voice rises in tandem with his enthusiasm. Nikos can feel his eyes bulge under their sockets, the blood vessels in his brain dilating and expanding.

'Religions have been born out of it; whole cultures rotated around its bloody axis; wars were waged for the procurement of fuel for its hungry engine. Empires fell, cities sank in blood and many, many thousands of men and women and children died the most horrible deaths, under the blazing sun, the hateful glare of the sky, on altars in high places and in hidden ravines, all the way back to Isaac, through the blood and flesh of Jesus, to the battlefields and killing fields, the smoke and crematoria fires of our own history and on until the earth itself becomes the ultimate sacrifice to the black gaping hole of space.

'In Palassos, it happens to be specific to centipedes. A chance spasm. A fluctuate of history and heat and breeding cycles. One of these things. Yet, a whole sub-rosa culture developed out of it.'

'You said on the phone there were anomalies. That this cult didn't fit the pattern.'

Nikos can see the Professor has a tendency for tangents and wants to get him back on track. This was no time for a history lesson.

'There are always anomalies. But this is something else. Ask yourself: how did a group of hippies, running away from civilisation, from war and their parents' expectations, end up as a centipede cult?

'Of course we know how easy it is for idealism to turn to its dark twin and become fanaticism. Look at the world around us, at many organisations which began as one thing and turned into something else. Idealism always leads to death and sacrifice because the world can never measure up to the abstractions we try and place on it. But why these hippies? Why this time? And why kill two children and *then* commit mass suicide? It doesn't make sense at all. It doesn't follow a pattern. There's no build-up like we find in other cults, no discernible threat from the outside like at Waco. And if they all died thirty-three years ago, why are you finding bodies now?'

TWENTY-FIVE

The building of the archives of the Archpatriach stands grey and silent in the early morning haze. Businessmen rush by in crumpled suits, sweat pouring over their brows. Tourists stand eyes agape, maps in their hands and a look of awe surrendering their faces. Dogs scurry through the backstreets, their mouths clamped over this morning's newest discovery, a day-old piece of souvlaki or a rat.

Hangovers have never been this bad.

Nikos stands on the steps of the building, massaging his temples, swigging from a bottle of warm mineral water, trying to still the persistent pounding in his head.

He'd made the appointment at the last minute. So far, for all his efforts, he'd been unable to unearth any information on the two priests. The records of the Church were notoriously sloppy and incomplete. Several phone calls had yielded nothing but promises to call back followed with sincere regrets that the material he'd asked for was missing.

He flashes back to Vondas, prone in the mortuary. The sense of relief that his body seemed to convey in death. The scars and mutilations.

He'd gone through the police records on Karelis's disappearance, but there wasn't much there. He'd been reported missing on 11 June of last year. His housekeeper had seen him the night before. She'd taken out his dinner and left him a cup of tea as she did every night. The next morning, when she went in to give him his lunch, he was gone. When he hadn't come back that night, she'd called the police.

A deputy had searched the room. He found nothing unusual and nothing missing from the priest's belongings; his wallet and ID card were still in his desk. Neighbouring monasteries and churches were contacted, but no one had seen the old man. And that was it. There was no follow-up. No one had even questioned Vondas on his former colleague's disappearance.

The archives are housed in a converted bank. The metal doors and barred windows give the place an aura of impregnability that Nikos is sure must have appealed to the Synod. It has all the solemnity of church but with the added reassurance of capital.

This morning, however, Nikos is not able to appreciate the delicate refinement of the marble work, the painted saints who stand rigid and true along the main corridor. It feels like there's a claw reaching up his back, under his skin, its fingers spreading across his neck and skull, each sharp and hot like a needle pressed into his brain. He stands, his hands placed firmly on the counter to steady himself, as the young priest in front of him telephones to announce his presence.

'You can take a seat,' the young priest whispers, pointing to a line of solid, straight-backed wooden chairs. They look more like torture instruments, but it's better than standing up.

It's been so long since he's been in a church, since his mother's death really, that he's forgotten how quiet it can be. The young priest receptionist is a study in silence. He moves through the air like a man in a film with the sound turned off. Nikos wishes, at that moment, for some piped music, something soothing and banal to take his mind off everything he's left behind on Palassos and everything which still waits for him there.

But there's only the silence of the empty halls, the long corridors and dark rooms, once the resting place of money and bonds and soft bricks of gold now housing no less mysterious treasures, the papers and files of the Archpatriach of Athens, the only centralised database of clergy in Greece.

'Detective Yannopoulis? A pleasure to meet you.'

Nikos takes the hand of the bearded priest standing resplendent above him.

'What is it we can do for you?'

The priest has one of those Old Testament beards, flowing down to his midriff, uncombed and greying, but he's only a young man – in his thirties, which at least seems young to Nikos. His gold-framed glasses sit at odds with his beard, giving him the impression of a slightly vain academic rather than an ecclesiastical archivist. His hands are small and move rapidly through the air as he points towards the main corridor, beckoning Nikos to follow him with a slight nod of his chin.

The room spins and twists out from under Nikos. He grabs the chair, takes a deep breath of air and sees the archivist nodding to himself, his lips pursed in silent commentary.

'Something I ate,' Nikos says but the archivist has already turned his back, his billowing black robes fanning out from under him like a raven's wing.

Nikos follows him through a long corridor studded with saints in agony. There are tortured saints with daggers in their sides, saints sitting serenely in cauldrons of molten lead while their tormentors gloat, saints strapped to wooden pulleys and racks, saints hung like meat, the flesh stripped off their body in ribbons, saints forced to copulate with animals, saints whirling in flaming caresses, saints with their skulls cracked and worms wriggling out, saints awash in blood and faeces dangling from gallows in town squares.

It all makes Nikos's head pound harder, the floor unsteady beneath him. He remembers why he stopped going to church. Those long Sunday mornings steeped in pain and guilt. His mother crying and praying to Jesus and receiving nothing but a life full of hardship and the most drawn-out and painful of deaths.

The archivist comes to a stop outside a large, barred door. He takes a key from a brass ring hanging on the belt of his robe and slowly unlocks the door.

Nikos follows him in and takes a seat behind a glossy wooden table. There's a green lamp and computer monitor, several phone lines and stacks of dusty books all with the same cover.

'I thought we were going to the archive?' Nikos says gently.

'No one outside the church is allowed into the archives, I'm afraid.'

'But it was agreed on the phone.'

'Not by me.' The archivist shakes his head slowly. His hands are intertwined in front of him, but he looks less like he's praying than rubbing his hands. The man Nikos had talked to had said there would be no problem, not for a policeman, not for a case this important.

'Well, if I ask you some questions could you go in and find the answers for me?'

The archivist stares at Nikos bemusedly. 'Absolutely not.'

'This is from the Archbishop?'

'I spoke with him personally on the matter. This being part of a police investigation. We understand the seriousness of your predicament, but I'm afraid the archives are sealed.'

The priest leans forward. He places his hands flat on the table, a stark wooden crucifix dangling from his neck. 'You understand it would be the same as if a priest came to you and asked to look into police files. There is a matter of protocol. Also, we do not believe you will solve your case in our files; therefore, it is not a matter of life or death on which perhaps the Archbishop can intervene. You do understand our position?'

'Perfectly,' Nikos replies. 'Is there anything at all you *can* tell me about the two priest-monks?'

The archivist leans back. 'It's not procedure, you understand, but after you phoned in your request, I did go and check what we had on them.'

The priest stares silently at Nikos. 'What I can tell you, detective, is that Theo Karelis and Laszlo Vondas both studied at the School of Theology in the University of Athens. Vondas was twenty-two when he began his course, Karelis was already in his forties. He'd been a schoolteacher before taking his vows. They were both ordained the same year. When Karelis was made Abbot of the Palassos Monastery in 1970, he requested that his old colleague Vondas join him. The church authorities could see no problem in that, and so Vondas was sent to Palassos. Remember, the monastery was well past its heyday at the time. We were thinking of shutting it for good. Not many monks wanted to go there. Even a monk wants to live within a community. So, when Karelis made his request, it was a relief to the hierarchy. The monastery could stay open. That, detective, is all I can tell you. The Archbishop doesn't know, so please do not mention this talk in future correspondence.'

The archivist leans forward, his hands stretched out in front of him.

'You're wondering perhaps why I told you this, and I asked myself this very question before you came in. I thought back to being a child and reading detective novels under the covers with this insatiable hunger which later became a hunger for God. I believe mysteries are allegories for God. That it is in mystery and darkness wherein we find the light and not, as supposed, the other way around.'

The archivist sits back and stares at Nikos. 'I wish you the best of luck in solving this mystery, detective, but I must leave you now.'

He gets up, moving in that same silent way as the receptionist, virtually floating around the table. His palm feels cold and hard like it was made of paper not skin when Nikos shakes it. 'Follow the main corridor out,' he says, 'otherwise you can get lost. This building is like a labyrinth with no solution.'

TWENTY-SIX

He's thinking about her when there's a knock at the door. He does a quick check in the mirror, making sure his hair's OK and that he looks presentable. In the time it takes to cross the floor, Jason thinks of her standing outside, arms reaching for him across the empty space. The press of lips and sway of hair.

But it's not Kitty at the door, it's Wynn. He's uncharacteristically grim-faced, the charming smile all but erased.

'I need to come in,' he says and does so before Jason can even reply, brushing past him and taking a seat on the bed. He smells of cigarettes and impatience.

'We need to talk,' Wynn says, and it's almost like that moment in a relationship when you realise you've been kidding yourself it's been going fine and then she says those words. Four words which only signify bad things.

'What about?' Jason asks, taking the only chair, sipping lukewarm Coke.

Wynn looks tired. His clothes are crumpled and hanging out all over the place. He's tapping one foot on the floor.

'The future,' he replies.

And though Jason has a good idea of what he's insinuating, he says, 'What are you talking about, Wynn? What's that got to do with you?'

He smiles for the first time since entering the room, and some of the old Wynn flames back. Which is preferable, Jason can't say.

'It's got a lot to do with me and a lot to do with Kitty.'

Like he knows he will, Jason clams up. The room's cold, but he can feel it burn across his skin. He tries to sit as still as he can. Fold down all emotion inside himself. This is the moment he's been dreading for so long. There's a certain relief as well as trepidation in his eyes as Wynn continues.

'Remember that first night you asked me to do you a favour?'

How can he forget? His loose tongue. His willingness to enter into deception. His fear of approaching Kitty directly.

'I need a favour back,' he says, waiting for Jason to nod, which he doesn't do, just stares at him.

Wynn shuffles on the spot, his shoes making strange creaking sounds on the tiles. 'Things are changing on the island,' he says.

'Things are changing everywhere.'

His eyes blink twice. The smile turns into something else. 'That's as may be.'

'I don't owe you anything, Wynn.'

'I could have said the same thing that night you asked me to stalk Kitty.'

It's like a punch to the stomach you know is coming but can't prepare yourself for.

'I didn't ask you to stalk her.'

Wynn shrugs. 'I'm not sure she'd see it quite that way.'

'What do you want?'

His shoulders slump, he reaches for a cigarette. The curl of his lips, and the way he's trying to hide it, tells Jason he thinks he's got him on the hook.

'I'm not sure what's going on, and I wouldn't tell you anyway, but let's say I no longer trust the people I work for. I think they have plans for me.'

'Who? The man with the huge jaw? The one you sent to harass Kitty?'

His reaction is worth whatever may come next. For the first time, Wynn looks stunned, speechless. It's almost like you can see his brain trying to formulate a way out of this.

'Well done for working that out.' Wynn's laughter takes Jason by surprise. He's reminded of the garrulous charmer of the first night. 'What I need is for you to help me get off the island.'

Jason isn't sure what to say. It's what he wants and what he doesn't want. Wynn off the island is good. But getting caught helping him leave . . .

'You trust me?'

'No. But I trust you want to keep certain things secret. Certain parties in the dark.' His teeth flash white, 'I've learned that you can always trust someone who's got something to lose.'

Jason thinks about Kitty. Murdered boys and girls. The sinkhole years swirling behind him. 'Find someone else.'

The words come hissing out like air from a punctured tyre. He can't quite believe he's said it, and it doesn't look like Wynn can either.

Jason stares at him. Wishing he was better at reading faces. He knows if he agrees now, it'll only be the start. These things only spiral down. It's a risk, but helping Wynn is a bigger one, letting him know he'd do anything to keep a secret.

'That your final answer?' Wynn doesn't seem perturbed, and it makes Jason feel as if he's made a huge mistake.

Jason nods, walks across the room and opens the door. 'Get out.'

TWENTY-SEVEN

He kneels by his mother's grave. He takes the handkerchief out of his pocket, dabs it with some bottled water and slowly, methodically, cleans the stone. The dirt and dust and bird shit are stubborn, and he scrubs until he's sweating, until every piece of dirt is gone from the stone and only the lettering remains. He tells her how much he misses her and how he wishes he could have made her life better as he stares out at the barren hill directly opposite him, the mountain rising like an angry giant from behind it, the Black Monastery a spot of white like a dab of icing at its summit.

The cemetery at Palassos has seen better days. The young people have left the island, in search of better wages and a better life on the mainland. There's no one left to tend these graves any more, and every week there's another piece of ploughed ground, another stone succinctly marking the arc of a life.

Grass grows wild across the graves, weeds and roots stick up out of the ground, the only things growing in this place. Most of the stones are broken, cracked and split like fingernails, whether by time or teenage antics, Nikos cannot tell.

He pulls the roots and weeds away from his mother's plot. He tramps down the earth beside it. When he's satisfied it's perfect and shipshape, he lights a cigarette and walks through the occluded path towards the big yellow earth-mover, abandoned now like a dinosaur stranded in a museum.

He checks the fresh mound of unearthed dirt, the long dark hole in the ground, because he's certain he's got the wrong place or the wrong time. It's supposed to be Vondas's funeral today, but there's no one here.

* * *

Nikos sits in the empty cab of the bulldozer and smokes until he sees the priest coming, first a black dot in the distance, gradually taking on the shape of a man as he nears, his face clearly perplexed, checking his watch and looking around.

'Seems it's just you and me.'

The young priest jumps at the sound of Nikos's voice. Nikos climbs down out of the cab and introduces himself.

'Then this is the right place?' The priest looks confused, like a child whose father hasn't come home for a few days. He's young, his beard still hugging his chin, his body rake-thin and wiry. He's suffused with nervous energy, his hands constantly jittering inside his robe, his foot absentmindedly tapping the floor, his eyes surveying the scene as if it had all been a mistake and somewhere over the next rise there was a group of figures, sheathed in grief and wailing, awaiting his entrance.

'I thought there would be a lot of mourners.'

Nikos nods. 'Me too. Guess people forget quickly enough.' He takes out a cigarette, offers the priest one. 'When's the body arriving?'

The priest cups his hand over his cigarette as he lights it. 'Any time now. I spoke to the funeral director this morning. I expected . . . I don't know what's happening here. You'd think the death of a village priest, an ex-monk, would bring everyone out. That's how it used to be. People just don't seem to believe any more. Every day there are fewer and fewer people in church. I used to think it was me, but now I think it is them. Something has changed in this world. I feel like the last cowboy or something, you know?'

They sit and smoke and wait for the coffin. The sun snarls above them. Nikos stares out at the blue ripples of sea, at the dark and dry hills surrounding them. He remembers the day of

185

his mother's funeral. His last day on Palassos before taking the post in Athens. The wind and rain that morning, the congregation of locals all tears and hooded eyes.

The funeral director sets up the coffin. He wheezes, splutters and coughs as he explains to the priest how to work the machine. He tells them he'll be back later.

'Suppose we should get on with it,' Nikos suggests.

'It feels wrong, you know, it being like this.' The priest looks genuinely disconsolate, still a stranger to the disappointments which constitute life.

'You knew him?'

The priest nods then shakes his head. 'Not really.'

He takes another cigarette and lights it off the old one, 'You'd think we'd have known each other better, but Vondas kept very much to himself. I always said I'd go and visit him but you know, there's so many things to do, you forget.'

'I don't suppose,' Nikos waits a beat, lets his voice drop, 'you would know of any reason why someone would want to kill him?'

The priest looks stricken, like Nikos had just questioned the blueness of the sky. 'Why would anyone want to do that to any man, let alone a priest? I don't think this is something any of us can know, detective, maybe even God himself doesn't.'

'I was thinking more in the line of threats, things like that. You never came across anything that may have fit that description?'

'I think I would be the last to know. There are always people who hate us. People who hate God because they fear Him so much. They know He can see into the labyrinth of their souls, and this makes them scared. But, no, I do not recall anything specific.'

They stand across the coffin, two men in a barren field of broken stones. Nikos thinks back to the archivist's words, how God was the greatest mystery of all, and he wonders how much they have in common, this thin young man and him, both circling around the unknown chambers of men's hearts in search of a thunder strike that would rip all the pain and suffering away.

'Do you know why Vondas would have been up at the monastery the night he was killed?'

The priest turns and examines Nikos's face. 'I heard he went back there often. You know how it must be, no? He spent his formative years there, it was a place of purity and silence. He was horrified that it had been turned into a tourist attraction.'

'Really?' Nikos lets the priest find his own rhythm, no point pressing him yet.

'Yes. There was quite a lot of controversy in the hierarchy about it. As you know, the monastery was closed down in the mid-seventies due to lack of personnel. That was when Vondas and Karelis both moved to town. They stopped being monks and became priests. Neither really adjusted to that loss, I think. In the late eighties a lot of these long-shut monasteries were being reopened by the tourist commission. There was money to be made. Vondas launched a petition with his higher-ups, said the monastery had to remain closed. He went to Athens. Sat in conference with the bishops. They dismissed his petition. The monastery was reopened as a tourist attraction. There were reports that he would haunt the monastery grounds trying to scare tourists off. Maybe that's why he was there that night.'

Nikos lets these new facts tumble through what he already knows. 'You said the priests never got used to leaving the monastery. How so?'

'Well, it was like they never did leave. They became hermits in their own abodes. Karelis in his house in the interior and Vondas in his room in town. Vondas refused to deal with parishioners, and Karelis was drunk a lot of the time.'

'Karelis drank?' This new information sets Nikos's mind wandering through all the theories and suppositions he's so far held.

'Yes. More than he should.'

'So it's entirely possible that he was drunk one night and fell?'

The priest looks around him as if his superiors had crept up unawares and were watching him. 'He had passed out several times. And once he turned up with bruising all over the left side of his face but said he couldn't remember where he'd got it.'

'So maybe his "disappearance" was just misadventure?' Nikos thinks of all the precipitous ledges and slippery cliffs on the island. Depending on the tides, his body could have floated anywhere in the Mediterranean.

'I hate to say this, but that's what we all thought when we heard he'd gone missing.'

Nikos stands silently as the priest intones the liturgy. Deep and mellifluous, his voice carries the dolorous melody across the bleak hills and fields as if presiding over a presidential funeral. The coffin is plain and chipped. Three goats stand like tardy mourners around the hole, watching with black eyes, as Nikos and the priest winch the coffin down into the waiting ground. The priest recites a short eulogy, waves his incense and crosses himself as the coffin touches the ground with a cold, bottomless sound like a ship sunk in deep sea trenches. There was nothing left to do now but wait for the bulldozer operator to come and fill the hole. Nikos and the priest share one last cigarette in silence, their faces drawn and lined, as they watch two blackbirds circling in the endless blue above.

TWENTY-EIGHT

'You can't keep a secret for ever,' Nikos tells her, and though it is the wrong thing to say, it's nonetheless true. This he knows. This he's kept hidden from himself all these years. Thirty-three years. A whole lifetime on the point of unravelling.

'You can try.' Alexia's eyes are like whirlpools. Eyes he's fallen into over the years, pools of escape from the humdrum of his days. Now they're blazing. Fear and anger make them shine.

'We should leave. Mother still has her place in Athens,' she offers, knowing he won't but she feels the need to say this, to exhaust all their options before the inevitable end of this thing.

She can feel it like a room closing in on her. The room of her past. She didn't think she'd have to enter it again, but how stupid can you be Alexia? She chides herself, knowing Nikos is right. Knowing all lies eventually come to the surface stripped of what made them so seductive in the first place.

'I came back here for a reason,' he says, stirring the sugar slowly into his coffee. There was a time, a couple of years back, when he was hemmed in by the routine of his days: stirring coffee, sun-dappled mornings on watch, the boredom of a life without surprises. He thought he'd go mad, but Alexia always brought him back. Into his life, their life, this life. And now . . . now he'd got exactly what he wanted. Excitement and mystery. But it was not what he wanted. Not at all. The fragile lies that held them together are starting to unravel, and he wonders where it will leave them. Together or apart? Knowing, either way, that the life they knew is over and he

189

feels a sudden stab of loss for those idle days stirring coffee, looking up at his wife, the smile on her lips telling of kisses past and future.

'They won't find out,' he says finally.

She sits down next to him. Her skin is tired from worry, lined and creased like the tablecloth. 'Who won't find out?' She replies, and her voice is little more than a whisper. 'The cops? The rest of the island? Or is it the writer and her friend you're worried about?' She tries to untangle her words from the spite and fear that produces them, but it's still there, palpable on her tongue as last night's alcohol.

'I won't betray you,' he says, and this she knows. 'For anyone. This life is more important than the truth.' He's made his decision. This is what his life comes down to.

She's washing the dishes downstairs. He hears them break and clatter to the floor. He tunes it out. He's in the storeroom again. He thought he'd put it to use as a workout space. Now he's here for the past. For things he'd thought long buried and forgotten.

Even after the first two murders, he wouldn't accept that this was the start of something that would eventually unravel his life. Coincidence and the poetry of random events seduced him, told him not to worry. But how many random events did it take before you started calling it a pattern?

For a while, he'd managed to convince himself it was drugs and money and murder. But he's been kidding himself. Again. The book in the priest's room. The things he's learned in Athens. The fear in every word Petrakis says. This is related to 1974 even though it can't be.

He hasn't even thought about that week for years. Sometimes images, the sound of someone's voice, will drift from the past and wash through him – but it's always been easy to shove it away, to pretend that life belonged to someone else. He stares down at the loose files and dossiers he retrieved from the station. Maybe in these quiet and bland pages there's an answer. A way to save them. He's saved her before with lies, now maybe he can do it with the truth.

The scribbled notes of a twenty-two-year-old. The rushed excitement betrayed by the slant of the words, their spidery connections and dense assemblage. He'd just graduated from the police academy. Life was different then. The colonels holding onto the last tendrils of power. The terrorists blowing up American businessmen in the streets of Athens. The summer of 1974.

He'd requested Palassos. All his friends at the academy wanted terrorist detail. That's where the promotions and connections were to be made. The fame and political leapfrogging. That was not what he wanted. Too many hands to shake, deals to make, principles to swallow. The police force was a de-facto private army the colonels used to diffuse and destroy the rising tide of leftist protest. He had no politics. He was only a kid. But he didn't like blood. Didn't like the rumours they'd heard at the academy about special hand-picked police death squads.

He got Palassos. His colleagues laughed. Chasing sheep to arrest them for not being as stupid as the locals, they said. Have fun.

The island hadn't changed. He'd only been away three years. His mother was ill. He could look after her and do his job.

He'd heard the rumours, of course. Teenagers in the hills. The deep interior. European and American kids. He knew the type. Had seen some in Athens. He envied them their freedom, their sense that the world held infinite possibilities in store. The American dream, he knew, was not money and success but the ability to begin again, to shed your old skin, leave your town or city and become someone else. In Greece you only became your father. That's if you were lucky.

He'd been manning the desk when they came in that summer day in 1974. He knew right away it was trouble. Their faces were whiter than sugar-dusted *kourabides*. Their breath short and raggedy. It took them several minutes to calm down enough to tell him what they'd found.

A boy and a girl. Illicit lovers in an island of gossip hounds and prurience freaks. They'd gone out to the ruins for some peace. Kisses away from the watchful eyes of the older folk. The ruins had always been a place for lovers. They had no drive-ins on the island. No one had a car. The woods were where kids went. It was where he'd gone with his first love, Lydia, and he still can't forget the buttery taste of her skin as he laid her down by the forest and caressed her hair, sucking in her breath like it was pure oxygen and he a man falling underwater.

The two teenagers in front of him didn't have a chance to kiss. They'd got to the ruins at sundown. Walked hand in hand through the forest. Whisper and anticipation. Blood rushing through their hearts.

Neither screamed when they saw it. It was just not something they could take in immediately. Two boys, seven or eight years old, were staked naked to the top of the stone altar which stood at the centre of the ruins.

They stepped closer, realised what they were looking at. The boy apologised to Nikos for throwing up all over the scene. Nikos nodded. He only wanted to know what they'd found.

It wasn't long before he saw it for himself.

After taking their statements and letting them go, he marshalled a couple of part-timers and headed with them towards the ruins. He'd briefed them about what they were likely to find unless this was all some big joke being played on the new recruit – and he wouldn't have discounted this apart from what he saw on the faces of the two young sweethearts who'd sat before him an hour earlier. This was how ghosts looked.

They came upon the ruins in the last glimmer of day's end. The stone monoliths blazed in the heat. The boys' bodies shone as if they'd been varnished. He heard one of the part-timers cough, then turn and puke.

They shone their torches on the altar. Nikos told them not to get too close in case there were still footprints or other evidence. He took off his shoes and examined the floodlit scene, a cigarette in his mouth to keep away the smell and flies.

The altar was about six foot long and three wide. It was made of stone and stood three feet above the soil. The centipede carvings and strange hieroglyphs were well known to him. Even now, years later, he can still see every little detail, smell the heavy musk of woods and blood and smoke.

The two boys were staked legs and arms akimbo on either end of the altar. Their legs wrapped over and under each other. Thick twists of rope binding hands and feet to the stone. There was blood all over the bodies but no visible wounds. It was as if the blood had been smeared or painted on. Their mouths had been sewn shut, the stitching faltering and ugly like a mock set of teeth. Their mouths had been stuffed with centipedes. The coroner said the arthropods had been alive when the lips had been sown shut. There was evidence of egg-laying in the warm, mucous-drenched throats of the boys.

Their hands, bound and tied, evinced deep defensive scars along the palms and wrists. The torsos were bruised and cut, with crude orange symbols painted across the rib cages and stomachs. The symbols were identical on both boys.

Where their genitals had been was a wide black cave. Whoever had done this had not only severed the genitals but had scooped the whole pelvic area away to leave a shallow repository for the live centipedes. They were writhing and scuttling in the depressions. He'd wanted to turn away, go back into town, drink off a bottle and forget this happened. He wanted to be anywhere else but here.

The cry made them all jump.

Nikos dropped his torch, and the sudden darkness swallowed him.

'Christ!' He said, turning to the blanched faces of his men. 'One of them's still alive.'

Then he heard it again. Not really a cry, more a whimper, the kind a small dog might make if someone stepped on its foot. He rushed to the altar.

Which one was it? They both looked as dead as each other. He knelt down and put his ear to each of their mouths, listening for the whisper of a breath.

The boy's eyes flicked open.

Nikos jumped.

The boy looked at him with an expression – he couldn't say what it was, not fear, pain, panic or relief – but rather something totally stripped of any human referent. The kind of look an animal gives from its trap.

He quickly set about untying the boy. The rope was thick with grease and centipede juice. The creatures crawled up his arm, and he could feel the tiny points of their teeth, but he didn't care. His colleagues were untying the feet when the boy leapt up.

His whole torso sprang like a figure in a pop-up toy. His lips moved frantically as he tried to open his mouth, eyes bulging when he realised his lips were sewn together.

Nikos carefully put his arm on the boy's head, stroking it in what he hoped was a placatory gesture. The boy's eyes spun in their sockets. The part-timers alternately cursed and praised God. The boy's chest pumped like an accordion as he struggled to breathe through his nose. Nikos took out his penknife. He would have to hold the boy still while he cut through the stitches. He turned to his colleagues and felt the boy fall from him.

The boy's head hit the stone of the altar with a thwack, like a cartoon sound effect on Saturday morning television. His eyes misted and rolled back into his head.

He knew the boy was dead. The tension which had sprung his body was totally gone. The amount of blood surrounding his pelvis was deepening. It had been too late. Too fucking late.

Later, he would think that if he'd hurried the two lovers along he might have got up there in time to save the boy. Later, he would think that he had killed the boy. The head hitting the stone, the final nail. Even after the coroner had told him the boy had been beyond saving, even then Nikos could hear, every night, when silence finally fell on him, that one lone thud like a full stop punched into the surface of the world.

The old-timers took over after that.

The boy was dead. They left him where he lay. Nikos didn't say anything to his colleague, the one who couldn't stop crying. It was something which didn't need to be said. As if the man's crying precluded his own. And that was good. For now, he had to go back into town and report this to his superiors. He remembered he'd only been two weeks on the job. How he'd thought the island would be quiet, pastoral police work.

They took his statement. They took the part-timers' statements separately. He could hear them crying in the next room along. He wanted to cry too, but he was in charge, first at the scene, and didn't want to betray his inexperience.

They took him off the case. He was glad and he was pissed off. Glad not to have to see those bodies again, to untie them, zip them into bags and carry them down the hill. Glad not to be the one who had to knock on a parent's door in the middle of the night and usher them into the nightmare which they would learn to call the rest of their lives.

But he was pissed off too. He wanted to be there when decisions were made. He wanted to see the people responsible caught, the sound of handcuffs clinking and the long journey back to the mainland.

The last bit he got. But alone. The next day, staring out at the splashing sea, hearing the boy's cry, heading back to Athens to meet the detectives there. Petrakis and his sergeant had sent him as liaison. Meet the detectives and coroner. Explain on the boat. Bring them back.

Rumours of the cult were already spreading. Almost as soon as he'd reached town. As if the story had been broadcast on the massive speakers embedded in the rock surrounding the harbour.

He'd spent the day going over his story while his superiors went back up to the ruins and sealed it off.

He'd argued. Shouted. Screamed. Said he was the one who'd got the call. He was the one who found the bodies. 'I'm part of this,' he told them. *I need to be part of this* was what he left out.

They told him it was procedure. He was still a rookie, on probation. This was too big a case. Any screw-ups would go straight back to Athens, and heads would roll down here. He listened. He knew they were right. But he couldn't bear it. The sound of the boy's final cry filled his head. The look in the boy's eyes was there every time he closed his own. An image tattooed on the back of his eyelids. He knew it would never go away. He wanted to do something, but they told him to leave it in their hands. They had experience. They knew the protocol.

He had no choice. He went back home. His mother lay wheezing in her bed. He didn't tell her a thing. He didn't need to. She saw it in his eyes, felt it in the gaps between the words he spoke. She took his hand and held it all night as he lay staring at the ceiling, putting off for as long as he could the moment when he would have to shut his eyes and face the boy again.

He took the boat to Athens. He met the detectives. Hunched chain-smokers with voices that sounded like flooded engines. Cold eyes and graveyard humour. They shared coffee, cakes and war stories waiting for the ferry. They spoke of mass murders in the highlands, Communist plots, decapitated diplomats. He thought of the boy. He knew he'd have to find out his name.

Petrakis and his deputy met the detectives at the dock, introduced themselves, smoked cigarettes and talked about the weather. He understood they needed to do this before they could do the rest.

Petrakis took him aside. Thanked him. Then said he wanted him here, at the dock, watching who got off the island. They gave him Michaelis, an old-timer, almost seventy, normally desk-bound. They stood by the boats for two days and took photos of everyone who left. They stopped tourists and interviewed them. Took down passport details. Checked under fingernails for signs of blood or hair.

It was boring. It was sun-smacked and useless work. They stood there and took names. They were as obvious as nuns in a mosque. No murderer would catch the ferry. There were plenty of fishing boats available at a price, or there to be stolen, to whisk anyone away to one of a thousand islands, or even further, to the beaches of southern Italy where they could disappear for ever.

Michaelis murmured darkly. The cult, he said. Those fucking hippies. He'd already made up his mind. Nikos wasn't so sure, but it was seductive. He wanted someone to blame. Someone to punish. He knew the boy would never leave him but perhaps if they caught the killers he could sleep easier.

The next day, he watched as Petrakis crossed the harbour looking punch drunk and bleary. Fucking Samsonites under his eyes.

'It's over,' he told Nikos and Michaelis. 'The fuckers escaped our justice but not God's.'

He'd asked him what he meant. Petrakis said 'Come, see. We need men to help clear up.'

They walked in single file like a procession of the dead. They climbed slowly past the forested hills and ochre valleys. No one said anything. They had left words behind. Entered a country of silence and horror. Each footstep one closer to something they didn't want to find.

Petrakis had briefed him back at the station. Him and eight other policemen on loan from neighbouring islands. He was no longer the one who'd discovered the terrible crime. He'd become part of the clean-up squad.

Petrakis had stood at the front of the main police hall. He'd been drinking. His eyes looked as cloudy as water-infused ouzo. His hands shook as he told them what had happened.

After marking off the crime scene and wrapping the boys'

bodies, they'd marched across the island. Petrakis, his deputy, the Mayor and a doctor. They knew about the hippies. There'd been rumours going around for months. Farmers had reported mutilated sheep and cattle.

They approached the camp with guns drawn, but there was no need.

At first, they'd thought the hippies had fled. Realising the import of their deed, they'd packed up and hidden in the interior – perhaps were already on board boats heading for different islands, scattered like shattered glass, never to be put back together.

But nothing had been removed. The fire still smouldered from the previous night. Dirty cups and half-drunk bottles of retsina stood like sentries around the camp perimeter.

Petrakis's voice choked as he continued. The air inside the station was hot and still. The policemen all sat, eager to hear more, the whine of the fan above like a constant reminder of their beating hearts.

Petrakis told how he shouted out to the hippies, in English, he didn't want them to think this was another rout. He told them they were policemen and had a few questions to ask. But there was no response, just the eerie crackling of dried wood in the ashes of the fire.

Petrakis went in first.

When Nikos got to the camp, it was exactly how Petrakis had described it. Nothing more than a few tents flapping in the wind, an old scar where countless fires had chafed the ground and a swooping view down to the sea.

Petrakis led. Nikos followed. Others behind him. No one talked. This was unusual; policemen always talked in these circumstances. Words to ease off the dread.

But that day there was only silence. And when Nikos followed Petrakis into the main tent, he thought this had all been a game, and, yes, the hippies must have fled, for the tent seemed as silent and empty as space itself.

The police lights made shapes out of the gloom. Slowly his eyes adjusted. Then he saw them.

They had been sleeping on the floor. Neat lines of sleeping bags. A poignancy in how ordered it all was. The odd paperback, a radio, some baby toys. The sleeping bags were occupied. There was silence as Petrakis walked up to the nearest bag and leant over. All the other policemen were now in the tent, and their lights illuminated the scene as if it was only waiting for a director to shout *Action*!

Nikos was closest to Petrakis as he gently unzipped the first bag.

The woman looked like she was sleeping. Her blonde hair flooded around her neck like spilled honey. A vague, uncertain smile clung to her face. Nikos was going to ask, *Was this some sort of joke?*, when Petrakis turned the sleeper's head towards him.

The bullet hole was black and big as a two-drachma piece. The hair was copper and tangled in a dark knot. The sheets were rust red.

'Every one of them.' Petrakis shook his head. 'Every single one. One gunshot to the head.'

Nikos peered down at the woman. She couldn't have been more than twenty. Will always be twenty, he corrected himself.

'Self-administered?' He tried to choke down the horror and anger which suddenly flooded him like sleep. Here they lay, peaceful as old men in mid-afternoon slumber. Peaceful and dead. There would be no clink of handcuffs. No trip to shore. No trial. No justice. Just this.

'No. We don't think so,' Petrakis muttered, 'There's one at the end. A man. Different angle of entry. The coroner will have to concur, but it looks like he was the leader. Looks like he killed them all and then himself.'

The question of why was on nobody's lips.

'We need to bring them back to town,' Petrakis added, this time to the other policemen as well. 'We've taken photos. We've checked the ground. Now it's up to the coroner.'

They spent the whole day and most of the night putting bodies into bags. They didn't have the real body bags they saw every night on the news, black cocoons coming back from South-East Asia filled with young men. As he was putting another limp dead kid into a fishing sack, Nikos thought how ironic it was: one of the main reasons the hippies had fled here was to avoid being shipped back from Vietnam in just this way.

They bagged all personal effects. They bagged books and journals and kitchenware. They bagged cigarettes and maps and postcards from home. They bagged shoes and socks and baby's diapers. They bagged bodies. They bagged everything the bodies left behind.

Two men to a body. That was how they did it. The slow descent into town. Nikos was at the front. He held some woman's head, the features still recognisable by touch through the shifting shroud of the bag.

When they reached town, they had an audience.

Everyone was gathering in the main square. Old men and kids, wives and butchers, fishermen and hoteliers.

When they saw the policemen bringing in the bodies, they cheered. They clapped and sang praises to Jesus. They wept and spat on the bags, and the policemen ignored everything but the task of bringing them into the fish market which, with its abundance of ice, was doubling as a morgue.

That night there was a party. The policemen were treated like kings. The townspeople bought them beer and ouzo and food freshly steaming from home. They sang hymns and national songs of courage and bravery. They drank through the night, and only Nikos thought about the thirty-five bodies lying on top of blocks of ice, two doors down.

The morning came like a sigh of relief. The islanders could go about their business. The savage murderers had come to their senses. Guilt and fear had trapped them like rabbits in sparkling headlights. They knew there was no way out for them. They did what they had to do.

And no one in town felt cheated.

No one apart from Nikos who had been waiting for the court date. The confession and sentence. The boy's face slowly fading from his eyelids.

And now, thirty-three years on, in the back of his house, he knows that he was cheated.

That it had all been too easy. Too pat.

And that something terrible had happened that day they sent him to the mainland to pick up the detectives.

Whether they had spared him or used him, he is yet to find out.

TWENTY-NINE

She loves being surrounded by books. The walls around her made of paper and glue. She enjoys the smell of them, these old volumes, the way they call to her. She could almost be at home, but she isn't. The strange writing which embosses most of these spines reminds her that she is not at home. The moaning of pipes and scream of scooters brings her back to what it is she's trying to do.

Solve a mystery.

Except she's not doing it within the confines of her text, not sending Lily out into the streets knowing she'll stumble upon the key that unravels everything. This is for real, and yet, however many times she reminds herself, it still doesn't feel so different from what she does at home.

Jason hadn't answered when she'd tried calling him earlier. His room was empty. No message for her. He might have disappeared off the island, packed his bags and got out while he still could. She's surprised, and a little annoyed, at how sad this makes her. How she was starting to feel things for him that were barely understandable to her. She remembers the kiss and how her lips trembled but she also remembers she's married and the ring is still there on her finger, marking out tan lines and boundaries.

Don feels so distant, as if she'd been stranded here for years and not days. Was it just the cigarette, the way he tried to cover up his lies? Or something deeper? Something about the island itself?

She'd thought about calling her friends, but all they'd want to hear about would be her and Don and not the things happening on Palassos; her agent and editor would only ask how the book was going. She'd realised that Jason was the only one she could talk to about this, and it makes her smile, the way they've become conspirators. It's why she's here, digging through these books and files, looking for more things she can tell him when they next meet. In between these walls of books, she feels present. Like a part of her has suddenly revealed itself. As if her whole life up to now had been lived in the past tense.

She bypasses the exhibits and goes straight to the library. She has her Greek crib book next to her. She's scanning microfilms from the island newspaper, haltingly making her way through the crooked characters of this strange language. The machine whirs and clicks like another presence in the room.

She looks towards the screen and there's the priest. She remembers the night he came upon them at the monastery. She'd thought his bile and snap were because he was hiding something about the murders. Now she sees it could have been pure fear. Knowing he would be next; maybe wondering if Jason and her were there to kill him.

The photo shows a younger man than the one they met, but it is unmistakably him. She always looks at men's eyes first. It's what draws her in. She never forgot the priest's eyes, like dark drums pummelled into cavernous sockets.

Kitty tries to place the information in the context of what she already knows. The admonishment that night up by the monastery. The priest's murder.

She wonders if the disappearance of Karelis, the older priest, has anything to do with this. It's too tempting a coincidence to ignore, but it may also be random. Both sets of murders, in 1974 and the current ones, happened in the vicinity of the monastery and ruins. One priest disappears a month after last year's murders and, a couple of days ago, the other priest is found dead by the monastery grounds.

Silence descends on her again. Now she has a theory, a place to fit the clues into, she delves into the material with added urgency. She flicks through archived photos stored in large, mice-gnawed boxes. There are enough weddings here to flood a chapel. Happy men and women in white, smiles and the rest of life filling their faces with serenity and peace. There are prize hogs and sheep. Farmers holding up vegetables so large they're no longer recognisable. Shots of houses and monuments and heroes. But there's nothing about the ruins or the '74 cult. Not even one photo.

She's disappointed. She was hoping the papers would have more information but it seems as if it's all been expunged. It still bothers her how anyone could know that the entire cult had killed themselves. How anyone could know how many people had been up there in the first place. What if they didn't kill themselves? What if one of their number suddenly decided to take things into their own hands?

She sits in her own silent cocoon, reading, flicking through images, processing all this new information. Her eyes fall on the photo of Karelis on the screen in front of her. The kind of priest who'd scare children into believing in Hell. His beard and eyes wired with righteous fury. His mouth twisted in angry pronouncement. She looks up, unnerved by Karelis's ice-cold gaze, and sees the smoke.

The main door is closed. A thick halo of grey-black smoke surrounds it.

She looks around. She's the only person in here. It's Alexia's day off. The kid who'd let her in told her to lock up when she was done. She gets up. The papers and photos go flying to the floor. Is it already hotter or is she just imagining it? She's not sure but she knows soon it will be. The smoke halo thickens, and she can hear the wood beginning to crack. The smell rich and pungent. The paint on the inside of the door blisters and pops. It's this sound that makes her turn and begin running.

She reaches the end of the room. There's a massive explosion, and then heat and light fill the room as the door finally gives and the flames come lapping like waves rushing through a break in a sea wall.

She's running now, but there's nowhere to go. Endless corridors of books. A labyrinth of books. She knows soon these volumes will be on fire and that nothing will stop this.

She coughs and retches. Her throat feels swollen and misshaped. She tries calling out as the room fills with banners of smoke, but the sound of flames is all she can hear.

She scans the room. Shelves and bookcases make her dizzy. Then she sees the fire escape at the other end of the room. She runs towards it.

She reaches the door. She grabs it and screams. Her hand sizzles and burns. She feels the skin peeling off her palm. She takes off her shirt and wraps it around her fist. The smoke rips through her lungs and it feels like someone's scraping a knife along the inside of her throat. She knows this will hurt, but it's her only choice. She grabs the handle again and turns.

Cool air rushes across her face. She almost says a prayer but instead she pushes harder. There's a bang as the door hits something and stops.

She can see the sky, the deserted street, but she can't open the door more than a couple of inches. It feels like there's a tank wedged in front of it. The tiny sliver of air is all she's going to get.

She stares for a second as if landed here from a dream. She feels the heat now, burning skin and eyes. Then she remembers. She forces herself backwards, away from the cruel sliver of sunlight and back into the black smoke.

Everywhere around her is the sick sizzle and hiss of burning books like a thousand insects talking at the same time. The bathroom is just ahead. She used it an hour ago and remembers the feeling of the cool breeze that brushed her face as she washed her hands.

The door, thank God, is open. She screams anyway because her shirt is not enough to dampen the heat. But inside it's cool. The fire hasn't penetrated this small room yet. Outside she hears the crashing of shelves as they topple to the ground.

She looks up at the window and begins to shake. She's trapped. There's no way out. Though the window is big enough for her to squeeze through, it's barred.

Smoke floods the bathroom. The heat rises. It's only minutes to go. She thinks of Don, or tries to think of him, because this, she now realises, could be the last few minutes of her life, and if she's going to die she wants to see her husband's face but, however much she tries, she can't picture him, and for a moment the panic at this is worse than her panic about the fire. He's just not there.

The smoke makes her cough. Rips her out of this reverie. She climbs onto the sink hoping it will hold her weight. She can feel the breeze now, the cool rush of air. She grabs one of the metal bars and pulls. Rust flakes off in her hand. She pulls harder. Nothing happens. Then again and there's the faintest of creaks. She uses both hands, steadying herself on the sink. She wedges her elbow to gain leverage. The bar groans, then gives way, sending her flying back down onto the floor. The room is blistering. The paint is popping and sizzling. She gets back up on the sink and pulls at the second bar. This time there's almost no resistance. The gap it leaves is just wide enough. She squeezes herself through, the rough iron scratching and tearing at her skin.

The fall is only one floor but she lands on rocks and garbage bags. Long thin streamers of pain shoot through her legs as she gulps the air like someone trapped in a dream of drowning. Above her, the sky is streaked with ribbons of black smoke, reaching up into the wide expanse of blue.

THIRTY

She's crying again. This time she won't let him soothe her. Nikos understands those days are over. He's told Alexia about the fire. She was coming back from town. She hadn't heard. Had been at the beach all day. These coincidences and lucky escapes unsettle him. What if it had been her normal . . . better not to think about that.

She hadn't taken him seriously at first, searching his face for some indicator of jollity or elaborate ruse. But there was nothing, and he didn't joke with her. The scope of their relationship had never allowed that. There was too much history, too many secrets. Things that kept them in the gravity of seriousness these shuttered years.

She became silent, folded into the very deepest part of herself. He made her countless cups of tea. Listened to her sentences, broken and fragmented now, as if the fire in the library had robbed her of the confidence of language.

He fell to lies. Hating himself but not able to help it. Those words falling from his lips: there'll be an investigation; we'll catch the culprits; rebuild; the library will be better than before. And then the worst lie: it must have been an accident.

She's in her room now. She'd asked him not to come in. It had been four hours. He sits in the storeroom, staring at the files.

Looking through them a couple of nights ago, he felt something was wrong. The way it had all fallen so neatly into place. His trip to the mainland. Everything wrapped up by the time of his return. And then his mother had died, and he'd transferred back to Athens, and the questions had stopped coming, he slept well, didn't even think about the island most days.

Coming back here, he thought that was all over. Thirty-three years. Too much time. He never dreamed he'd be the one to dig back in. Unearth ghosts he'd buried. Take back all the lies he'd told himself.

He tries not to think about it, but he knows that somewhere in here lies the answer to why his wife's place of work now lies smouldering. Perhaps even to the bodies recently discovered on the island. There were so many things he'd left unsaid for so many years in silent supposition. How much did he actually know? More than he thought he did, or less? He flashes back to the book in the priest's room. The word NO scrawled all across the text, across Karelis's face. The feeling of being cheated he'd had that day coming back from Athens, the cult already dead. He knows that there is only one person on the island who can answer his questions.

Petrakis sits slumped in his armchair like he's a part of the design. Over the years his snarled body has moulded itself to fit into this tatty rattan chair.

His mother sits in an old wheelchair at the other end of the room. She doesn't move. She hasn't moved for eight years since the stroke. She's catatonic like sculpture. Nikos can smell the unchanged diapers and death stink. Despite being Mayor, the old man has chosen to live like this. He has a villa on the other side of the island, but he spends his nights here.

Petrakis had sent him to the mainland that day. Petrakis had wanted him off the island.

'Thought you might come.' The old man says. His features seem to have dwindled since Nikos saw him a few days before. It's as if they were made to fit a much smaller face. Petrakis looks mummified, and, with all the ouzo and armchair residence, he may as well be.

208

'You have any idea what's going on?' There's no time to waste on formalities. They were never friends.

Petrakis snorts. His shoulders involuntarily jump. It's not a shrug but a sign of something Nikos can't decipher. Perhaps just nerve damage, old age.

'Yeah. I killed those tourists. Priest too. Can't wait to get up off my armchair and do another.' His ensuing laugh is filled with a sinewy up-gust of phlegm and tar. He sounds more like a broken-down machine than a man.

'They burned down the library.' Nikos says, watching for surprise to etch itself on the old man's face but there's no movement at all.

'Doesn't surprise me. Your wife smoking in there all the time.'

'She was on her day off.'

'Lucky for her.' Petrakis snorts.

Nikos wants to leave. The room suddenly closes in on him with its miasma of decrepitude: the unwashed clothes and spoiled food; the stink and fog of stale smoke.

'Why did you send me to the mainland?' It's out. The first time he's asked this to someone other than his wall. The things you suspect are often the last things you want to know.

Petrakis leans forward. It's an effort for him and a sign the old man's upset. 'To pick up the city detectives.'

'Bullshit.' It comes out with more force than he intends but he's glad. He wonders if he'd asked this question years ago, would the recent murders still have occurred? He can see Petrakis's face shade with uncertainty. 'What happened when I was on the mainland? What did you do at the camp?'

The old man leans back. Takes another long gulp of the misty liquid. 'You think I can remember? That was thirty-three years ago. We did what we did. That's the way it's always been on the island. You would have done the same.' The sarcasm makes the sentence sound like a slap in the face. 'You need to investigate the present not the past. The killer isn't a ghost. Someone's got it in for us. They're using this to bring back memories of '74. They want to tear this island apart. Force tourists to stop coming. None of us wants that, not even you.'

Nikos moves forward. The smell of the room fills his nostrils. He looms over the old man. 'That's bullshit. None of this makes sense.'

'What? After all these years you still think things make sense?' Petrakis laughs loudly.

Nikos spools back to what the Professor told him in Athens. 'You had a bunch of middle-class European kids who suddenly decide to kill two boys and then commit group suicide? This isn't how cults operate,' he pauses. 'Had they been threatened by the locals?'

'They did what they did. No one bothered them.'

'I talked to someone who knows about these things. He couldn't understand it either.'

'You really think you can ever understand what lies deep in another man's heart?'

'No, but we're talking about cults, not individuals; there are patterns and structures. They turn inwards, close in upon themselves. They don't murder kids. These were normal European teenagers. What made them change so quickly?'

Petrakis smiles. 'Maybe it was the deep interior that called to them. You know the tales, Nikos, you know the forest isn't what it seems. There have always been things we can't explain on this island.'

Nikos leans back. 'I'm going to find out what happened that night.'

'Find out what? There's nothing to find out and a lot to lose.'

Nikos ignores the taunt, is about to leave, come back later when the old man's not so sozzled, when the front door opens.

Dimitri, Petrakis's son, walks in. First thing he does is notice Nikos. Just stares at him. Nikos smiles.

'What the hell are you doing with my father?' Dimitri's hand reaches down, settles into a back pocket.

'Just catching up on the good old days, weren't we?'

The look Petrakis gives him could be from a 1940s B-movie; all overplayed malevolence and spitting hate.

'Your father was just telling me some interesting things.'

Dimitri moves forward, crowding Nikos's space, his jaw weirdly angled and solid. 'I think it would be better if you leave. Papa's drunk. He doesn't want to talk to you.'

He's always drunk; he never wants to talk. Nikos is about to say these things when his nose wrinkles. He coughs and smells the air again. For sure.

'It was good of you to help put out the fire,' Nikos says.

Dimitri looks towards his dad, but the old man is staring out the window.

'The fire in town. You weren't one of the men putting it out?'

'I don't know anything about any fire,' Dimitri says.

Nikos smiles. 'No, of course not.'

THIRTY-ONE

There's something about Jason that makes her uneasy. As they walk up the cracked and broken street towards his hotel, she can't understand why he seems so distant, so uncaring. And then she can't understand why she expects him to be these things.

She's told him about the fire. She can still smell it on her hair and skin, despite two hot showers, but it serves as a reminder. This is not some story you're concocting nor some Nancy Drew kick. This is everything that's just happened.

He'd tried to talk her into going to see a doctor, held her hand when that hadn't worked, told her how sorry he was for getting her involved in all this.

As she'd landed outside, shuddering and smoke-choked, she finally realised the fire was no accident. Someone wanted her dead.

'You don't know that,' he says, and she can tell he'd prefer it to be an accident. That facing up to the danger they're in is something he's trying to avoid. He can smell the smoke on her but not the need to be unburdened.

George shakes his head, spitting out some loose tobacco. 'Wynn was looking for you.'

The word is like a stake driven through Jason's lungs. 'What did he want?' He hates the way his voice sounds, wonders if Kitty's picked up on it.

George's eyes look sad and weary, 'I don't know. He seemed . . . he seemed different. Desperate somehow. Maybe this would be a good time for you to leave the island.'

'I can't leave yet.' He watches the older man's face crumple like a handkerchief pushed quickly back into a pocket. George shakes his head. 'Last ferry's at five. Then everything closes down. Biggest night of the year tonight. Christmas and New Year rolled into one.'

The world spins again. The humidity drops from the sky like an anvil. 'What are you talking about?'

'You don't know?' George doesn't wait for an answer, 'Tonight the island celebrates its release from captivity. Our own local independence day. You know this was the first island to become independent from the Ottoman Empire?'

Jason shakes his head, not at all sure what this has to do with him and Kitty. He stares at the tablecloth as George continues. 'This night, of all nights, is in memory of the last night of the battle. The burning of the Ottoman fleet in the harbour.

'The sultan had sent ships to ring the bay, to stop the untaxed trade. Firebrands and militia from this island, from the deep interior, swam in the dark waters and boarded the galleons. They primed them and blew them. The Turks flew into the air like sparks. Cannons were erected and set upon the Ottoman army garrisoned inland. They buried the captured Turks on the beach. Buried them so that only their heads stuck up out of the ground. They left them to die and rot, a line of heads blistering in the sun. A warning to any others who thought the island was up for grabs. Tonight is not a good night to be in town. Tonight is for the locals. There will be a lot of men from the deep interior. They do not like tourists. They understand what will eventually happen to them.'

* * *

They walk through the winding main street. Kitty feels as if she's in a daze. The lights and colours seem to bounce off the beautiful dying blue sky. The sun's over to the west, disappearing blood red and baleful behind the dark torn teeth of the Peloponnesian mountains. There's still an hour of light left but soon it will be shadowed by the encroaching night.

'What do we know for certain?'

He stares at her, the sun a backdrop isolating her face as if it were superimposed on the landscape, the red lips and fire-hazard eyes. They're sitting in a waterfront taverna watching the people gather, the intent faces and hungry eyes.

'That the current murders seem to exhibit the same MO as those from 1974,' he says.

She swivels her fingers like an ex-smoker whose amputated limb of a cigarette still holds a phantom twinge. She puts both hands on the table. Spreads the fingers like the opening of a Chinese fan. He's staring at the newly polished nails, wondering when she had time to do them, were they for him, or just something she did for herself?

'We know that thirty-three years ago, hippies, mainly from Europe and the States, settled in the interior of the island. Then two local boys are found murdered. The hippies are blamed. There's whispers of a cult and evidence of mutilated animals strewn across the island's interior.'

He's surprised at how confident he sounds narrating this story when his own words fail him constantly.

'The day after the discovery of the bodies, the police and some of the village elders climb up the mountain to confront the cult. I think we can safely assume they were armed. Furthermore, I think we can assume they went up there for a very different reason than to arrest the cult.'

'You think they went up there to kill them?' Kitty sounds surprised, but she's not. She's considered this theory herself and found it the most plausible. But she likes the feeling of surprise which comes from finding out your co-conspirator's thinking along the same lines, and she pretends this is new to her.

'Yes. But when they got there, the job was already done. They find the whole cult in their beds, neatly dead with a single bullet hole in their skulls. This must be a shock to them. The obvious one, of course, these dead kids, the vast number of them, but more than this it must leave them with a feeling of unresolved matters. Some might think justice was done, but others, I'm sure, felt justice was cheated. These islands always liked to enforce laws themselves, and the hippies took that prerogative out of their hands.

'Then the bodies are taken down the hill into town. They're bagged and shipped to the mainland. The case is closed. The two boys are dead, but so are the killers. Everything goes back to normal.'

It makes more sense when he puts it into words; the seduction of narrative pulls him along, making him see things clearer than before. He signals the waiter for another Coke and continues, 'Then, thirty-two years pass. . . . there's another murder with a similar MO to that of the two boys. Specifically the centipedes. The ritual mutilation. The carvings on the rocks nearby. But the victim is a young tourist, probably involved in the drug trade.'

He leans back, takes a drag of the hazy air, letting the facts fall into place. In the distance two ships pass by each other, honking greetings, then disappearing round the edge of the opposite island.

'George told me that both the murdered locals were dealers.' He watches Kitty take this in. 'I think Wynn knows all about the 1974 cult murders. I think him and Dimitri, the guy with the jaw, are using the MO as cover to take over the drug trade. Maybe Vondas saw them committing one of the murders. He was always up there by the monastery, it makes sense. Wynn has to kill him. Maybe that's why the priest doesn't fit any pattern.'

Kitty takes a swig of her drink and lets it roll around her mouth as she contemplates this. 'I had another theory.' Her chin lifts, catching a last gleam of sun which makes it seem made of marble. Jason nods, watches as her body swells with air and speculation.

'What if Karelis never disappeared?'

Jason stares at her. He's not even considered this.

'What if Karelis is behind the recent murders?' Her breasts nudge the table, her hand shakes. Jason hasn't seen her like this all holiday.

'Why?'

'Revenge.'

'Revenge for what?'

She smiles, 'For closing down the monastery. For turning away from God. What if Karelis blames the island for what happened in 1974? The murders. The closure of the monastery. The move away from belief and towards material pursuits. Doesn't it strike you as weird how unreligious this island is compared to others? Normally there's more churches, the streets are empty on Sundays. I remember thinking back when I was here as a student, how religious these islands still were, how they seemed trapped in a time warp.

'Karelis sees the monastery close down. He's helpless to do anything about it. At the same time, the developers move in. Money and expansion become the only goals. He wants to take revenge on the island. What better way than to replicate the centipede murders? On one level, these murders are all about ritual and the world behind the world. They're a statement of faith even if that faith is a corrupted one. I think that would appeal to him. One the other hand, it's the perfect way to get back at the island, at what he sees as its soulless heart. One murder is an accident, even adds to the allure of the place. Two murders is a place to avoid.'

'So they framed a drifter.'

'The island subsists on tourist revenue. They hate us coming here, but they have no choice, it's either that or starvation. An arrest is made, and everyone goes back to sleeping peacefully.'

Jason tries not to stare at her hands, the way they describe shapes in the air when she talks, the way they settle millimetres from his.

'Karelis goes into hiding after the first two murders. Probably in the labyrinth. Then, when they frame the drifter, he realises he has to do it again. He resurfaces, and maybe Vondas sees him. He has to kill Vondas too now. Once you start along this path there's no turning back.'

Kitty takes his hand. Her smile is faded like a sun-scorched postcard. Silence envelops them even though the town is filling up; people are screaming and laughing, but they could be on another continent as far as Kitty and Jason are concerned. She leans forward, and, while normally he never picks up on these things, something about the air, the restaurant, the thrill of crime and detection makes his senses more aware, and he leans into her, and their lips touch once more across the red chequered table, and this time they hold, and her soft flesh presses against his, and he's sure he can hear her heart beat, or is it his? And then her lips part ever so slightly, and he can feel the first tentative touch of her tongue, and he meets it with his, and there's electricity there and heat and peace and bloodrush. And though they stick to that, the tracing of each other's lips, it's enough, and when they pull back simultaneously there's no feeling of loss or divorce, just that this is a foretaste of things to come.

THIRTY-TWO

The harbour is crammed. Engorged by locals. Dressed in black. Carrying candles. Waiting for the last breath of the sun.

All around them the crowd gathers.

They leave the taverna and walk along the promenade, past the huddled groups of villagers, all eating the black candy symbolic to this festival, staring wide-eyed at the harbour, expectancy saturating the air with fever and anticipation.

They stand among the locals as the sun arcs down behind the mountain. The town is snuffed into darkness. Candles flicker on like torches. Everyone is holding them.

They look around them. Trying to see a familiar face; Nikos, or at least some drunk British tourist to reassure them. But there's no one.

They've been hemmed in. The crowd has got denser, no longer a collection of discrete groups but an almost featureless mass. Kitty looks out towards the water. It's only now she realises the boats she's seen from far-off were not the usual yachts and pleasure-cruisers but older boats, wooden boats – schooners, she supposes they're called.

It's getting fully dark. People are coming from all parts of town, spilling out of streets and alleys like black volcanic flow.

They're penned in. People crowd around them and press them nearer to the dock's edge. Eyes lock onto theirs and don't let go until they've passed. Kitty feels slivers of panic burn through her. Hands and fingers touching her legs and brushing her breasts.

The crowd begins chanting. An old song. Words, archaeological and mysterious, the melody long and slow and sad. The wind wails and snaps around the harbour. The wooden schooners trail light like fishing lines as they circle the main boat. A loudspeaker from somewhere on the cliff begins intoning an eerie liturgical canto. On the bandstand a four-piece brass band punctuate the words with honks and snarls. Kitty looks at Jason. They smile, both acknowledging the absurdity of the situation.

The candles all blow out at once. They are shrouded in darkness. The press of bodies against them. The deep breathing and slitted looks.

Then it begins.

A rocket arcs over the boat's mainsail and explodes into the stars. Showers of red and green umbrella down onto the harbour. The liturgy sinks deeper as more people sing the dolorous melody. The brass band sounds like it's playing a funeral waltz. The horseshoe cliffs reflect and amplify the sound.

Kitty looks around, fascinated. The faces of the people are frozen in a medieval tableau of sin, penance and suffering. She's about to call Jason when the world explodes. Her eardrums scream with feedback, and her eyes close to bright brilliant glare.

Her ears are still ringing, but her vision's adjusting. She sees the fire. Illuminating the main boat. Slowly engulfing it in its caress. People cheer and scream and raise glasses to the night. Kitty and Jason can't move. The chanting grows furious, as if somehow the collective power of the town could usurp history, take out the new invaders just as devastatingly as the firebrands of old took out the Turks.

The boat burns upon the water. Ripples of flame surround it like a halo of gold. The crowd cheers and whoops. Kitty looks closely and – yes – those are effigies tied to the mast, flames licking at them like the tongues of hungry lovers. She watches mesmerised. Unable to pull herself away. To even think of herself beyond this moment. She understands now how shared awe and wonder can make us forget ourselves for a while, disappear into the warm soup of the crowd. Something in her aches. The way people subsume to something bigger than themselves. It is almost like church.

The effigies whirl and dance in the flames. They look so real. She thinks of witches in the hills and dark deeds in forested places. She tries not to think. To let herself fall. But she's always there, watching herself in silent commentary.

'Christ, I think someone's up there.' Jason's pointing to the effigy on the far left. His face is drawn. Teeth clamped down tight. Kitty scrunches and focuses. The effigy's moving, flailing, fighting against something.

'It's just the wind and flame. It's like Guy Fawkes,' she whispers into his ear.

They continue watching. The music gets louder. The crowd crams tighter. Kitty tries to hold her claustrophobia back, to forget these people amassed around her. Stare at the sea. The boats. The burning water.

The main mast finally cracks, and the sound reverberates through the harbour as it collapses aflame into the dark swell of sea, where, for a moment, it lights up the underwater trenches and then is swallowed by the blackness.

The crowd wails. The crowd cheers. The crowd cries out for more.

She watches them. They look back at her. She feels they know. Know everything. That perhaps this ceremony is for their dead and that, later, the retribution will come. She feels silly for feeling these things, knows it's her imagination usurping reason but she's helpless to fight it.

When the boat sinks, when the sea collapses in around it, the harbour shakes to a resounding cheer which leaves only darkness in its wake.

The crowd does not disperse. It drinks from small dark glasses and glares at the foreigners. The celebration has turned into something else. The singing gets louder, more impassioned, and she can now see pain and fear among the faces as if the very words coming out of their mouths bring them back to some atavistic defeat which has crippled and bent them for so long.

They watch the last boats leave the harbour. They watch the crowd empty-eyed with the realisation that now they are back to their lives. That every moment of awe has its end and that the trick is to somehow carry it back into your day-to-day.

The crowd holds dense and tight like rush-hour passengers. Jason tries to move forward, but it only brings grunts, incomprehensible mangles of sentence as if, in all this awe and wonder, language has deserted the islanders.

And then the screaming starts.

Where it begins they can't tell. One moment it's all chanting and singing and the next there are people screaming. The crowd moves as one mass. Bodies shift and twirl and fall.

Jason grabs onto Kitty but they can't move. The crowd presses tighter. The brass band's playing but all of a sudden the trumpet drops out on an off-key screech and stops. They turn towards the bandstand and watch as the musicians drop their instruments, looking down at something in front of them with barely concealed horror, and jump into the crowd.

They hold each other tight. They watch the crowd move slowly, like ripples in a cornfield, a ribboning away from the bandstand.

'What the hell's going on?'

Kitty turns to him. His eyes are wide and bulging. There's nothing she can say as the crowd groans and shudders, and she's pulled away from Jason, her hand ripping out of his as if they were both swimmers suddenly chanced upon opposing currents.

Jason tries to reach for her, but she's gone. The crowd closed up again. He's carried along by the momentum, his feet barely touching the ground, as the villagers head away from the bandstand.

His head turns and swivels trying to locate Kitty. He's pushed along by the crowd but he can't see where there is to go. Everyone is heading away from the bandstand. The mass of people shoves and crams and heads for the water. He sees a cigarette kiosk buckling under the weight of movement and then collapsing as people rush into the space it leaves. He sees women and children falling, the crowd rushing over them oblivious, only one thing on their minds. For a moment, he wonders if this is part of the ceremony; people are waving their arms and flailing as if in the throes of religious ecstasy. It reminds him of mannerist paintings of supplicants and flagellants, roped out along a dirt road, fighting their own skin and bones as if demons resided within.

A women falls in front of him. She grabs onto his hand. Her nails rips across his palm, and she loses grip. She is swallowed by the many-legged crowd, churned under its feet, not even time enough for screaming. In the gap that opens up, Jason twists and jumps and pulls himself out of the stream only to be immediately taken up by another one, a rip tide of black-clothed celebrants wheeling out towards the harbour.

His ribs feel crushed and bruised. His shirt is torn and ripped from his body. He's on higher ground now, and he can see the centrifugal pull of the crowd. Moving away from the bandstand towards the water. Already people are jumping in, their arms windmilling as they crash into the blue water.

He gets pulled up and almost falls himself, only managing to grab hold of someone's shirt at the last moment, and he's whirled again, facing away from the water, back towards the bandstand. He passes a wall perpendicular to the sea, and sitting on it are thirty or forty cats, skinny and shivering, watching, their haunches taut, tails like question marks rigid behind them.

He pulls and scrambles and manages to find his footing. He turns, and there's Kitty, a deep red scratch across her face and her hair tangled around her eyes. He reaches out and manages to grab her. They both pull out of the stream they're trapped in and come crashing against each other like two ends of an elastic band.

'Thank God.' He wipes the hair from her forehead. She takes his hand. Then they're both swept up by the crowd again as it tries for the high ground, away from the bandstand and the sea.

'What the hell's going on?'

'Look.'

The ground is moving below them in a rush, but he can't miss the slivers of orange carpeting the cobblestones. The crowd lurches, shifts and staggers. Centipedes wind in and out of the cracks, climbing dresses and limbs. They pass by an abandoned wheelchair covered in centipedes, torn strips of clothing, a row of women on their knees praying, centipedes crawling across their outstretched hands.

The floor below them is sticky and dark. Their shoes stick and squelch as the crowd rushes onwards. They pass by the group of donkeys wildly chomping and writhing against their tethers. Their manes covered in centipedes. The donkeys finally break through, swivel-eyed and crazed, bellowing like madhouse inmates as they stampede towards the water, people falling like cornstalks in their wake. The animals jump into the sea, their heads trying to gain air, their heavy saddles and mantles dragging them down, until there's only their eyes wild and uncomprehending and then a few bubbles breaking the surface of the water and they're gone.

Jason brushes off the centipedes climbing Kitty's legs. They jump and bite. Little needles in his skin. She's holding him tight, trying not to look at the ground. Jason can see the red welts and bumps appear on her skin. He can feel the poison cruising through his own veins.

He grabs Kitty's hand, pulls her roughly. He can see a break in the crowd. He swivels, and something rips in his back, but the momentum is enough, and he carries Kitty with him and they both land, clear of the crowd, on the hard sticky cobbles. They get up immediately and begin to run, their feet slipping and sliding on the wet street. They head away from the crowd, towards the bandstand. Kitty gives Jason a puzzled look. 'It's the only way,' he manages to shout above the maelstrom of noise. He can hear Kitty's breath, short and ragged behind him. They run past the bandstand, instruments abandoned, sheets of music flying in the air.

Jason turns suddenly when he feels an arm grab his, locking tight.

'This way. Quick.'

He sees George's face, contorted by the effort of holding onto him, sees his beard, his dark eyes.

They follow George, keeping close, as he passes by fallen women and kneeling men, prams left abandoned and children's toys covered in centipedes. They wind through small, deserted back streets, and, just as Jason begins to worry, begins to wonder where George is taking them, this unfamiliar part of the island, the deep blackness – just when panic is rising like too much food in his throat, just when he is about to scream, wrench his hand away – they turn a corner, and there's the hotel, serenely quiet in the dazzling spotlight of an almost full moon.

III

THIRTY-THREE

Nikos walks through a town less familiar to him now than when he first stepped off the boat. He nods, greets, says hello, but in every face he watches for a sign, some signifier that they're hiding something.

The town seemed subdued after the boat-burning. No one had died, though several almost drowned, and the doctors were deluged with people wanting treatment for bites. But the centipedes left as suddenly as they'd appeared. He'd seen locals crossing themselves that afternoon, standing in front of the statue of St John the Silent, asking for contrition, for a blow to open their hearts up to God. They would stand there all day. What happened was explainable by science not fear and faith, he knew.

The rubbish gets collected once a week on Palassos. Tuesdays. Two days away. Sometimes being in a small town has its benefits.

Nikos didn't think to bring gloves. His hands are caked in oil and scraps of food, some half-digested, left to rot in the garbage these last few days. He's had to jump into the dumpster. Not only can he see better, all the way to the bottom, but he's also hidden here in case some villager should stroll by, wondering why their Chief of Police is elbow deep in week-old rubbish.

But he knows how the island works. How overconfidence and a sense of security breed recklessness. He's counting on it. It's been four days since the fire in the library. Four days since

Petrakis's son walked in stinking of kerosene and denying all knowledge of that fire.

Nikos knows Dimitri, knows Petrakis raised him spoilt and lazy. Is counting on this as his hands sort through fish entrails, empty bottles of ouzo and sodden toilet paper. The heat outside is terrible. Inside the dumpster it's worse. And the smell. He wishes he'd bought something to cover his face. Takes off his T-shirt and wraps it around his head like an anti-globalisation protestor. It makes things better. But only a little. There's the overwhelming stink of rotting mutton, fermented alcohol, stale cigarettes, vomit and . . . he feels his pulse fight up his neck against the tight strangle of the T-shirt – yes, a faint trace of kerosene.

He finds it three minutes later. Lying near the bottom. Just as he thought, Dimitri too lazy to get rid of the kerosene can anywhere but in the dumpster behind his own house. Why should he? His dad was the Mayor after all, who would even bother looking?

He climbs up and into the fresh air. He gulps at it as if he'd just emerged from deep water. He drops the can and vaults the dumpster, landing winded on the cobblestones.

He looks around, but no curtains shimmy, no windows creak. It's dinnertime, after all, and people are eating, talking, watching TV with the volume so loud it's a health hazard. He stands, does a three-hundred-and-sixty-degree check and allows himself a moment of pleasure as he takes the can and puts it carefully into a plastic bag he removes from the back of his jeans.

Just as he'd thought. Dimitri set the fire. But why? This proof in front of him isn't much good without that.

The houses in this part of the village are terraced. As if each has climbed onto the shoulders of the other trying to scale the heights, away from the stink and heat of town. Nikos crouches, one house up from Petrakis's. He can see through the window that leads into the main room, hear the dead hum of the TV as it's turned on, Petrakis's heavy footfalls as he comes back from the toilet.

He gives him a minute, thinks of Alexia back at the house, panic trembling on the edges of her smile that morning. The way she's turned distant and sulky, all walls and empty space. He wonders how she's coping. Never the one to air her fears, but, over the years, he's learned to read them, the smallest twitch, the lines around her mouth, the way she would answer a question.

His head snaps up. From inside the house he can hear Petrakis shout and curse Jesus, his voice loud and brandy-trembled, and Nikos knows he's seen it.

He was hoping the old man wouldn't be too drunk. Wouldn't come back in, not even bothering to turn on the lights, and slump in armchair or bed until morning. Then he would have had to wait here all night, and already his calves feel like they're filled with burning needles.

But Petrakis *has* seen it. And, now the cursing and shouting have stopped, Nikos can hear the faint beep of phone numbers being punched, and then, as he'd expected, the angry voice, gruff and ungiving, growling into the phone: 'Get over here right now.' There's obviously some argument because the next thing Petrakis says is 'I mean it,' and the slamming of the phone is like a thunderclap.

He can see the back of Petrakis's head as he sits on the sofa. Waiting. Staring at the rusted and stinking gas can that rests, neatly centred, on top of his dining table.

It was easy getting in. Another boon of small villages. No one locks their doors or windows. Even now with all that's going on.

Petrakis's mother gave him a shock. He was sure he saw her mouth twitch. But she was frozen as always. It was only his imagination. Her eyes bored into the back of his head as he placed the can on the table.

Five minutes later, and Dimitri's scooter rasps and stutters to a halt outside the house. The young man is dressed in a pink

T-shirt, red jeans and white shoes. His hair's gelled and slicked and looks like it's made out of patent leather. Clubbing. Out harpooning the tourist women when his mobile rang, Nikos guesses, hence his reluctance to come see his father at this hour. He's sweat-soaked, dark half-moons on his shirt, and out of breath as he waits for his dad to answer the door.

Nikos thought of broaching him earlier. Taking him in for questioning. But Dimitri wouldn't have given over that easily knowing his dad would spring him within the hour. There would have been nothing to gain, and, if Nikos has learned any lasting lessons in his years as a policeman, it's knowing which battles are worth fighting and which can be won.

It doesn't take them long, as he suspected it wouldn't. His view is a good one. The light inside Petrakis's house is as bright as supermarket-aisle illumination, shadowless and supreme like the light of God. From where he is, he can see every movement and hear the words flung across the room as if the window were a frame and it's a Punch and Judy show he's watching.

Dimitri walks in, swagger and petulance boiling and bubbling. He can't wait to ream his old man out, shout at him for all this hassle, but Petrakis just points to the table, and Dimitri, halfway through the first admonishing sentence, turns, stares, his words grind to a halt, and he just stands there shaking his head as if he's watching a dog levitate.

'What the fuck is the meaning of this?' Petrakis shouts, and Nikos realises he could have heard the conversation all the way back at his house, so loud is the old man's voice. A loudness that masks uncertainty and fear.

Dimitri keeps shaking his head as if this is all just some strange dream he's walked into and he's certain any moment he's going to wake up from.

'You fucked up again, you idiot,' the old man shouts, and Dimitri raises his head, all too aware now that this is really happening and that an answer is required of him.

'. . . rid of it,' he mutters weakly, so much so that Nikos only catches the last three words.

The scream of flesh against flesh makes Nikos jump. It's an unnatural sound that cuts cleanly through the stillness of night. Dimitri reels from his father's slap. He almost stumbles, putting his hand to his reddening cheek in a look of shock that's almost cartoon-like. As if all our actions turn into clichés when life surprises us.

'Got rid of it,' Petrakis mimics, his voice juiced with venom. 'What the fuck is it doing here then? Walked here by itself? Jesus, if you weren't my son I'd think you were fathered by a mule.'

Dimitri's body language is all acquiescent slumber and shrug. He seems smaller than he did a few minutes ago at the door. His head is valiantly trying not to hang down, but it's failing. His shoulders respond and angle in towards his back. He starts shuffling until Petrakis screams, 'Stand still and fucking answer me.'

'I threw it in the bin just like you told me.'

And there it is. That's enough. But Nikos continues listening.

'Our bin? The bin out there?' Petrakis turns and points to emphasise how stupid he thinks this course of action is. Dimitri, in that instinctual human way, follows his gaze, and they both stare out the window directly at Nikos.

Nikos falls flat to the ground. Breathing hard. Small stones poke his chest and neck.

'You put it in *our* bin?' Petrakis wonders unbelievably, as if it's the stupidest thing he's ever heard of. Nikos realises they didn't see him. The light in the room, the darkness outside, the only thing which could have given him away was his sudden movement. He's forgotten even the basics, he realises, all the stuff drilled into his head out on the mainland so long ago.

'And how the fuck do you suppose it got here?' Petrakis's voice is coming under control now, the rage and incredulity fighting against the tight mouthful of vowels and consonants.

Dimitri shrugs, moves out of view. 'It was there when you came in?'

'Are you on fucking drugs, you imbecile? That's what I just fucking told you. Someone snuck in while I was at dinner and put it here. Someone who knew what to look for in the dumpster.'

Dimitri shuffles back into view. He raises his hand to the old man's shoulder, a placatory gesture, father to son, but the old man brushes it away. 'We're fucked,' he says. 'Why didn't you get rid of it somewhere else?'

'It's just a can. Could be any can.' Dimitri says quietly. 'Nothing tying it to the library.'

Petrakis shakes his head, turns and slumps into his armchair. 'You think if it was just any can someone would have gone to the trouble of taking it out of the dumpster and placing it here? On my fucking table?'

'No one saw me at the library. I made sure.'

Cigarette smoke clouds the room as father and son take a moment out from accusation to light cigarettes, puffing so furiously that Nikos suspects in a moment he won't be able to see a thing.

'You can't do anything right, can you?' The old man says, a litany familiar to all sons, the critical barbs of the father's displeasure and failure pushed onto the son. A dynamic Nikos counted on.

'I tell you to do one small thing. One thing, and you fuck it up. Bring it all back to me. Didn't I make it clear how important this was? What was at stake here? Did you do this to spite me or are you just a fucking retard?'

THIRTY-FOUR

She's staring at the screen. Words pouring from her fingers. The computer humming in the still white room. But she isn't writing. The world of fiction seems like a misplaced dream now. These things dripping from her fingers are facts, bold and stark, black marks on the white page. She stares up at the walls of her hotel room thinking how strange and yet oddly exhilarating it was to find yourself in the middle of life and somehow not recognise yourself; the distance between the person you want to be and the person you are ever widening. She'd dreamed about Jason this morning. His hand on her skin. The brush of lips on her breast, the hairs standing up on the back of her neck. How could you control yourself in dreams? Was that the person you really were or only its darkest outpouring?

Jason was back at his hotel, gathering his things. They'd spent the night there. George had found a spare room for her. All night they could hear screaming, crying, yelling, expressions of disbelief and wonder in the streets outside.

The morning was quiet and the town empty. The centipedes were gone. The aftermath of the boat-burning cloaked the streets in dry smoke and ashes. She hadn't slept. She paced her room, wall to wall and back again, but could not find the peace she needed to close her eyes. She thought about Karelis instead. Was last night part of the priest's revenge? There was a certain symmetry to it, she couldn't deny, the whole town gathered together for this one evening of celebration and ritual, as if history had usurped faith.

She'd had her breakfast with Jason, neither of them saying much, then said she had to go back to her hotel, take a quick nap, and check some things out on the Internet.

She searches seminary records and religious chat forums. She manipulates her parameters, tries different spellings of Karelis's name. Comes up with nothing. Short, dry biographical nuggets that only obscure the man further. She scours local papers and websites dealing with monasteries. She scans and skim-reads. The light from the screen stabs her eyes. Her fingers start to ache. Words buzz like insects around the screen. Words lined up in a row like mourners at a funeral.

It's amazing she doesn't miss it.

She reads it twice before it even clicks. And then she has to read it again. It's small, almost inconsequential. It's history, there in black and white. It's a witness, mute and immutable, but it almost slips her notice.

Because it's not about the cult or the priest.

She'd given up on getting any direct hits. She'd entered *Palassos 1974* into the search engines of all the Greek papers she could find, both mainland and island. Of course there were features about the cult, running commentaries and leaders. But they only told her what she already knew. They laid out the facts, the numbered dead. They printed photos of the two boys. They speculated and tried to make sense of this thing to which no sense would ever adhere.

She'd almost given up, packed her things and gone back to bed, when she spotted it.

She gets up from the table, walks around the room, as if by physically moving away from the computer she would gain the perspective she needs. She wishes she smoked. This is what cigarettes are for, she thinks, these moments in between moments. Then she rereads the article.

Two more cases of the virus were found on the island today. A health official from the mainland stressed that these were

'isolated' cases as the stream where the virus was found has been purified and is now safe to drink and bathe in.

It is thought it was the farmers' practice of dumping dead sheep into a landfill that bled into the creek that caused the virus which, for the last couple of months, has swept through the village.

Though it is not fatal, several people have been hospitalised with severe stomach pains and cramping. Doctors at Athens Memorial say that all the patients are doing well and, indeed, most have returned to the island.

When asked how two new cases were found when the stream had been apparently sanitised, the health official was quoted as saying, 'There are always anomalies. We did our best but sometimes that's not good enough. These people were living in the interior where the virus was more rife. Also, they are not native islanders and therefore probably had less resistance than the locals did. They have been evacuated to Athens where they will be treated.'

When asked if any more cases were likely, the official said, 'no.'

Her heart's racing. A sharp spike of pain starts under her ribcage and shoots through her arm. Her fingers fumble as she scans through back issues looking for a follow-up article. The date on the first article is a week before the murders and mass suicide. It's the words 'not native islanders' and 'living in the interior' that jump out at her.

Twenty minutes later she finds it.

One Dead and One on the Way to Recovery

The recent virus that swept the island of Palassos has claimed its first victim. An unidentified man of Northern European extraction died last night at Athens Memorial hospital.

While the virus was not lethal, the man's body was, according to the coroner, so ravaged with drugs and alcohol that the virus managed to cripple the immune system.

The man is yet to be identified though he is obviously not Greek, in his mid-twenties and, from his appearance, one of the hippies that have come to dominate our landscape these past few years.

The other patient is said to be recovering and due for release in the next couple of days.

The article was dated the day before the murders of the two boys. Two days before the cult's suicide.

A survivor.

This is what's been at the back of her mind for the past couple of days. The stone lodged in her shoe. She'd thought it was someone who'd left voluntarily, then changed their mind and come back. It's always bugged her how anyone could have been certain that all the members had killed themselves. Now she knows. Two were sent to the mainland before the murders of the boys and the mass suicide. One died in the hospital but one didn't.

Did the survivor come back to the island before or after the mass suicide? Did they come back to find that everyone they'd known was dead? Would that be motive enough to take revenge thirty-three years later?

She doesn't think it has anything to do with Wynn. Jason seems pretty convinced, but she's noticed he has his own issues with the drug dealer. She still thinks Karelis is the most probable suspect. His disappearance the major fact against him. But now this new knowledge opens up fresh paths and trails in front of her. If the survivor is still alive; if they're still living on the island . . . could they have a stronger motive?

She reads the article again. She jots down names and dates. She brings up a listing of mainland hospitals. She scans the screen until she finds the number for Athens Memorial. She calls and asks to speak to someone in the hospital's PR department. She tells them she's writing a book about the 1974 cult. The man on the other end of the line's never heard of it.

'That's OK,' she says, 'I just need to clarify some information.'

She gives him the dates of admission of the two cult members. The reason for the interment. The man says he'll do his best and call her back.

She slams the phone down. The files are probably all gone by now. The man sounded as if he was going through the motions, but before despair totally takes over, the phone rings, and it's the man from Athens Memorial. He tells her what a wonder the new computerised filing system is, proud like a father of his newly born daughter. She bites her nails. She chews her bottom lip. The impatience courses through her veins like poison. And then it's all over, and she's not certain at all she's heard him right and so she asks him to repeat the name again, and when he does, she just drops the phone and stares at the flickering screen in disbelief.

THIRTY-FIVE

They spend the night together. But it's not the way he thought it would be, nothing like it, yet, despite the fact all they do is hold each other's barely clothed bodies beneath the thin sheets, it's better than anything he could have expected.

They hadn't talked much in the lift up to Kitty's room. He'd arrived to find her pacing the floor of the lobby. Her phone call had been urgent and breathless. He'd come as quickly as he could. She took him upstairs. She said there was a survivor. She showed him the article. She showed him the photo the man from Athens Memorial had emailed her.

He wakes to the smell of fresh-brewed coffee and the sight of her, a slip, a pair of flip-flops, hovering over him, stating quietly, 'It's time.' He doesn't want to move. Wants to freeze-frame this moment and reside within its borders.

But there are things to do. They both understand.

He stares at the grainy photo again as if the morning would bring a different result, but the face is the same.

He makes the phone call. Asks for Nikos. Alexia's voice sounds a reduced version of itself, struggling to find words. Jason wonders if he's just woken her or if her tired slur is the result of not having been to sleep. She says Nikos isn't around. Unavailable all morning. It's the result they want, surprised that something, at least, is going their way.

Alexia's face shows no sign of surprise when the door opens and she sees them. 'He's not here,' she says, then adds, 'he was looking for you.'

Kitty and Jason stare at each other. Certainty slips like water from their hands. The clang of a ferry horn tries to pull them back from this choice they've made.

'Actually,' Kitty says, her voice soft and measured, 'it's you we wanted to talk to.'

* * *

Nikos frowns. He's sure he's just heard the front door open, but maybe Alexia is only putting out some trash. He ignores it, looks back down at the files and clippings spread across the floor of the storeroom. All night he's been here. Trying to connect the dots, to find out why Petrakis wanted the library burned down.

There's more to the events of June 1974 than is told. That he's certain of.

His mind slips back to that summer, Petrakis the newly appointed Chief of Police. The way they sent him back to the mainland. What did they do that night up on the promontory?

He goes back to the library. Was there something inside that jeopardised the official version of events? Some document or note left at the bottom of a box in the basement? And then it hits him. Not something but someone. He slams his fist into the table. The pain burns through his arm.

How did Petrakis find out? What does he think she knows?

He's puzzling over this, trying to make sense of the incongruity of the fire and the murders when he hears voices, urgent and terse, coming from the other room.

* * *

Jason slowly takes the print-out of the hospital photo out of his pocket, flattens it with his palm and lays it on the table in front of her.

Alexia looks down at her younger self as the door opens and Nikos enters the room.

'What the hell's going on here?' Then, without waiting for an answer, Nikos stares down at the bad printout laid flat on his coffee table. His hand rests on his holster strap. It worries the leather as he looks across the room, at Kitty and Jason, then back to his wife.

Alexia sits at the table, her face collapsed into her hands, bitten nails and dry skin, unable to hold her quietly shaking head. She's muttering something, but they can't make out what it is.

Nikos lets out a long, measured breath and reaches for the table. His left hand leaves the gun. There's something in his face, not quite relief but not far from it. A cessation of tension that relaxes his eyes and jaw. He picks up the newspaper clipping and scrunches it. 'Where did you find this?'

'Hospital records.'

Jason stares at Kitty, amazed at how in control she sounds. He's still holding her hand, and in his palm it's shaking like a wind-blown flag.

'Did you break into my room? Alexia would have told you why I was there at the library. Did you think I'd found out who she was? Did you burn down the library to protect her? How many people would know it was her day off?'

Nikos stares at them for what feels like hours. It's less than a minute. Then his face breaks into a huge grin, and he laughs. This is more frightening than his previous expression. If it's supposed to relieve the tension in the room, it doesn't.

Alexia turns to her husband, 'You didn't?' she asks, her voice small and awkward in English.

'Of course not.' And there's something in his tone, like he can't quite believe his wife would accuse him of such a thing.

'You've got this all wrong,' he says, 'Jesus. You actually think I set the fire?'

'Considering we just found out your wife was part of the cult, the only survivor, what else were we supposed to think?' Kitty's words come out in short, rapid bursts, 'Is that why the murders haven't been solved?'

'What are you talking about?'

There's something in Nikos's face for a moment, and then

it's gone. He looks at Alexia, and there's only the faintest of nods but it's enough.

'She has nothing to do with this. The murders. Any of it. Blame me if you want to.'

Kitty leans forward. 'I'm not interested in blaming anyone, I just want to know what happened.'

Nikos sits there and stares at the wall.

'They sent me to the mainland to pick up the detectives and bring them back to the island. This was the day we found the boys' bodies.'

Jason can hear regret weigh down Nikos's words. He watches as the detective fiddles with his empty coffee cup and sighs, a strange exhalation that's both relief and frustration. Then Nikos takes his wife's hand; a look passes between them, the faintest curl of a lip and squinting of an eye. The coffee is strong. Alexia made it while they sat there in silence. Now the sound of their sips is like a minor explosion in the still room.

'I met the detectives in Piraeus. We took the ferry. The main-landers headed straight for the bar. I couldn't follow them. I could still smell the boy's blood. Every time I closed my eyes I could see him, his eyes beckoning me, then rolling back in his head. I needed air. I didn't want to spend the ride talking shop, sharing bad jokes and political gossip. I wanted to be alone.

'The sea was terrible that day. One of the stewards told me the deck was closed, too dangerous. I flashed my badge and walked out into the white wailing sea.

'It felt good. The way the water hit my face. I stood there and screamed the boy's name out into the ocean.

'"You'll ruin your hair." That's what she said. The wind must have died down because I caught her words like she was whispering them in my ear. I turned around and saw the most beautiful woman I'd ever seen.'

A smile breaks through Alexia's grim expression, quickly hidden, but somehow her face is softer when it falls back into place.

'Only a young man would think that, right? The most beautiful woman?

'She said I had lovely hair, and it was a shame to get all that salt and wind in it. She looked radiant, her eyes fierce black orbs. She looked gaunt and sickly. This too. But it just seemed to make her shine more. Her hair was cut short – later I was to find out it was because of the hospital – but at the time I thought she looked amazing, like Mia Farrow in *Rosemary's Baby*.

'We began to talk. She told me she was returning to Palassos. "Really?" I said, "That's strange, I don't think I've seen you around." She told me she lived up in the interior. She was part of a hippy commune. She must have seen my expression when she said this because her face froze. "What's wrong?" she said. "You think I'm some kind of freak?"

'I didn't know what to say, what to tell her. We only suspected, after all. There was no proof yet that the commune had killed the little boys.

'We both stood there in silence, against the chop of wind and spray of sea. She told me about the virus, her month in the hospital, watching her fellow islander die in the bed next to hers. Her conviction that she too would die in that anonymous military hospital.

'For a moment, I thought of Charles Manson, I'm ashamed to admit it now, and the angelic faces of his lipsticked killers rose in front of me. I told myself keep talking to her, you're a policeman, she doesn't know this yet, find out what you can, interrogate her now when she thinks you're trying to chat her up – but another part of me knew this was only an excuse.

'We talked about the island. I edged around asking her about the cult. She said it was nothing. An experiment in self-sufficiency. "Come up and visit," she told me. "Everyone always thinks the worst when they don't understand something."

'I knew I had to tell her. Not because I was a policeman – I should have kept my mouth shut, pumped her for more information – no, because I was a man, and in the twenty minutes we'd talked I felt something I'd never felt before.

'So I told her what we'd found. The rumours. The evidence pointing to the cult. What I was doing on the boat. Who the men drinking in the bar were. I said she should keep a low profile, stay in town and check into a hotel. Don't go up there, I told her. Not until we sort this out, make whatever arrests we need to. Two months I'd been a policeman and already I was breaking all the rules.

'I don't know if either of you have come across a moment like that – when you make a decision and you know that decision will irrevocably change your life regardless of whether you are right or wrong?'

He looks at them, sees them both nod involuntarily, wonders how many times they've made such a decision since being on the island.

'I gave her the keys to my flat. I told her she'd be safe there. Take the spare room, wait it out. There would be an investigation even if the cult weren't involved. She kept denying vehemently that anyone she knew could have done such a thing. Even if they were innocent, I told her, even then there would be a lot of hostility among the locals. It wouldn't be safe for a while, not until the matter was cleared up. She tried to argue with me, told me she had a duty to the people up there – they didn't know if she was dead or alive, if the virus had taken her. I said the whole interior would be crawling with cops. The cult would be interviewed and probably arrested. She could do more to help them on the outside. She was Greek; she could melt in, pretend to be a mainland tourist.

'She cried when I told her about the bodies of the boys. She screamed and raged when I told her she was better staying away. But we agreed. Somehow, among the lash and snap of the waves, the noise of the boat, we agreed, a few days at my place, a room of her own, and then we'd see where to go from there.

'Of course, by the time we got back to the island, everyone in the cult had committed suicide, and all the loose ends had been neatly tied up.'

'You kept the secret for thirty-three years.' Kitty's voice is unreadable, the words clipped and sharp as broken glass.

'The room in the museum,' she says, sliding forward on the chair, watching as Nikos puts his arm on Alexia's knees, an involuntary gesture of protection. 'The room full of cult memorabilia and history. Damn it, I should have realised then.'

Alexia slowly raises her head. Eyes red-rimmed and watery, she nods.

'When I came back with Nikos I knew there had to be some kind of memorial,' she says, her voice rising now. 'It was the only way I could enshrine them. The only way I could get away with it. I had to look at those lies every day, polish the glass that sealed them in. But at least the commune wasn't forgotten.'

'But your friends killed two boys, how can you . . . ?' Jason's tone feels unfamiliar to him, hard and crunchy like gravel.

Alexia shakes her head, mutters *no* into the shelter of her hands.

'They wouldn't have committed suicide,' she says, 'and they would never have killed anyone, let alone two boys.'

The atmosphere in the room has changed. The story, unburdened, has deepened the silence between Nikos and his wife. As if the years of shared secrecy had kept them glued together.

'What do you mean they never would have committed suicide? Isn't that how most cults end up?'

She stares at Jason. 'You don't understand.'

'Make us,' he replies.

And so she tells them. Words buried so long ago she's amazed they're still there. Names and faces she's consigned to wherever you put everything you never want to think about again, but here they are, rushing through her like a river in late

244

spring. A part of her has always wanted to tell this story. To defend what they did, what they were – Nikos has never really asked her much, perhaps too scared to find out – and she's glad because this is the only story she knows, and it is one she managed to hide and imply through the photos and articles in the museum but a story no one ever read or understood. A story that is the story of her life, part one.

'I won't bore you with background; the how and why and who I was. Everyone has their reasons to disappear. More so, then. The colonels ran the country like it was their personal interrogation centre. My dad, God forgive him, helped them. I'm sure he didn't have much choice. Lawyers were co-opted as easily as anyone else. He always said they had something on him, that he was only trying to protect us. But this means nothing, right? Not to a twenty-year-old girl, her head burning with all the music and rhetoric coming from America.

'I just walked out. A small bag filled with the few things which still meant anything to me. A photo of my parents at the Eiffel Tower, a copy of *Howl* and a cassette of *American Beauty* by the Grateful Dead.

'It was summer. Getting exit visas from the country was too difficult. I took a boat instead, always wanted to go to the islands, saw my chance. I withdrew the money I'd saved for a car, bought tickets and spent three months island-hopping. I ended up in Palassos. This is where I met Frank.

'We clicked the way young people do. He found out I had that tape, he had the same one – that was enough for us to become friends and spend afternoons on the beach talking about what was happening in the world, the counterculture, the Vietnam War, the reign of the colonels. I expressed my antipathy, told him my dad was a collaborator. He seemed very interested in my politics, my desire to disappear from the world of bombs and bodies. That's when he told me about the commune.'

Alexia stops, reaches for a cigarette, lights it and continues, her words brushed with smoke and years.

'It was always a commune. You need to understand this. Only after what happened did people start calling it a cult. That was never what we called ourselves or how we saw each other. There was no leader. The four Americans who'd set up the camp were in charge of all practical disputes, but there was never an ideology, a belief, apart from the fact we'd all got sick and tired of the world we'd been born into and wanted something simpler.

'Frank had been with the first three. They'd all been members of communes back in the States. He'd told me about the cops' dirty tricks, the burning of their camps, Nixon, COINTELPRO, the constant harassment. They'd left the country and, after months of travelling Europe, ended up here. No one bothered them on the island, and when they bumped into like-minded people in town they invited them to join. You could leave any time you wanted to. Pray to any God you so wished. No one cared. As long as you did your share of the gardening and housekeeping, you were left alone.

'We were all kids. We grew our own food, raised goats, sang songs in the evening and kept to ourselves. A few of the villagers helped us out with food or basic supplies at first. Then, as more people came to the island, something shifted, and we had to become more self-sufficient. We began to get strange looks in town, curses only I understood, the sole Greek-speaker amongst them.

'We wanted to see if we could make it on our own. Like me, most of the people there had come from middle-class families. We'd grown up in safety and comfort. Our lives had been handed to us on a platter. We wanted to know if we could survive without our parents. Without the support system of our backgrounds and hometowns. I think we did pretty well.

'Then the virus swept through the island, and everything changed. Some of the members began to get paranoid, said it was a plot by the islanders to clear us off. Kill us if necessary. But no one really believed that. We knew the townspeople had come down with the same virus.

'When I became sick, Frank took me down to the village. I spoke Greek to the doctor, and he immediately sent me off to the mainland. The rest, I'm afraid, you know.'

She sits back, looking almost smaller now, as if the story has been a cyst kept inside her all these years. Nikos takes her hand. She pats his, says something in Greek and turns to Jason and Kitty.

'No one was suicidal. No one believed in the apocalypse or any other cult prophecies. If we'd been asked to leave the island, we would have left, found somewhere else to set up. There's no way anyone I knew would have committed suicide.'

Jason leans forward, lowers his voice. 'You're so sure of that.'

Alexia nods. 'It's impossible. Not only because no one even thought about suicide . . . and my God, there's no way they would have done anything to a couple of boys, that's really beyond imagining, but . . .'

'But . . .'

Alexia tilts forward to make sure she can be heard, 'But, apart from all that, no one had guns. No one. It was exactly the kind of thing we were escaping from. That was one of the only rules we had. No one was allowed to bring firearms into the camp.

'Tell me, because my husband can't, even after all these years,' she shoots Nikos a look that speaks of unanswered questions and bedroom silences, 'tell me, how can thirty-five people kill themselves when they don't even have a gun let alone any ammunition to perform the task?'

THIRTY-SIX

He watches his wife, the way she's almost released now the story has been told, and how her body catches up to this new state of affairs. She sits straight, not crumpled in her hands or staring down at the floor. There's a faint hint of amusement in her voice.

'It really is nothing more sinister than that. People want it to be. They have this romantic vision of cults, but it was just a bunch of people growing vegetables, living communally, making breakfast for each other.'

'Then why keep it a secret?'

Nikos looks at Kitty, 'No one likes loose ends. I didn't want her to become one of those. To always be hounded by her past, by people's suspicions. I believe we all have the right to start again, to wipe the clock.'

Alexia had always insisted the cult was innocent of the murders. Nikos believed she believed this, but he also knew you could never really know anyone. They'd left the island the following summer. In Athens, it all began to fade, to become like the dust which was once the mortar and stone of the city's temples and palaces. They'd gradually stopped speaking about it. It became a room they never entered. He hadn't wanted to know more. It was enough that in the worst days of his life he'd found someone to cling on to, something that would remain through the erosion of years.

But if the cult had really been innocent of the murders? Then he was as complicit as the killers themselves. Ignorance was no mitigation. Following orders had lost its charm. Protecting the one you loved above your responsibilities to the community was what got the world in this awful mess in the first place.

'I think you need to look for Karelis.'

Kitty's words take him out of the well of his thoughts. 'Karelis?'

Kitty smiles. 'He "disappeared" after the first two murders. He and Vondas weren't happy about the reopening of the monastery and ruins as tourist attractions.'

'That's not much to go on.'

There's something about the theory that forces Nikos into the present moment. He remembers the castration scars on Vondas. The defaced pages of the book about the cult. The blacked-out photo of Karelis. The priest's words at the empty funeral.

'The killings all happened up by the monastery. He knows about 1974. Maybe Vondas and Karelis disagreed on how to stop tourists coming to the monastery. We talked to Vondas that night. I didn't tell you, but he made it quite clear we weren't welcome. He pretty much shooed us off the site. But maybe that wasn't enough for Karelis. Maybe he went further and Vondas found out.'

'You're saying he killed his colleague?' Nikos's expression is a mixture of interest and disbelief.

'If he killed the others then he's certainly capable of that. When Vondas approached us, he seemed to come out of nowhere. I'm convinced now he was hiding in the labyrinth.'

'The labyrinth's been closed for years,' Alexia says, but there's something else in her face Jason can't quite read.

'We saw fresh footprints leading into it that night,' he replies. 'It would make sense that Karelis would know the way. An easy place to hide. To "disappear". Close enough to the ruins to get away quickly.'

Nikos finally lights the cigarette that's been dancing between his knuckles for the past fifteen minutes. Alexia gives him a look, crumpled features and heavy disappointment, but he just shrugs and puts the match to the end of the cigarette. The sizzle fills the room. He shakes his head. Could he have been wrong again? Their theory resonates on enough levels, and he's annoyed he hasn't thought of it himself. But Petrakis ordered Dimitri to torch the library. This he knows for certain. Whether it has anything to do with the current murders, he's not sure, but he knows he has to see Petrakis again. Has to learn what happened that night and what his own role, unwitting though it may have been, was.

He gets up. Alexia seems reluctant to let go of his hand, but he leaves her no choice.

'I'm going to follow what I know,' he says to Kitty and Jason. 'We have only your speculation about Karelis. That's not enough for me, I'm sorry. I have to find out what happened that night in 1974.'

THIRTY-SEVEN

The monastery is quiet and picture-postcard pretty. The sun reflects off the blinding white masonry. Jason stares at the sea below, the dark swell of waves breaking against the rocks, the circling of small white birds above the foam.

Up here it still smells of sea, salt and tang but with the added touch of burnt wood. A reminder. Why they're here. Not tourists any more. That, a whole world behind.

The breaking of a branch startles Kitty.

Jason looks out into the black trees. 'Animals,' he says, much too quickly.

They move closer to each other and follow the path that leads down to the labyrinth. The ground is scuffed with footprints, one set reappearing, taking prominence over others.

Though it's still light, the canopy of trees covers them in darkness as they approach the gate. Jason knows it's too high to climb and they'll have to turn back. He senses Kitty knows this too and that she's counting on it as much as he is.

But when they reach the gate, it's swinging open.

A silent rush of air, blown against their cheeks, comes from the dark inside of the mountain. The same pair of footprints go beyond the gate and lead up to the entrance.

'What if we get lost?' he says, but it's only for punctuation now. The footprints are fresh and deeply embedded into the soft earth.

She takes the first step, then a second, and she's lost to him. Shrouded in the perfect darkness of the cave. He follows. Feels the soft moist earth beneath him, the chill of the stone walls, the lure of the dark.

'We don't know what we're looking for.' It's the last objection he can muster, standing in the dark chilled air, the light rapidly fading behind them. Kitty's right next to him, but he can't see her. Ten feet into the cave and they may as well be at the centre of the Earth.

Kitty pulls something out of her jacket. A disc of light appears on the opposite wall, shedding enough illumination for them to see that they are in a small cavern, round-roofed and about the size of an average living room. The walls curve a foot above their heads, and they can hear the faint trickle of water in the distance. The earth beneath them is soft and damp. Two paths stretch into further darkness in front of them.

They walk slowly, the torch scouting the ground as if it were a blind man's cane. The path is easy to trace. The footprints deep and well defined. *As if we were meant to follow*, Jason thinks uneasily.

They take turns and backswitching lanes, and, after a while, they're no longer sure where they are or if they're still headed in the right direction.

The air is soft and damp like something crushed up against your face. There's the steady hiss of the sea, a constant rush of white noise like a motorway in the distance. The passageway is only about three feet wide. Occasionally the walls buckle and lurch, and they have to press tight through the space, the wet rock like a tongue against their skin. Sometimes another path emerges out of the dark, and they stop and check their route. The walls whisper and groan. They make noises like an old abandoned house. They say you will never leave. In the flicker of torchlight, Jason can make out ancient graffiti; names and pictures scratched into the surface of the earth.

They walk for another half-hour. Jason keeps checking his watch. The thought of what they'll do when the torch's batteries run out is something he keeps pushing to the back of his mind.

Then Kitty stops dead. The torch goes off.

'Do you see it?'

He squints, follows the direction of her outstretched hand. He's not sure what he's looking for and, at first, doesn't notice it. Then he does. A small aperture of white at the end of the tunnel.

'It must be the exit.'

He can hear her breathlessness, the fear she's been hiding from him. The way the light is flickering, he's not so sure she's right, but maybe there's a tree in front of the entrance, the flicker just sunlight filtering through its branches. He tells himself this so that all his other thoughts will stay silent.

They walk towards the light. It's further than it seems. The ground is rough and littered with stones. They're careful not to trip or stumble, both knowing that a sprained ankle down here could be a death sentence.

As they approach the light, her pace speeds up. Then she stops. He can read her disappointment in the way her body slumps. He feels it in the pit of his stomach though it's something he'd suspected.

It's not sunlight, and it's not an exit.

Kitty stands at the entrance to another cavern. Jason walks up beside her. He can feel her breath like hot wind on his neck. The flickering light comes from candles. Hundreds of burning candles.

THIRTY-EIGHT

Arresting him had been the easy part. The guilty were never that surprised when they were caught. He'd got there early. Dimitri was still heavy with the previous night's drink, his movements slow and clumsy, the rattle and crash as he'd stumbled to the door. Seeing Nikos there hadn't been a shock. Perhaps he'd been waiting for this moment since his dad ordered him to set fire to the library. Or perhaps he was still too drunk to realise what the policeman wanted with him.

Nikos took him down to the station. Explained why he was there. Locked him in one of the two small cells.

Job done, he walked slowly to Petrakis's house.

Petrakis opens the door, and his face folds like a cheap camp bed.

'We need to talk,' Nikos says calmly, the voice he uses to tell relatives that someone has died, 'about your son.'

Petrakis doesn't move from the doorway. He's almost as wide as the frame. 'What about him?' he snaps, but there's something else there, underneath all the machismo and bluster. It's not concern for Dimitri, Nikos can tell.

He steps forward, and, for a moment, it seems like the older man won't budge, like this might end up in a pushing match, but Petrakis catches something in Nikos's glare and, without a word, turns and walks back into his house.

Nikos follows. The old man slumps down on the couch.

'What did he do?' Petrakis finally says, his voice devoid of interest. 'Got drunk again did he? Beat up a tourist?'

Nikos shakes his head slowly. 'I'm afraid this time it's more serious than that. He's been arrested for attempted murder and arson. We know he burned down the library.'

Petrakis springs up from the seat. 'Bullshit.' His voice is dry and grazed, like sand blowing in a storm.

'We have footage of him setting the fire.' This is where the whole thing will either fly or fail. He doesn't know when Petrakis last visited the museum. 'You never noticed Alexia put in CCTV, did you?'

He watches Petrakis's face take in the lie. His eyes seem to go back in his head and then his body slumps and Nikos knows he's fallen for it.

Petrakis doesn't even try to deny it. 'That dumb fuck,' he says instead, his body falling into the armchair as if it were a coat he could wrap around himself. Shaking his head. 'That dumb, stupid fuck.'

Nikos gives him a cigarette. Lets the old man light it and go through his options. The way he's dragging on the cigarette, Nikos knows Petrakis is making the only choice he can.

'He'll get fifteen years, maybe a little less depending on the judge.' He can't help enjoying this moment, but he doesn't let it show. 'Maybe they'll let him out for your funeral, maybe not.'

'Awww, fuck!' Petrakis slams his hand down, unsettling the ashtray. 'Get me a drink,' he shouts, and Nikos gets up and goes into the kitchen. Give him time and silence. Let him think it through.

'That's not what I'm interested in, though,' he says when he comes back, notices the spark of interest uncrumpling the Mayor's face. 'I want to know why the priest had to be killed. Why all the others?'

Now Petrakis's face is a jumble of incomprehension and . . . is that relief? Nikos wonders for a moment if he's got this all wrong.

'What?'

'You heard me.'

'I heard you, but I have no idea what you're talking about.'

'That's crap. I know you sent Dimitri to burn the library when Kitty was inside, and I know he killed the priest.'

Petrakis bursts out laughing. Nikos thinks the old man's snapped. But then he quiets down, snickering to himself.

'That? You think I did that? You were never a good cop, Nikos, only just passable. You haven't improved either.' The old man's laugh bounces against the walls of the room.

'Why then?'

Petrakis shakes his head. 'Not that easy. First you need to promise me something, then I'll tell you.' He looks at Nikos, his eyes squinting, 'You really don't know, do you?'

'Know what?' Nikos spits, suddenly aggravated by the old man's petulance.

Petrakis allows himself a crooked smile. 'What happened up on the mountain thirty-three years ago.'

They stare at each other. They both have something the other needs.

'What do you want?' Nikos finally says, but, of course, he knows.

'I want you to promise my boy will be all right. That you won't press charges. I know he's a fuck-up. I know what he is, goddamn if I don't. You think I haven't spent the past twenty-five years rueing the day I put my cock into his mother? But he's my boy. And he only did what I told him to. He fucked it up, sure, but he didn't kill any priest.'

Nikos thinks it through. Why not? After all, his word isn't binding, and there doesn't seem to be another way to make the old man open up. Nikos has a suspicion that this is a story Petrakis has been dying to tell him for years. As long as he thinks it's just about the arson, he'll talk – no point mentioning the real reason yet.

'You remember how young you were back then?'

The question takes Nikos by surprise. For a moment, he's not sure what the old man is talking about, and then he is.

That day on the mountain. Finding the boys. Crying in front of the other cops. Two months into the job, and he makes the worst discovery in the island's history. He remembers the way Alexia's hair blew in the wind on the ferry. The shape of her emaciated body against the white hull of the boat.

'Green too,' Petrakis adds, delighted now. 'The way you came down that mountain, it was as if you'd found Jesus Christ himself murdered. You know we had doubts about you beforehand, well, this did nothing to alleviate them. Your own sergeant called you "mainland pussy". Doesn't want to dirty his hands doing real work, rooting out Communists and terrorists. Came back here to take it easy.'

'I never knew you all thought so highly of me.'

Petrakis sweeps his hand through the air as if clearing a table. 'No one wanted you in charge of this. You were too young, and your politics were suspect. Someone needed to go to the mainland, hook up with the Athens cops. You fitted the bill.'

Nikos leans forward, grabs the old man's hand and squeezes. 'I know all this. Tell me what happened on the mountain.'

Petrakis pulls his arm away. Surprising strength for someone his age. He settles back into the armchair like an estranged uncle telling a bedtime story.

'We found the boys exactly as you described them. I kind of understood your attitude then. It was, and still is, the worst thing I've ever seen. I was there with the Mayor, Theo, the Sergeant and the old doctor. We looked down at the boys, and we wept, yes, but not for them. They were dead. We wept for the town, for what would become of it when this leaked out. You see, we knew immediately who was to blame, and we knew it wasn't those hippies up in the camp.'

Nikos stares at the old man, unable to say anything. His mouth starts making the right movements, but nothing comes out. His heart bumps against his chest. Sweat pours down his neck and face. He can feel its sting in his eyes but now's not the time to wipe them. He takes two deep breaths.

'It wasn't the cult?'

'Cult?' Petrakis laughs, 'There was no cult. That was all after the fact. But it was a good story, no? Even you believe it, right? To this day. It was such a good story, the kind of story people wanted to believe, so it was easy to persuade them.

'No, they were just a bunch of hippies. Fucking reds and wasted layabouts. Good for nothing. You think that bunch of miserable drop-outs could ever belong to something as disciplined as a cult? You think they could even put a decent camp together let alone a system of belief? They were misguided idiots. Lucky for us they happened to be in the right place at the right time. Very lucky for us considering the consequences if the truth had come out.'

'You set them up?' Nikos grips the table's edge, feeling his fingers sink into the wood. It's everything he's suspected and everything he's denied.

Petrakis nods, 'You did too. We all did. It was necessary. The island wouldn't be what it is today if we hadn't done that.'

'You're fucking crazy.'

Petrakis ignores him. 'We knew you wouldn't understand. That's why we sent you away. You should thank us, really. We did what we had to do, but if you think it's been easy living with that secret to take to bed every night, well . . . we did you a favour. We kept you innocent.'

'You didn't want a policeman with "dubious politics" to have one over you, you mean. You didn't want me to be able to blackmail you later. That's why you sent me away.'

'Does it matter why?'

This is all wrong, and Nikos is tumbling through time, unearthing conversations long forgotten – seemingly meaningless then, now making perfect sense. That feeling that he'd been suckered in. The years of not knowing. Of suspecting. Of paranoia. All coming back to him now as he sits facing the old man.

'Who killed the boys?'

Petrakis's leer is as ugly as a squashed piece of fruit. Saliva leaks out the corners through thin, bloodless lips. His eyes are blazing. Nikos realises the old man's enjoying himself.

'We'd had problems before. This is how we knew. We were islanders not big-city people. We thought that certain things would disappear once we buried them. We never suspected they'd come back to haunt us. Remember, this was the mid-seventies. These things weren't so well documented then. There was no way to understand them in the way we do now. To know that these people never stop. Not unless they're stopped.'

'What are you talking about?' Nikos, totally confused now, trying to keep up with the old man's scattershot narrative.

Petrakis leans forward and grins. 'The priests liked little boys.'

THIRTY-NINE

They're in another cavern. This one is smaller and lower than the previous ones. Three paths branch out. They all lead into darkness. But that's not what they're looking at.

The smell is richer here, as if it were squatting in their lungs, and they both try and breathe through their mouths. They gag and retch. It's much hotter in this cavern. There's the sound of buzzing flies, the click of beetles against the walls, the steady dull hum of the Earth.

In the corner, up against a wall, is something that initially they cannot make sense of.

The fact that it's a shrine of some sort is evident, but its placing here, deep in the labyrinth, wrenches it out of context and makes them mistrust their senses.

There's an altar. Or what passes for one. A small folding table in the centre, propped up against the wall. The candles resting on it burn and flicker. There are four photos, decayed with age, yellow and willowy as old parchment. They all show the same face.

A young boy smiling bemusedly at the camera. There is a playfulness to his face which sits at odds with the bare wall the photos are affixed to.

But it's the teddy bear that draws them in.

At the centre of the display, just below the photos, is a well-loved, raggedy teddy bear, the kind only a kid having grown up with, and spent nights with, would cherish.

The bear is moving.

Kitty's torchlight illuminates the centipedes. Their orange

backs absorb the light. They weave in and out of the bear's body, out of its eye sockets and into its mouth, causing it to lurch in a slow, stuttering manner.

Kitty steps back. The heat is terrible, scorching suns, dense thick air. The smell is worse. When she looks down, she sees that the ground is moving.

Jason grabs her, but there's nothing they can do. The floor is one massive carpet of centipedes. She can feel how cold his skin is against hers. His breath sharp and punctured. She thanks God she's wearing her trainers and not flip-flops.

Her torch light is like a scythe cutting through the centipedes. When she aims it down at the ground, they scamper, their legs scuttling in all directions. They seem larger than the ones they've seen before, even at the boat-burning. Kitty arcs the light, watches as the orange curtain parts to reveal the buckets placed underneath the altar.

There are three of them. Their positioning is deliberate and ritualised. Small animal skulls encircle them. The buckets are made of brass, tarnished deep and dark like Byzantine icons.

Jason catches a glimpse of the putrid mess of grey and red before it goes dark, the torch clattering to the floor, as Kitty turns and throws up in the dust behind him.

Jason picks up the torch and bends down near the buckets. The stink is almost solid, so thick it feels in the air. It's hard to tell what's centipede and what isn't, but after a few seconds his eyes adjust and he realises what he's looking at.

The torch illuminates the first bucket. He looks at the tangle of intestines and dark black chunks of organs. He remembers how all the bodies were found eviscerated, and he swallows his own vomit as it rises sharply in his throat.

'Fuck. Fuck. Fuck.'

She doesn't answer. She's trying to keep her mouth shut. She's trying not to breathe. Dizziness sweeps through her, but she knows to faint here would mean falling into the centipedes, letting them wriggle and burrow into her.

They look up because they can't keep looking down. The boy looks back at them accusingly. He doesn't seem to be smiling anymore. They sweep the torchlight across the wall. Next to the photos, at the top of the shrine, there's a postcard of a fishing boat taped to the rock. Jason reaches forward and pulls it off. On the other side there's writing. He and Kitty scan it under the light, but it's all smudged, a kid's scrawl, shaky and angry, the card broken through several times.

As their hearts steady and their nausea becomes just a normal part of things, they study the other objects on the shrine.

There's a ring, gold or bronze, it's hard to say. A faded photo of an old man in traditional Greek costume. A torn and bleached-through section of a red dress. A bunch of flowers, still alive, left in the past couple of days. And four masks hanging as a border to the whole shrine.

Kitty points the torch at the wall. Stares at the masks. They're dried and desiccated skin. They're the faces of the victims. Preserved and hung for display. They're small and shrivelled, but there's no mistaking them. The boys hang on one side and the girls on the other. Their mouths are open in what could be a smile or a scream.

They take one more look, just in case they've missed anything. The candles cast shadows across the walls. The whole room seems to be in motion. They're about to leave when they hear something from the back of the cavern.

It's faint, at first, but in their silence it rises like an approaching thunderstorm.

It's the sound of a man's voice. It's the sound of laughter.

Equal parts phlegm and bile, the sound bounces off the walls, turning the one voice into a multitude, a demented chorus that weaves its way into their heads. Kitty grabs Jason's hand, feels it sweat-slicked and hot in hers. He looks at her, sees the squint of her mouth, and there's no need to ask if she's heard it too.

She hands him the torch. He holds it in his hands as if trying to ascertain its function. The laughter rises and crests like a wave.

'Hello?'

His voice sounds weak and unravelled. He wishes he could pull it back into the cavern of his throat. Kitty nods, acknowledging the things he can't say.

There's no reply to his greeting, only more laughter.

The switch feels soft under his finger. He slides it across, and light pools at his feet. His trainers are covered in centipedes. He can hear Kitty's breath stop in her mouth, the slow exhale of her fear.

He raises the torch. A disc of white hits the opposite wall. They don't see anything but the wall. They move closer, forcing themselves, one step at a time.

They see his hair first. Then the metal poles and manacles. They stop in front of the man. His laughter sounds further away now even though they're right next to him.

The torch lights up his face, but there's only darkness there. His beard is matted and black with dirt. His hair is ragged and dishevelled like an old mop. His laughter is high and tight, like a malfunctioning car alarm. He's chained to the wall.

Jason takes another step, and the prisoner's eyes flick open.

'Who are you?'

There's no reply. The prisoner twists his head, his eyes pinpricks punched into the shoreline of his face. He looks like a dungeon-room Jesus, but there's no mercy in his gaze.

His arms are hoisted above his shoulders. They twist and turn as he continues to laugh. His left shoulder is dislocated, and his arm turns in an elliptical circle, the bone pushing against the sallow skin. His wrists are encased in silver hoops which are welded to a metal pole attached to the wall. His clothes are torn, and there are scabs and bites along his legs and bare feet.

It's only when they notice what's around his neck that they recognise him.

FORTY

'What did you say?'

'I said the priests liked little boys.'

Nikos needs Petrakis to repeat this last statement. To make sure he's heard him right. Because if he has, then this whole thing . . . he's been thinking about it wrong, and people have died because of it. He flashes back to the funeral, Vondas's room, the book on the cult. To what Kitty said a few hours ago.

'Oh, it was well covered up. But we knew.' Petrakis draws out the words as if they were strings on a kite. He watches Nikos's face, enjoying the look of surprise and horror that suffuses it.

'There had been incidents. Reaching four years before the murders. Stories we were told. Marks and bruisings. But things were different then. No one talked about sexual abuse. No one even mentioned it. And priests? They were, forgive the expression, sacrosanct.

'Of course, nowadays, every priest is guilty of molestation until proved innocent. Back then, the idea that a priest, a man of God, would do such things . . . it was unthinkable. It was like saying God was guilty.

'These days, it's different. People no longer have the same quality of faith. They go to church, say their prayers, make their tithes, but their hearts are empty. You tell them this or that priest was a paedophile or rapist and they'll shake their heads at the tragedy of it, but not one of them will really be surprised. Back then, God was infallible. And so were his emissaries. You might as well accuse God of molesting boys.

'But after four years, we'd heard enough rumours, covered up enough complaints – we knew who the two priests were and what they did – but as long as nothing big happened, there was no way we were going to shake the boat. What if we were wrong? Imagine that. Accusing priests falsely. We would have been locked away ourselves. And besides, how could you prove these things? Even now, same problem. But then? Who would take a child's word against a man of God's?

'And that's not even looking at the big picture. If one priest was sentenced, then all priests were. To being human. To being slaves of their own desires. God was an essential commodity in the days of the generals. People needed to believe in something more than their shitty lives. They needed to be able to rise above the repression, depression and fear. You think the generals would have allowed us to prosecute a priest?

'So. We knew the two priests – Vondas and Karelis – had this proclivity. We knew they'd been friends in the seminary and that Karelis made a special request for Vondas to join him at the monastery in 1970. We knew all this, but we also knew there was no way we could arrest them for it.'

Nikos sits listening. He can't believe it and yet has absolutely no reason to doubt Petrakis. The delight the old man takes in telling him how wrong he's been all these years is proof enough. His mind is skipping possibilities and speculations like a search engine. The empty funeral. The death of the priest. The vandalised book. This all begins to fit into the frame. The things which he always thought were outside this case he's now realising are at the very heart of it.

'So, you didn't do anything to the priests? You just let them get away with raping and killing those boys?' His anger startles him, and he knows it's not just the boys he's thinking about but the hippies who had to pay for this crime. And his own wife, who's had to live for years with the possibility that her friends were killers.

'We didn't let them off that easy. But, as I explained, there was not much we could do. The island was falling apart as it was – the fishing dried up, the youngsters leaving – imagine what would have happened if they'd found out their own priests were murderers. That would have been it. I wasn't going to let that happen just to satisfy some righteous sense of justice. Justice is what's right for the most people at the time. I made my decision. It was the right one.'

'Even now you're sure of that?'

Petrakis actually takes a few seconds to think this through, the first sign of self-doubt that Nikos has noticed.

'Even now,' he says finally, and his voice is as heavy as a judge's pronouncement.

'Tell me what happened.'

'We went to the monastery. Straight after we saw the boys. Vondas and Karelis were praying in the chapel. Trying to ask God's forgiveness? Or just praying they wouldn't be caught?

'When they saw us, they gave themselves up. They could read our expressions, the blood-splattered clothes, the guns in our hands. Vondas said something to the older priest, but they didn't try and run, I'll give them that.

'Of course, we needed proof. And, I guess, maybe we did want to get back at them. To hurt them some.'

The glint in Petrakis's eyes says it all.

'You tortured them?'

'We only gave them back some of what they'd given out to the boys.'

'What did you do to them?' Nikos's voice comes out through clenched teeth.

Petrakis leans in closer. 'You really want to know, don't you? Well, OK. There's no shame in it. I don't spend nights worrying about what we did.

'Of course they were beaten a bit. Guns and sticks. Enough to let them know we weren't going through the motions. Then we asked them about the boys. They began blabbering, denying everything, praying to God. Can you believe that? They actually began to pray to God to save them.

'We tied the priests to chairs. We sat them next to each other in front of the altar. In front of God. They were stripped naked. You remember Theo, the sergeant?'

Nikos nods, the bitterness rising in his throat like backwash.

'You know he was on the mainland before coming to the island? No, you didn't know that, did you? Worked for the colonels. He'd done this kind of thing before. Knew how to extract information. How to administer pain.

'My God, even I had to turn away, remind myself of what these two priests had done, tell myself some humans give up their right to human rights when they step over a certain line. Still, their screams echoing in that empty church didn't make me feel better. You ever seen a man castrated? Perhaps you can imagine. This was after they confessed everything. Confessed to things we didn't even know about. Molestations and rapes stretching back years. They confessed to every sin they'd ever committed as if they were at the gates of Heaven and Peter their interlocutor.

'They said the two boys had stayed behind that day. The priests caught them smoking in the gardens. They took them back in to scold them. They hit them, and, I guess, that's where it started, where they felt their blood rise. Desire took hold of them. They kept whacking the boys, telling them they were wicked and that God would punish them. They stripped them and beat them with bibles and sticks. The blood must have set something off. Vondas told us this; he was beyond embarrassment or concealment then. He said they took the boys. And took them again. Writhing in the blood and screams and pain. He said they totally lost control, but, even as he said it, I could see a glimmer in his eyes, reliving that moment, that one moment in his life when he'd done what he truly wanted, and you could tell he didn't regret it at all.

'When they were finished, they realised one of the boys was dead. The other boy started screaming. Vondas said both him and Karelis knew what had to be done.

'They strangled the other boy. They then had a problem. By nightfall, the boys would be reported missing. Everyone would know they'd gone to the monastery for the weekend. The priests remembered the hippies living in the mountains. They knew the stories. Realised they could use them.

'And so they began to think. And the story they made up, it was so good, so logical, that I think even they began to believe it. As you of all people know, denial is an extremely useful thing.' Petrakis's glare is like a hawk's.

'Just get on with it.' Nikos feels the blood drain from his face. He can see the satisfaction in Petrakis's eyes. He only wants to get this over with now.

'They took the boys out to the ruins. They did what they had to do with their bodies. The centipedes were a final touch of the bizarre. They were all over the mountain and monastery, and it seemed just the kind of thing a cult would do and the last thing on earth a priest would. They improvised a story out of necessity and fear. They planted the bodies and hoped the story would hold. That people would only need to move that one small step from what they already suspected about the cult.

'Vondas told us all this, and then Theo finished his work. The doctor cauterised their wounds. Told them they were getting off lucky. That it would bring them closer to God. Old man had a sense of humour, I'll give him that. Kept a cigarette in his mouth all the time he was treating the wounds. Went along with everything we agreed. Kept his mouth shut till the cancer ate it away. By then it was too late for deathbed confessions. The man couldn't even speak after they removed his tongue.

'We knew the priests wouldn't talk just as we knew we couldn't do anything more to them. But we believed they wouldn't be a problem any more. Didn't have the tools even if they still had the desire. We left them there, passed out, lying in their own puke and blood.

'But we still had the problem. What to do about the boys? Who would take the blame? We went out to the woods. Sat and smoked and passed a bottle of brandy we'd liberated from the monastery. Got blind drunk. Only reaction to events we could think of. And maybe it was partly the drink, maybe partly the dark of the woods, the unnatural quiet after the screaming crescendos of the priests – that's when we decided what to do. No, realised what we *had* to do. What needed to be done to keep the community whole. And, with that, to also clear the island of the little problem we had. The hippies. The fucking hippies.

'You wouldn't understand how it was. They represented everything we were fighting against. They lived up in the mountains and thought they were better guardians of the island than we were. They didn't realise we needed to make money to eat, we didn't have their trust funds, we needed to fish and exploit the island for what it could give us. This, you have to understand, was survival not revenge.

'We all sat there in the deep forest, drinking steadily. We decided we could play on everyone's feelings about the cult. The priests gave us their idea. And we saw how two birds could be killed. We knew we were the stone.

'I don't think we ever said it out loud to each other, but it was there in the way we looked at one another, in the things we didn't say, the objections we never raised. Someone had to pay the price, after all. Otherwise, without resolution, this thing would haunt the island for ever.

'Theo radioed for some more men. A couple of deputies and some of the locals we knew we could trust. When they arrived, we explained to them what we'd found. How every sign pointed to the cult. The ritualisation, the proximity, the cold-bloodedness. They believed us – after all, who else would do such a thing? Not normal islanders, no, but a bunch of weird Americans living out in the open? Everyone could buy that.

'They didn't have a chance. They were sleeping, and never even heard us enter the clearing. The deputies had brought more guns and ammunition. We explained that this needed to look like a mass suicide. We told the angry village men that if we arrested these people – and, with their numbers, there was no guarantee we'd get them all – that if arrested they would go to trial. There would be a big international outcry. A conviction was possible but not guaranteed. We let the men make the choice we'd already made for them. We detailed what had been done to the boys, the mutilations and sexual abuse. We wanted each man to have that picture in his mind when he entered the tent. We didn't want any wavering or second thoughts.

'Then we went into each tent, and we killed them. The ones who woke up had no chance. The ones still asleep never knew what hit them. It took less than five minutes.

'The next day, you came back with the mainland detectives, and they too wanted to believe the story we'd made up for them. They saw what had been done to the boys, and they knew no Greek could have done such a thing. They wrapped it up with a ribbon and took the package back to Athens.

'There never was a cult, you see, but there was the belief in one, and that was enough. We gave people the ending they wanted and secretly intuited. And . . . and we thought we'd got away with it. Thought that until last year when they found the first body. The ones of us left, we knew what it signified. We knew it couldn't be a resurgence of the cult, because there never was a cult in the first place. Still, it scared us. If someone had found out . . . we still had lives we didn't want to lose. We thought it was Vondas, you see. Vondas and Karelis finally taking their revenge for what we did to them that night. But then Karelis disappeared, and Vondas got killed.'

Nikos doesn't say anything to that. He runs his fingers through his moustache, thinking it through. 'And the library?'

'The library had too many archives. Too many things about the hippies, the cult, that whole period. When your wife set up the cult exhibit, we all got nervous. But it was nothing, just another display. Now though, with the murders continuing, with that fucking English writer poking her nose into things, talking to Vondas – who knows what he might have told her?

Well, you see it was better that it burned down. We didn't know what was in the archives, what someone with enough perseverance would find.'

'Is that why you broke into Kitty's room?'

'Dimitri saw her talking to your wife and to Yanni. We didn't know what she was after. What she'd discovered. We had to make sure. Protect the island.'

'You're saying you had nothing to do with the centipede murders? With the four teenagers killed?'

Petrakis looks towards his mother. His head is shaking. He seems slighter, his unburdening a thing of the body as much as of the conscience.

'You think it's in my interest to kill tourists? To kill our boys and girls? What could I gain from this? Tell me? You can't, can you? I don't know who killed those tourists and our children. It wasn't us. It's someone who wants to get back at us. If anything, we're next.'

Nikos smiles.

He takes out the cuffs, watches Petrakis's bemusement like a stain spreading across his face. 'You'll be safe in the cells,' he says.

Petrakis's mouth makes shapes, but there's nothing coming out. His face flushes red. Nikos hopes he's not going to have a heart attack. He's waited for this moment too many years.

'You're under arrest for attempted murder and arson. That's the library. You're also under arrest for intent to distribute and smuggle methamphetamine.'

Nikos watches Petrakis's face run through his options. He looks ten years older than he did a few moments ago.

'Bullshit,' is the best the old man can come up with. 'You think any of that will stick? This is the end of your career,' he shouts.

'Your son was very cooperative.'

'What did you say?'

'When we arrested Dimitri, told him how many years he'd be serving for the arson and attempted murder, you should have seen him. You would have been proud. Spilling anything he knew, fucking begging us not to ship him to the mainland. He told us everything. How the drugs are manufactured in your villa on the other side of the island. How you co-opt mules and dealers. He gave you up, and you know what?' Nikos waits a beat, 'He was happy to. Don't think he likes you that much. Just another failure to chalk up, Petrakis.'

The old man closes his eyes. He leans back into the sofa and takes a deep breath as the handcuffs go on and Nikos leads him out of the house, through the streets of town and into the station.

FORTY-ONE

The dog collar is faded and torn, but there's no mistaking it. The beard is rust red and the skin black with dust and dirt, yet Karelis keeps laughing. The smell is stronger than at the altar, and, as they carefully make their way towards him, they see the bucket he uses for his needs, overfilled and surrounded by a halo of flies. The contents of the bucket are in motion. The torch reveals large centipedes crawling in and out of the human waste, gorged and fit to burst. Centipedes cover the floor and crunch under their feet like dry leaves.

Kitty looks at the priest's wrists, cut, scabbed and infected. There are sores all over his skin, dirt covering every inch of exposed flesh.

Jason tries wrenching the pole out of the wall, but it doesn't budge. The rough metal tears at his fingers, and when he looks down he's bleeding. The blood drips onto the priest's face. Karelis' tongue emerges from the tangle of his beard and catches the drops.

'We have to get him out of here,' Kitty says.

The priest is looking at them, but it's the look of an animal. Uncomprehending, sensing only danger, not needing to know more. He struggles against his chains, the sound of metal grinding against bone.

'It's OK, we're here to get you out,' Kitty says in faltering Greek.

Jason reaches for the old man's wrist, feels along the metal for an opening.

'It's locked.' He bends down, examines the floor, picks up a rock and puts it back down. Finally, he finds one just the right size. It fits in his palm. He motions the priest to turn away.

'Shine the torch on his wrist.'

He stands there in the spotlight, measuring, sizing, getting his nerve up. In one clean arcing movement, he brings the flat edge of the rock down on the rusted lock. There's a spark, and slivers of metal fly across the room. He does it again, and this time the sound of the lock breaking ricochets against the roof and walls like a gunshot.

Jason loses balance, dropping the rock, falling towards the priest. Karelis looks up at him, teeth red and rotten in the fading light. The priest laughs then, with the broken lock still attached, swings his arm in a circle. It's too fast a movement for Kitty or Jason to react. One minute the priest is still, the next it's a whirlwind of motion as his arm completes the circle and comes crashing down onto Jason's thigh, the rusted and sheared metal of his manacle cutting cleanly through Jason's jeans and embedding deeply into his flesh.

Jason screams. His head spins. The priest slashes again with the broken metal, hitting the same point, unleashing a geyser of blood as Jason steps back, stumbles and falls.

Kitty watches all this. It's like she's there and she's not there. She sees Jason lean down to unshackle the priest. She sees the old man lunge. The broken metal sparkles in the torchlight. Then Jason is on the floor, holding his leg, stemming the blood, a red fountain arcing into the air.

She bends down and takes his hand. It is both cold and hot and covered in a thin layer of sweat. She hears him moan. 'It's going to be OK,' she says, but there's no conviction in her voice. The priest chuckles behind them. His beard red and wet, his eyes bright and burning.

'Christ, it hurts,' Jason moans, and she nods though she knows he can't see her. He's lying on his back, his left hand wrapped around his leg, above the knee. It's like trying to hold onto a handful of water. The dark black blood pours between his fingers and around his hand. She doesn't want to think the word 'artery', but there it is, and she knows there's barely any time left.

The priest continues cackling, his back against the wall. 'You fucking asshole,' she screams, 'he was trying to help you.'

She takes off her shirt. The cold air scrapes against her skin. She folds the shirt, wrapping it around Jason's leg. He's as cold as the rock under her feet. Cold as the air.

She takes the end of the shirt and tightens it. Jason screams. His back arches, and she nearly loses him. 'It's OK,' she whispers, her hand stroking his forehead. She tries to find words that will make him feel OK. She looks into his eyes. His mouth opens, but no sound comes out, just an echo of his breath. Her shirt has gone from canary yellow to deep dark red.

His eyes roll back, and he falls limp into her arms.

'Jason! Wake up!' She screams, grabbing his other hand. She pinches it hard. His eyes flutter and open. The blood is coming through the shirt now. Deep black puddles lie at her feet.

'Kitty?' His voice is less than a whisper. She feels his palm tighten against hers, but there's hardly any strength left in it.

'This is going to hurt,' she says, and before he can reply, she yanks on the shirt, tightening the tourniquet. He screams, and his body twists. The blood squeezes out either side of the shirt. She feels his body vibrating, a slow tremor that turns into an explosion, and she almost loses hold of his hand.

'Jason!' She's screaming into his face. His eyes are misty and unfocused. The blood is warm and sticky on her knees. The priest cackles to himself in the corner.

'Jason? Can you hear me?'

He takes her hand, pulls her towards him. He can feel the softness of her body make contact with his, feel her warmth flow through him. His head is full of light. 'It doesn't feel like anything,' he says.

She forces a smile, nods her head. 'I need to go and find Nikos. I need to find a doctor.' She looks down at his jeans, stained red from thigh to ankle now, and she knows there isn't enough time.

He looks up at her. Takes everything he has to focus. Her lips. The shape of her mouth. The words mean nothing. Her eyes say it all. He knows.

'Go.'

She leans down, straining to hear his words. His hand feels cold and dry. His breath dark and bitter. 'No,' she whispers. 'I'm not leaving you.'

She thinks he's laughing, she's not sure, it's not a sound she can make sense of, but his lips are curled in a smile.

'Get a doctor. I'll be fine.' He tries to smile again, to show her it's no big deal, but a wave of pain buckles his mouth and tears through his face. He feels himself falling, falling out of his body and into the soft wet earth. It's like the first big dip on a rollercoaster, the ecstasy of weightlessness before the plunge.

She hesitates. Stares down into the whirlpool of his eyes. It's as if he's moving further away. 'I'll be back as soon as I can.'

He watches the back of her head. The black waterfall of hair. The sway of her leaving. She looks back once and then disappears round a corner into the darkness.

He lies there, the warmth of his life leaking over his legs and sinking into the moist earth. He stares at the corrugated roof of the cavern, traces the lines and cracks until they spell out names long forgotten, lovers lost in memory, days gone to the mist of time. He can hear the priest cackling, the echo transforming his voice into a choir of voices, his own Greek chorus to usher out his days.

It's too late. He wishes he'd told her when she held his hand, when she cupped his shoulder and whispered her breath into his lungs. But she's gone, and so are all the paths and possibilities of his life. He'd never told her what he felt towards her, the deep burning awakening of something within himself, the fire that sparked from his fingertips every time they touched. He wants to kiss her lips once more, just once. So many things he'd intended to do, say. So much left unfinished. It rises in him like a fire, ripping through his stomach, collapsing his lungs, burning his head. He should have told her that he could see a future where they would fit each other like missing pieces of a puzzle. But he'd been so terrified of her rejection, the look on her face, the cold words she would utter. So scared of so many things all through his life, and now, lying here in the pool of his own blood, all the fear was gone, but it was too late.

He thinks of the manuscript back in his room. He's never even mentioned it to her. It would be cleared away, he supposes, along with his other belongings, trashed, compacted and forgotten. Maybe that was better, but yet it felt like another thing lost to the world. He remembers a bright diamond-studded night in London, the books he'll never see again, music he'll never hear, the dog he never had, the house with curtains and children. His life seems to be summed up by everything he hasn't done. He grinds his hand into the floor, the sharp stony ground underneath him, and it feels good, to feel pain, to feel anything again.

He says her name. Kitty. And again, but there's no sound coming through his lips. He can hear water rushing somewhere in the distance, the heartbeat of the world. The scampering of cave-dwelling creatures. The laughter of the priest. The last words she said. The way her lips didn't quite meet when she closed her mouth.

And then he sees her. A shadow emerging from the gloom. Hair electric and black. She's walking towards him. She's at the end of a long tunnel. There is light in her hands, a soft white light she cradles like a baby to her chest.

He begins to fall. The ground tilts and swerves under him. His breath catches in his chest. He can hear it wheeze and sputter, try and fail. His head rests on the ground. His eyes stare at the cavern's ceiling. The priest is quiet now. There is no one in the room but him. No one in the world but him. And then not even that.

FORTY-TWO

It's here somewhere. He's sure of it. It's been here all along. Thirty-three years in a box, the box sitting like an unexploded bomb in the station's basement. The way secrets can reveal themselves to you.

You were never that good a cop.

Petrakis's words come back to haunt him, and, finally, he has to admit there's more than a little truth to them. Was he always a bad cop or was the importance of hiding Alexia's identity more important? Were the two even so mutually exclusive as he'd like to think they were? If he'd presented Alexia to the authorities that first day, if he'd allowed her to tell her story, explain how the cult could never do such a thing, how they didn't even possess guns – if he'd done all that, would things still have played out as they did?

He's glad she's out. They haven't been talking much recently. She's become the shadow he sees in the corner of his vision, floating from room to room like a silent cleaner. He knows she's retreating into some part of herself she thought she'd lost, but he doesn't know how to stop her or whether he should. There's something in these silences that prevents him from worrying. It's the silence of a secret brought out into the open after many years, not the silence of betrayal or disappointment.

Petrakis's words rumble through his head. The worst thing is, he believes him. The story of the priests turns everything upside down. The clues have led him down the wrong path. They only showed a tiny piece of a much larger puzzle.

He thinks back to that day at the morgue: Vondas's body, the fury in which he'd been attacked. This was revenge, not business. This was personal, fuelled by cold anger and bad memories. He rubs his temples, the headache a constant pulsing presence behind them. Who would have a good enough reason to extract such revenge? There's only one person he can think of.

The files and papers he holds are lies. He can barely stand to touch them. His own report on the discovery of the bodies – was that the last truthful piece of information to come out of the past?

Coroner's reports. Pages of interviews with locals. Deputies' reports. The summations of the mainland detectives. All lies.

He places them to one side. He knows what he's looking for, and he knows it's somewhere in here.

It's a file he's read countless times. A report on the relatives of the murdered boys. He'd skimmed it and put it away. He'd thought it was irrelevant, background work. He'd been wrong.

He finds it at the bottom of the fifth box. He takes out the four pages of badly typed transcript, faded, almost invisible now. There are photos of Yorgi and Constantine, the two murdered boys, serene in their frames. A list of living relatives: aunts, uncles, siblings and cousins. He divides the papers into two. He puts the Constantine material to one side. He notes Yorgi's father died two years before his son. The only relatives he'd had were his mother and older brother. He stares at the faces, wondering if he's looking at the killer.

He re-reads the names, and it still doesn't make sense. And then it does.

He takes out his phone. He has to warn Kitty and Jason they're looking for the wrong man. But before he can dial, a tone notifies him there's a message. He puts the phone to his ear and hears Kitty's voice. 'We're going to the labyrinth. Don't worry, we're not going to do anything stupid.' The call was left over an hour ago.

He immediately calls Elias, tells him to prepare some men and meet him by the gates of the labyrinth. He takes the file containing the information about the deceased's next of kin. Once they secure the labyrinth, he'll make the arrest. He wants to get as much evidence as he can first. This time, there can be no mistakes.

The scooter rasps and stutters as it carries him away from town and into the interior. He thinks about all the fuck-ups he's made, past and present, as he climbs up towards the monastery.

He can see Elias and the deputies sharing cigarettes, laughing and joking outside the entrance to the labyrinth. If he's right, they won't be laughing or joking long.

They stand at the gate, shuffling their feet and hunching against the wind, as he explains what happened in 1974. He takes out the report and shows them the name. Says it's different now, but it's the same man. They take deep breaths and shake their heads as they listen. They can't believe it, and he catches them glancing back towards the monastery with fear and revulsion.

They take photos of the footprints leading to the gate. They scour the ground. Nikos takes out his torch and is about to enter when he hears a strange sound. He tells the others to shut up. There it is. Definitely. He can see Elias has heard it too. Footsteps, hurried and irregular, coming from inside the cave. They draw their guns. The footsteps get louder. They can hear breathing, grunting, feeble attempts to catch the air.

Kitty comes running out, hair ablaze, her body dark and half naked, pitted by scratches and welts like an army of red ants decorating her skin.

A shot goes off. Kitty stops dead as the bullet ricochets against the wall of the cave. She's staring at the policemen, but Nikos can tell she doesn't recognise them.

'It's OK. It's me. Nikos,' he shouts, turning to the deputy who fired the shot, making sure he's got the message too.

Kitty's skin is scratched and bleeding. She's not wearing a shirt. Her bra is dark with blood. She looks from face to face trying to make sense of this strange group. They're all taut and rigid, feet apart, more like diagrams of men than flesh and blood.

Nikos steps forward, holstering his gun. He treads carefully, feeling Kitty flinch as he puts his arm around her shoulder. 'It's OK now,' he says, his breath falling softly on her ear, 'it's over.'

Kitty looks up at him. Her eyes look like they're dissolving. 'It's not OK,' she whispers, and he catches her as she collapses to the ground, her body slick and sticky with someone else's blood.

FORTY-THREE

He leaves Kitty with one of the deputies. Her face is blank, and her eyes stare into the distance as if she's watching a movie of her life. There's nothing he can do for her now. He radios the paramedics, warns them what they're likely to find. He tells Elias what he wants him to do. He instructs the other policemen to start searching the labyrinth.

He takes the bike into town. He speeds around curves and almost loses the road several times. As he revs the engine, he notices curtains shimmying, doors being silently opened, men stopping in the street to watch him. The news of Petrakis's arrest must have already spread through town. News travelled faster than CNN in small communities.

The smack of wind on his face makes his eyes water. The houses and people blur by. He feels the motor hum below him. A slow cyclic purr. He knows it's the end of this thing. He's surprised, but not really, at how despondent this makes him feel. He knows by now that the case is all in the hunting. When it's over, it leaves you wasted and spent, empty-eyed and hollowed, like a political candidate the night after an election. Normally, there are other cases to sink into, a new mystery to make special the days, but this time it's the last one. There's nothing after this but the rest of his life. And this thought terrifies him more than what he's about to do.

He leaves the scooter a few blocks away. He walks the rest of the distance, watching the light slip and fade behind the distant Peloponnese. Shopkeepers and customers emerge from shops as he walks past. They stand like wooden Indians by the doors and watch him, their faces betraying neither hate nor respect. He fixes his eyes straight ahead.

He passes by the tavernas and clubs hugging the shore. Here the looks are darker, filled with mistrust and antipathy. Waiters and owners, clubbers and cleaning staff, watch as he walks past, some shaking their heads, a few spitting on the floor in front of him. The island will change now. This he's sure of. Whether it will survive these changes, he can't say, and, to his surprise, he doesn't care. He and Alexia will be gone by the time the case is wrapped up. He knows their life cannot be what it was. Maybe this time they can leave the island for good.

He walks past the museum, nothing now but a heap of black ash pollinating in the wind. Scraps of books and maps and faded photos rise in the late evening breeze and twist like dust devils across the cobblestones.

He passes the church, its white steeple an obscenity against the square, regimented houses. He used to walk past it, envy the sense of peace and escape from the world. Now it only reminds him of events up at the monastery. Petrakis's story rushes through his head like a compressed vision of hell. He bites down on his tongue, thinking about the two boys, the priests, but most of all thinking about the deception. Petrakis's pathetic attempts to justify shifting the blame onto the commune so that they could murder them.

What would have happened if they hadn't sent him to the mainland that day? Would he have joined them? He curses Petrakis for having seen into his heart so easily, for giving him the easy way out.

He stops outside one of the bars and lights a cigarette. He watches as Elias drags out a handcuffed and bruised Wynn. The drug dealer is shaking his head, blood dripping from his eyebrows and nose, still fighting the restraints which will keep him company these next few years. Elias stops and nods at Nikos. Nikos acknowledges him and turns away.

Petrakis and Dimitri are already in facing cells, their mutual loathing boiled down into that tiny space. Spiros, back in

Athens, will be pleased. The drug trade will be curtailed for a while, though it won't be long before someone takes Petrakis's place. Nikos knows there's a hundred Wynns just waiting for their chance. But he did what he was sent here to do. The drugs are gone. Now there's only one thing remaining.

Nikos walks in to the bar. The lights are flashing, the music is blaring, and the revellers are twisting and twirling on the diamond dance floor. The place is busier than usual tonight. Nikos stands there and surveys the room. He can see a girl passed out on a table, two men running their hands up her legs like they were the keys of a piano. There's someone throwing up in a corner. Dancers with eyes like teddy bears, all pupil, unblinking and empty. There's a lot of people wandering around, looking distressed, asking others if they have anything to spare.

Nikos sees him as he's crossing towards the bar. He doesn't stop. He calls the waiter and orders a double, no ice. His whole body is quivering with energy, fear and madness. He takes the drink and slowly lets it slake his desiccated mouth. He wants to make this moment last.

The glass in his hand is empty. The cigarette gone. He tips the waiter and recrosses the dance floor. A scarlet-haired girl grabs him as he passes and pulls him into her. She's smiling and laughing, but when she looks up into his eyes her face drops, and she lets go of his hand. He watches her spin on the dance floor, a burning flame like some fabled Djinn crossing the land.

He turns away and walks over towards the far booth. He sees him sitting where he always sits, a glass of ouzo half empty in front of him. When Nikos enters, he looks up, and it's a look not of surprise or fear but a quiet contentment that almost throws Nikos off balance. He'd expected fake outpourings of innocence, an attempt at running perhaps, but not this quiet and silent resignation.

They stand there for a moment in the hot stuck air like two figures in an improbable still-life. The fan buzzes overhead, casting blade-shaped shadows on the walls. The singer on the stereo is singing something about going home.

'You know why I'm here,' Nikos says, and his voice sounds strange to him, as if he'd pressed the wrong button on a tape recorder.

George takes a deep swallow of ouzo. His lips smack against each other. Thin tears of alcohol dribble from the glass and moisten his beard. He stares at Nikos and lights a cigarette. His hands are steady, and his movements measured as if he were the one giving Nikos benediction and not the other way around. 'Sit with me. Have a drink,' he points to the chair facing him, 'you're going to arrest me and get all the credit, it's the least you can do.'

Nikos finds himself sitting down. This is not what he planned. But there's something inviting about the empty glass, the beaded bottle in front of him and the chance to make this last just a little bit longer.

Nikos pours himself a beer. He checks over his shoulder to make sure the deputies are guarding the exits. He looks at George. He's trying to see the ten-year-old boy from the photo in the relatives-of-the-deceased file. But there's nothing there. No indicator that ten-year-old Alex Mavropolous and George Mavers were the same person. He'd taken his brother's name, Yorgi, and anglicised it the way his mother had done with their surname.

'I don't understand how you, of all people,' Nikos breathes out. The months and years of frustration come down to this one moment. 'You lost someone yourself to murder, your own brother. How could you do that to other families? You know the effect it has. What it does to a life.'

George looks up into the air. His beard is all Nikos can see of him for a moment.

'Don't tell me you wouldn't do the same? If it was your brother those priests raped and killed that night? Your blood?'

Nikos thinks about Alexia. The years of lying and subterfuge. He thinks of the ten-year-old boy in the file, how carefree and open he looked, and the man in front of him now, all shadows and darkness, and how once they were the same person until a blow had struck them apart for ever.

'I wouldn't kill anyone,' he says, for himself more than for George.

George finishes his ouzo, rubbing the back of his hand against his lips. 'Don't be so sure. You don't know until you know. And by then it's too late.'

Nikos tries to imagine, but it's impossible, like trying to picture a concept that doesn't exist. 'And you never thought about what you'd become? About punishment?'

George's abrupt laughter startles Nikos so badly he's halfway to his gun before he realises it's benign.

'What? You think God exists?' George shakes his head as if at a small child professing a belief in unicorns. 'After all you've seen, detective, you really still believe?'

George doesn't wait for Nikos to answer. His tone is no longer one of amused condescension.

'They took more from me than just my brother that night. Much more. You don't realise that at first. One day you look at yourself in the mirror and you're not who you thought you were. And the worst part is you don't even remember that other person. The man before.' There's no remorse in his words. He's so certain of the rightness of his actions that Nikos has to remind himself that George killed four innocent teenagers as collateral damage to his revenge.

'You feel better now?' Nikos finds himself surprised that he genuinely wants to know.

George's shrug could be interpreted as anything. 'The priests are dead. I'm happy about that.'

The air hums around them with music and insects. The stars seem too bright, lost in a massive blanket of darkness. Nikos finishes his beer and lights a cigarette. He knows George won't be so willing to talk later, when they're in different surroundings. 'Why did you pick those particular teenagers? It's been bothering me.'

George waves his arm across the dance floor and the town beyond.

'Look what happened to us. You grew up here. You remember the place it was. Look what they made it into. Noise and drugs is all the tourists want. I had to kill someone for the plan to work, so it was better that I killed someone who was doing the island harm. It didn't take me long to realise Petrakis was behind the drugs. I knew killing his mules would send the message directly.'

Nikos feels the night close in around him, a swaddling heat filled with guilt and recrimination.

'Why not kill him first?'

'I wanted him to suffer. Suffer and remember. Karelis too. It's good to have time to reflect on your sins.'

'I thought you didn't believe in God?'

'I don't, but everyone else does.'

Nikos stands and places the handcuffs on him and with a single, unheard click shuts down the past thirty-three years of fear and silence.

Eighteen months later

The rain washes everything away. The gutters are filled with the dust of crumbling houses, getting smaller every year. The rivers of rain run through the town, sweeping empty beer cans, fast-food wrappers and cigarette butts into the hungry swell of the sea.

There was not much cleaning up to do any more. This was the off-season. The empty grey days of early winter. The ferry boats had stopped. The tavernas and clubs boarded-up for the season. The streets empty of everything but rain and skinny dogs rubbing their noses in the garbage cans behind the restaurants and bars.

Everything feels off these days. The weather. The town. The sea itself. But most of all him.

Nikos sips his coffee and stares out at the rain. The drink is too hot as always, the machine no longer working as it should. The police station is empty, the clocks ticking in the silent room. It's almost ten in the evening, and, instead of the lights flashing from shore, the distant detonation of dance music, there's only the sound of the rain as it hits the cobblestones and rushes back towards the sea.

He turns and sits down. There are boxes all over his office, stacked on the floor and on the table in front of him. He's in the process of packing up his life once again. Squeezing every-thing into a small cardboard receptacle which he'll take with him to wherever he goes next.

Luckily, there's not much to pack. He's been in the job just over two years. It had been a time of stripping, not accumulation. He looks around the dusty office, the posters of places he'll never visit, the crime sheets and photos, the chair that always ruined his back. Everything has been tied up. The trial is over. The case closed. The drugs are, for the moment, gone. There's nothing left for him to do.

He spent the last month in Athens, giving testimony and watching as George took the stand to receive his verdict. Now there's only the boxing of these loose ends, the papers, files and statements that are meaningless now. He takes another sheaf of reports and squares them against the table before putting them neatly into the last box. All that's left are his pens, note-books and the framed photo of Alexia resting on the table.

It's been eighteen months since he's seen his wife.

She didn't come back the day of George's arrest, and she didn't come back the following day. He'd had the whole town searched, the houses and clubs and cafés. Then the interior, the monastery grounds and labyrinth. No one had seen her. No one knew where she'd been that day.

Two months later, he received the postcard. It had been mailed from Argentina.

She said, 'By the time you receive this, I'll be in another country.' She said, 'Sorry.' She said that the years together were all she thought of now. She told him there were things he might never understand. That she wanted a clean break. From the island. From history. From him. The last she didn't say, but it was there between every line. She said they made mistakes. They should have come clean at the beginning. That now she had to start again, and Greece, and everything there, could only serve as a reminder of terrible days.

She wrote how she still thought about the hippies, the time they shared together and, most of all, about Frank. She broke his heart by telling him how when she was stricken with the virus, she lost Frank's baby. She said she loved him, always had done, but some things, some people, stayed with you for ever.

Her handwriting made him cry. Made him remember little notes she used to leave attached to food, *I know you'll come back late so I prepared this for you.* In her handwriting are years of shared memories and a life he cannot return to.

He read and reread the postcard until he could tell where every mark and discolouration was. The handwriting small and cramped as if she'd contracted events, trying to fit the whole narrative onto the edges of the postcard.

He looks back down at the photo in his hand, the empty station around him. He fingers the rough gold edges of the frame, stares at his wife, smiling, ten years ago, happy on the steps of the Campanile in Venice, her eyes filled with wonder and possibility. He snaps the frame off, and the glass breaks, cutting a deep furrow in his palm. He wipes the blood on his shirt, takes the photo and carefully places it inside his wallet. Drops of blood spot Alexia's face.

He starts taking the boxes out, one by one, into the main hallway. He'll get one of the deputies to drive them over to his house in the morning. For now, everything's packed. He hadn't wanted to do this during the day. Didn't want everyone congratulating him and wishing him the best of luck. Some things you had to do alone.

He's just putting the last bit of tape on the last box when the phone rings. The answering machine will pick it up, he thinks, but then, out of habit, he looks at the display and sees an international prefix.

'Palassos police, can I help you?'

'Nikos? . . . Is that really you?'

Her voice floods him with memories and emotion. He almost drops the phone.

'Kitty?'

She laughs, 'I thought you'd forgotten me,' she says, but her voice is deep and languid and he almost doesn't recognise it.

'Is she . . .'

He can hear her breath, slow and steady on the other end of the line.

'No,' he says, and that's all there is to say about that.

He accepts Kitty's condolences, finding himself buoyed by her voice, the memory of their last few days together on the island when they comforted each other in what they'd lost. She asks him if he's received her letter yet. He says he hasn't. She tells him that everything important is in there.

They talk about mundane things for a while. They talk about everything that doesn't really matter. She tells him about the late December sunshine, and he tells her about the rain, even holding the phone out towards the window when she expresses disbelief that it could ever rain in Palassos. She tells him that she's stopped writing, about her upcoming divorce, and then she asks what she's called up to ask him about.

'I was there every day,' he says, surprised at how comfortable he feels talking to her about these things, things he's kept locked up all these months. 'They sentenced him to life. No parole.'

'He give any reasons for what he did?'

'Too many,' Nikos murmurs. 'He had justifications for everything.'

'And Dimitri?'

Nikos thinks back to the other trial. Dimitri had been good to his word. His confession was worthy of Augustine. Petrakis simmered next to his attorney as Dimitri laid out the whole drug-supply network in return for a reduced sentence. Petrakis didn't say a word as the judge gave him thirty years. As he was being carried out, he'd turned to his son and whispered, *You're as dead as me,* before being dragged back into the steel and metal world he would spend the rest of his days in.

'He's gone. Petrakis too.'

'And . . .' Kitty's voice stutters a bit, and Nikos momentarily thinks they've lost the connection, 'What about Karelis?'

'He died in the hospital. Heart attack in his sleep. Doctor said that as soon as he stopped having to survive, his body just gave up.'

Nikos pauses, thinks about the misery and blood caused by the actions of the two priests, the exponential nature of their crimes.

'You don't mind talking about this?'

'No, not at all.'

'What I still don't understand is how George knew it was the priests?'

Nikos flashes back to the courtroom, George in a jumpsuit sitting next to his lawyer, his hands pressed against his beard, his voice logical and calm as if he were the judge.

'He said he knew as soon as he heard about his brother's death. He said the kids all knew the priests had this proclivity. But he was ten, there was nothing he could do; the next month his mother moved them to England. He came back to Palassos three years ago only to bury his mother. He saw Petrakis, the town elders, saw how rich and respectable they'd become, how his brother had been the sacrifice that allowed the island to prosper. A Faustian pact. That's when he decided to get revenge.

'When he kidnapped Karelis, he made him confess everything. Karelis told him all about that night at the monastery when they killed the boys. He told him about the visit from Petrakis. George put one and one together . . .'

'Did he kill Vondas?' Kitty sounds breathless, as if waiting for a doctor's prognosis.

'Yes. He wanted to save him till last, but he'd heard Vondas had spoken to you, to other tourists up at the monastery; he was worried that the disappearance of Karelis and the resurgence of the murders would unhinge Vondas, force him into some kind of confession.'

'He didn't try to deny any of this?'

'Not at all. He was . . . he was proud.' Nikos pauses. He hadn't intended on telling her, but there's something in her voice.

'You know, it's strange you calling because a couple of nights ago I had this dream, and when I woke up your face was in front of me.'

'Was it a good dream?'

Nikos remembers waking sweat-drenched and heart fluttering, a feeling of utter dread inside him.

'In the dream, my father gave me a box. He told me never to open it, but of course I did. Inside the box was God. He was small and shrivelled and alone. He kept trying to turn his face from me. I told him I would free him. I remember I was crying. I put my hand in and gently pulled him from the box. But when I opened my palm and looked, I saw that somehow I had crushed him. Suddenly, all the lights went out, and we were plunged into darkness, and I knew, the way you just know things, that this was the real darkness and that it would last for ever. Then I woke up and saw your face.'

They talk some more, and then Kitty says she has to go, and Nikos listens to the dead tone for a few seconds before putting it down. He stares around the office, the tables and computers and faxes. This is everything he never has to do again. Tomorrow Elias takes over. Spiros has already approved his early retirement. He stands there and smokes one last cigarette.

He takes the box of personal things with him. He carries it in his arms as the rain drenches his hair and clothes. He locks the door of the police station for the last time, looks up at the broken crucifix and crosses himself.

It's almost midnight, and the town is asleep. It's the opposite of what it was during the summer. Now only the sea, the weather and the islanders remain. He walks past the boarded-up tavernas and clubs, past the grocer shops and martyred saints kneeling in the square. The rain drips from his eyebrows into his eyes. His feet slosh and squeak on the cobbles. The box feels like it's disintegrating in his hands. He follows the promenade and then starts walking on the soft wet sand. He reaches the little jetty and walks through the rain and wind until he's at the edge staring at the deep black rippled sea. He takes the box and flings it into the water. It explodes in a shower of paper and photos. The box darkens and sinks. The papers spread out like dead jellyfish, an army of white ghosts cresting the water.

He turns and walks back home.

He stands outside his door and wipes his shoes. He remembers he forgot to put out the rubbish. He takes out his key and turns the handle. The letter from England is waiting for him. It's funny how these things happen, he thinks, as he picks it up and shakes off the rain. The house is quiet and cold and damp. There's no sound but the insect hum of the refrigerator. He takes a beer out of the cooler, slumps down onto the sofa and begins to read.

A year and a half. I can't believe it's been that long, Nikos. Staring out at the leafy boughs caressed by wind, at these windows which haven't been cleaned in months, I sometimes think back to that day I made my decision to go to Greece. I think about the life I led and the life I now lead. There doesn't seem to be any connection between the two.

I stopped writing. But you know that. It's been over a year, and I haven't even talked to my agent or publisher in that time. A couple of weeks after I got back I disconnected the phone and answering machine. My life is simpler now. I take pleasure in what I can, the slow evening cigarette and cup of coffee that I would never have allowed myself before. I sometimes wonder what Don would say if he passed by the old house, saw me on the porch with coffee and cigarette, listening to music, watching the day fall. But I don't wonder about it often because there's work to do.

It's been the hardest thing I've ever worked on. But that's as it should be.

Remember that backpack you helped me with from Jason's room? Well, I didn't open it for six months. I put it in a special room in my house I rarely use. Then, one day, it was time.

There was a pile of clothes and toiletries. Each object so filled with the longing of going away, I couldn't bear it.

There was an iPod which I listen to every night. Sixty giga-bytes of Jason's music. I put it on shuffle, and in the sequence of songs, sometimes I think he speaks to me. Other times I'm sure of it.

There was a copy of my latest novel. It felt strange in my hand, like some alien relic. There was also an invite. From my last book launch. On it, in his cramped handwriting, was the word *Palassos*. I stood there and stared at it for the longest time. I remembered having mentioned to my agent where I was going, and then it struck me: Jason must have been at the launch. He must have followed me out to the island. God knows why! Nikos, I can almost hear the cop part of you going off like a fire alarm, but I swear, it didn't feel like that to me at all. I know Jason's actions should make me feel weird and uncomfortable. I know this is not the way most people behave, but I can't help it. It only makes me more protective towards him, thrilled too that he'd gone out of his way to meet me. I've kept the invite. I placed it on my mantelpiece when I took down all the photos of Don.

There was also a manuscript and hundreds of pages of notes, synopses, chapter titles and character summaries.

I spent a few months going through it. I added what I could from notes he'd made between the lines, on the edges of the margins. I know you'll think me crazy, but when I was rewriting Jason's words I could hear him speak to me in a way he'd never spoken to me on the island, and I knew this was the real Jason and that he'd finally found his way out of the labyrinth.

I finished his book. I sent it to an agent I didn't know. I signed off my emails with *Jason*. She sold the book to a mid-level publisher. You'll find the cheque in this envelope. Please give half to Yanni, the old man who lost his son; the rest can be used to rebuild the museum.

The book came out last week. The PR department have explained that Jason is out of the country, uncontactable, not interested in promotion. The non-publicity gave him far more publicity than if he'd been here to do interviews and radio slots. You would have loved it, Nikos. Everyone focused on the mystery behind the mystery.

On a cold December morning, the sky gauzy and grey, I walked past the windows of Foyle's and saw it there. I stood in the street and stared at the cover, his name embossed in gold. I thought about the swirl of sea and stars that night up by the Black Monastery, the heat of his lips on mine, and I stood there in the howling rain, smiling, knowing that something had finally turned out right.

Nikos carefully folds the letter and places it on the table. He'll read it again later. It's good to have things to look forward to. He picks up Alexia's postcard which rests next to it. Her handwriting takes him back to other days. The letters are faded, the stamp's come unstuck, and the card's almost falling apart from repeated handling. But he doesn't need to read the words to know what they say.

He expected another postcard from his wife, but it's been over a year and there's nothing. He stays in his room most days. His life has become circumscribed by the walls of secrecy that held them together for so long. By the memories he can't bear to let go of. The smell of her fingers, the dark curve of her ankle, the way she always knew when he was lying. Things lost to him. Memories, reminders of the past, ruins.

He's retired now, and he makes lists of the things he wants to do when she returns. He sits in his room and stares at the wall. He tells himself she'll come back. That she'll see he's forgiven her. And he waits. Hoping that one day the door will open again, his wife will step in, and his life will resume.

Acknowledgements

Lesley Thorne, my agent, without whose support and editorial skill this book probably wouldn't exist.

Angus Cargill, as great an editor as any writer could ask for. Alex, Katherine, and everyone at Faber who welcomed me so kindly. It's due to them that this book looks so good.

Damian Thompson, for being there in the worst moment and for Phoenix and many other kindnesses.

Leah Middleton and James Pusey who made some trenchant points about the manuscript which improved it considerably.

Sally Riley and everyone else at Aitken Alexander for their great work in selling my words across the world.

Matt Thorne, Richard Thomas, Nick Stone, Ali Karim, Mike Stotter, Toby Litt, Lee Child, Pete Wild, Louise Welsh, Beverley Cousins, Poisoned Pen Press, John O'Connell, James Sallis, Matt Dornan, Barbara Franchi, Don Winslow.

Rose Dempsey, Bailey Korrell, Luke Coppen and everyone at the *Catholic Herald*, Willy Vlautin and Dave, Dan, Paul and Sean from Richmond Fontaine, Jim Butler, The Grateful Dead.

My mother and father.

And . . . Jane for everything these sentences cannot say.